THE CALL OF THUNDER

Hidden Heroes Series Book 1

Sarah Blynne

Sarah Blynne Writes

CONTENTS

To my mom, the real hero.

OLAVAR LAGOON

MACAPHIN VILLAGE

PALUSO MOUNTAINS

ARBOL FOREST

PALUSO LAKE

ARYTHICA

VODA CAVE

ARBOL RIVER

PALUSO SNOWFIELD

AGURA OCEAN

KILLIOS TRAINING CAMP

STONELAND HILLS

SNAKE'S CANYON

VOLARE OCEAN

CAL-LÉA

SABBIA DESERT

SOLMA HILLS

SIRO

SABBIA TOWN

LUNA ISLAND

VULCA MOUNTAIN

REMOS ISLANDS

BARTO LAKE

BENA LAKE

KINGDOM OF PETROS

ALBERI JUNGLE

BELT CANYON

DARK WOODS

KETRA FALLS

MONTANHA PEAK

DOUMA LAKE

KETRA

CHAPTER I

"*D*avid, what's happening out there?" Mama's voice wakes me up. It's early morning and her tone indicates something is very wrong. I get out of bed and lean my ear against the wooden door.

"Cal–léa is being raided!" Papa says in a panicked, rushed tone. "We need to get Havanna to safety!"

The way he says it makes my breath shake.

Mama bursts into my room and scoops me in her arms with haste. "We have to get you out of here, Warrioress."

"What's going on?" I ask with genuine fear in my voice.

"Backers are looking for you," she answers as she grabs something out of my nightstand and rushes into the living area. "We need to send you to a safe place to hide."

"I don't want to go!" I scream, holding onto Mama for dear life.

"I know, but you need to be safe." I can hear the tears in her voice.

Dread and nausea course through my entire body. I need my parents. I don't want to go anywhere without them. Who will I live with?

I don't want to leave my best friends, Foss and Dahlia, either. I want to stay and play with them in the city square. I want them to come over and play hide-and-seek out in the street. I want to climb up the tree in our backyard and tell stories until the sun goes down.

All of that is slipping away from me.

Bolt, my Bennaru that has served our family for centuries, follows closely behind Papa in the form of a white mouse. Mama holds me as we rush outside the house into the cobblestone street, dimly lit with lanterns from the other homes. At the end of the street, the bright light of lit torches illuminates the street, signaling their approach.

"We have to hurry," Mama says, panicking. She sets me to my feet and hugs me so tight I could burst. I don't care, though. I need to hold onto her as long as I can.

"We will come for you," Mama promises. "Bolt will take you to Ketra and we will meet you there, okay?"

My face covered in tears, I nod. I've never heard of Ketra, which makes me even more afraid of leaving. I'm only ten years old. I'm not ready to go to a strange place without my parents.

Papa then holds me tightly, his metal knight's armor pinching my delicate skin with his squeeze. I don't care. He's comforting me and I don't want to leave him.

"We love you, Warrioress." He kisses me on the head. "We will find you. I promise."

Mama gives me one last hug, sobbing with all her might into my shoulder. Papa hugs me too, body shaking.

"Kora, they're coming," Papa warns her, grabbing her shoulder. "I have to ward them off."

Papa unsheathes the sword he carries on his back and charges down the cobblestone street toward the chaos, his armor clamoring together as he picks up speed. The Backers are nearby with the glow of their torches reflected on the ground and shining through the darkness of night. This town, with only a couple thousand people, doesn't take up a lot of space. Whatever damage occurs will appear as if it took up the entire area.

From a three-story stone building a few blocks away, smoke rises to the sky and fills my nostrils. The echoes of people screaming in terror and crackling noise of burning wood will no doubt be ingrained in my mind in the days to come. The clashing sounds of sword fighting is one I recognize very well, but it scares me to think that people are fighting for their lives and may end up losing them.

This is Cal-léa, the most peaceful place there is. Fights don't ever happen. The word "fight" is never spoken.

Bolt's mouse legs grow and extend into horse legs in jerky movements, hooves popping out at the end as he comes to standing, while his body balloons as if bulbous bumps are finding room under his skin to create a muscled torso and chest that is well-known on horses. Hair sprouts on his tail and his mane in one full burst. Mama picks me up and sets me on his back, but does so in a way that makes me think she will pull me back down on the ground and change her mind. But then I feel Bolt's strong spine and mane on my face and I know I'm really leaving. My crying fits don't change Mama's mind.

"Take her to Ketra," she tells Bolt. She then hands me a couple pieces of brownish parchment paper, one of which I'm guessing is the poem from my nightstand. "Don't ever, ever lose these," she commands. I put them in the pocket of my soft nightgown.

"I don't want to go," I cry.

"You have to," Mama sobs. "I'm sorry, but you have to. Bolt, hurry! Go! Stay out of sight!"

Bolt takes off in a gallop while I cling weakly to his maned neck, my body limp from crying so much.

I sit straight up in bed, my heart racing and I'm sweating all over. I had that nightmare again. The one that will haunt me for the rest of my life. The fact that I never saw my parents again after the fall of my hometown still comes for me even ten years later.

It's still nighttime; the tall torch in the front corner of my hut burns brightly, which means everyone else's torches are burning outside too. I remind myself that I'm in the village of Ketra, not fleeing from Cal-léa. The white-inked olive branch tattoo on my right forearm reminds me where I'm really from.

Willing my heart and mind to slow down, I look around my hut. Everything is made of wood or straw, including the weapon rack next to my door that holds an emergency sword and shield. The only things that aren't wood are the fireplace, hearth, and stove with a cast-iron pot next to the main door.

At the foot of the bed is a dresser and perched on top is a glass jar with Twinkle Fireflies. Immediately, I feel much calmer. They move so elegantly, floating dots of yellow light without a care in the world. The tension in my muscles dissipates, reminding me to be as at peace and carefree as they are. The Fireflies come from my secret hiding place in the village and it's always a glorious sight to see them flying around.

I open the top drawer of the nightstand next to my bed and remove two folded parchment papers my mother told me never to lose—just to make sure they're still there. They lie in the near-empty drawer, safely untouched.

This type of nightmare happens often and trying to fall back asleep will be pointless. There's only one thing I like to do when I can't sleep and it involves effort and sweat. A bottle of Sleeper's Brew just isn't going to cut it.

I rip the linen sheets and thick white-yarn blanket off my body and put on a pair of tight black stretchy pants, a black V-neck short-sleeved shirt, and leather combat boots. I tie my shoulder-length brown hair back and off my neck. The shorter the hair, the more it stays out of my face in a fight. I grab the jar off my dresser and step down from my loft to the front door. The view of my village stops me in my tracks and I take it all in.

Ketra is beautiful at night, all one hundred forty yards of it. Growing up, I was told stories that it was formed as a haven for refugees and escapees from war. It sits on the side of a tall mountain, Montanha Peak, three miles straight up from the village, far from other civilizations. The torches are lit and all is quiet, save a few faint sounds that are unique to Ketra, including chirping crickets and Clucks. The noise I love the most, though, is the rush of Ketra Falls and the flow of the Ketra River. A forest of tall trees borders the village where the obnoxious calls of Cawjays blend in with the sound of water. The entrance is hidden behind hanging vines within the trees, so hardly anyone ever comes across here. A short walk on beaten earth and grass leads to a sandy beach on the edge of the ocean.

If water didn't kill me, I would enjoy the beach a lot more.

My mother once said if I completely submerge myself in water, it can put my whole body in shock from the electricity that runs through me. When my body tingles to the point where it cramps and burns, I know I have too much exposure to water. The only way to remedy that is to quickly dry myself off before the sensation gets worse.

I lift the lid off the glass jar and let the Fireflies escape, dotting the dark sky with their bright yellow light. They know where to go; they know I'll come back for them.

With the empty jar in hand, I make my way to the training grounds. The grass is kept extremely short to mark the area, and off to the side are two rundown, open sheds with full weapon racks. We have plenty of guards to protect the village from intruders, but a lot of citizens enjoy having combat skills when it's necessary. Jael, Ketra's chief and my mentor, told me once, "I can't be the only one in charge of protecting everyone." As a trained warrior, I do what I can to help her in that effort.

There's a plethora of weapons of all sizes to choose from: swords, axes, spears, bows and arrows, clubs, flails, even throwing knives. I grab the one I'm most proficient with—the sword.

It's my favorite one. A golden crown at the tip of a brown handle. The hilt is gold with two tiny rubies on each side and the lightweight blade covered in engraved swirls can do a world of damage.

I methodically swing my sword around and enjoy the whooshing sounds the blade makes as I slice it through the air. I pretend to fight an enemy, particularly a Backer. Picturing them in front of me makes me swing and stab harder. They're the reason I have to live my life in hiding. Something as simple as exploring the Dark Woods outside the village is forbidden for me. Coming out of a hiding place means more exposure for the Backers to hunt me down for my powers. Not to mention the fact that Dormants can spring from the ground at any point and hunt me down too.

Every single day, it saddens me that I have to hide myself in order to be safe. I want a sense of normalcy where I can live just like everyone else.

With the memory from ten years ago in my mind, I stop what I'm doing and open my right hand. An etching of a lightning bolt stares back at me—something I've had since I was born. Normally, I wear fingerless gloves to hide it, but with no one around, I can finally free my hands from such stifling captivity. Although I was born with the Strike ability, I was raised to never use it, as much as I desperately want to. Using Gridlock was out of the question until I came to Ketra, and even then, I had to limit it.

Along the side of the training area is a line of trebuchets with sandbags on the slings. This is normally used for archery practice, but I never use it for such. I launch one of the slings and the sandbag whips into the air. While it flies, I stretch my hand out and use Gridlock. I freeze the bag in its place, a soft vibration tickling my hand when doing so. The bag follows the motion of my hand as I move it back and forth in the air.

I concentrate as much as I can to maintain control of the bag. Before my head begins to hurt and the pressure builds behind my eyes, I break my gaze from the object and it plops on the ground.

I follow this routine when I release the slings on a couple more trebuchets. I freeze the bags in the air, then they plop on the grass. The next time, I refill the slings with more sandbags, then run and release multiple slings quickly. As the bags fly, I catch some of them with Gridlock just before they hit the ground, then aim my focus on the ones still high in the air. Then, before my head hurts too much again, break focus and let them fall.

The annual target competition is coming up in a couple days. The village's most anticipated event helps warriors-in-training hone in their aiming skills. The rise of the morning sun slowly wakes up the world with the chirps of birds and a gentle breeze. Aria, my best friend, asked me yesterday if I wanted to practice sparring with her later in the morning. She wants to fine-tune her reflexes and become quicker with her movements in hand-to-hand combat. She decided to join the target competition, so she also wants to practice for that. Observing my own training over the years to improve my fighting skills, with or without weapons, motivated her to learn the same thing. She relies on me for help since I was raised by a trained military warrior and she has no one else to teach her.

After leaving everything the way I found it in the training area, I returned to my hut to try and sleep for a bit. That effort proved futile—as I knew it would—tossing and turning just to get comfortable. I once again threw on my black training outfit and met up with Aria.

The training grounds had already filled up with more people when I came back. The men dressed in breastplates, boots, and thick pants in preparation for practice and the women wore the same black attire I'm wearing now, but with the addition of chest armor.

After a couple hours of practice, Aria and I are sweaty and sore. She stands in front of me, her smooth, brown skin glistening with sweat and her black curly hair tied back behind her. She keeps her arms up, ready to keep going, her eyes fierce and determined. I'm exhausted from training early this morning, but I push onward. Pushing myself is ingrained in my blood.

From the corner of my eye, I see Victor, a young, new resident who started living in Ketra in the last couple months. Any new residents to Ketra are kept under strict watch by the guards and Jael to make sure they're trustworthy and they prove they're not here to harm anyone, and Victor passed with flying colors. He took on a job cleaning huts for a living, and he does a decent job. While he's not working, he practices for the target competition. Right now, he's stretching his arms across his muscled chest in preparation. My eyes rake him from handsome top to manly bottom.

"Hi, Havanna," he greets me with that shy, dimpled smile that stops me in my tracks every time so I can admire it. I have to admit, his light brown skin and black hair swept to one side make him very attractive from my point of view.

"Hi, Victor," I greet him back, my heart doing a weird flutter in my chest. I can't figure him out. He's a very handsome man who's around my age, and he's very kind and polite to me, but I'm not sure if I should let myself feel more for him and risk feeling like a fool when he tells me he doesn't feel the same about me. There's always a chance he could just be a nice man who doesn't find me attractive. It's a confusing limbo to be in.

My whole life is confusing.

Also in the corner of my eye is Darius, the object of every girl's affection and the bane of my existence. He's supposed to be practicing for the target competition, but he would rather flirt with three other girls who are pawing at him and giggling. He's a player and he thinks he's the best thing to ever have been born. Anyone with that attitude automatically lands on my "hate" list.

He soaks up the attention like a sponge, flipping his shaggy black hair back and forth in a way he knows makes girls swoon. To me, he will always be known as the boy who threw me in the ocean because he thought it would be funny. I remember that moment like it was yesterday.

It was the first time I met Aria.

I was still a new resident of the village. Darius and some other boys grabbed me by the arms, laughing in my ear while walking me out to a deep part of the water, and dropped me in. When I slapped my hands around seeking rescue, I saw Aria in the distance. My skin turning bright red caused her to take action. As I was fighting for my life, she ran at top speed through the sand toward Darius and shoved him over with such force that his breath was knocked out of him. The boys watched in awe as he thumped on the sand, then watched as she dragged me out of the water. I was afraid she would have figured out who I was and that I wasn't like everyone else in the village; I was scared she would tell everyone. Later that night, though, when she came to my hut to check on me, she said, "I know you're different, and that's okay. I'll still be your friend." I knew at that moment that I could always count on her.

Aria becomes distracted in our training when she sees girls flirting with Claeron. Standing next to Darius, he smiles when they talk to him and he shines his boyish, charming smile, running a hand through his dark blonde hair that's longer on top but shaved on the sides. He seems to enjoy the attention, but it's agonizing for her to watch.

I want to empathize with her, but not while we're in the middle of training. To teach Aria a lesson about distraction, I crouch and sweep a leg under her feet, causing her to fall straight on her back with a thud. Seeing her lying there, wincing and groaning in pain, I'm taken back to the injuries I've endured in my training, laying on the grass, drained of energy while Jael loomed over me and yelled, "Pain waits for no one!" In her mind, allowing exhaustion to take over wasn't an option.

I've lived by those five words my whole life.

"Are you okay?" I ask.

"Yes," she replies with strain. "I deserved that."

I extend my gloved hand and help her back to her feet. "No matter how much you like someone, they can't be the ones to distract you from danger," I advise her in a low voice, patting her shoulder encouragingly.

"I know. I'm sorry." She turns back to Claeron while wiping her face with a towel and sighs. "I just . . . I thought he liked me . . ." she says despondently.

Thinking back to when we were children growing up in this village, Claeron seemed to always have a fondness for Aria's no-nonsense attitude and loyalty. He may enjoy the attention from other girls, but it's obvious that he's always had eyes for her. He has yet to tell her that, though.

"Just tell him." I flap my arms to emphasize. "You've waited long enough."

"Hey, Havanna!" I hear Darius's annoying, insufferable, arrogant voice call out to me. Without hiding how much I hate him, I slowly turn, glaring. "I see you're being mean to your trainees again," he comments with a smug grin. Why the girls in this village like him, I have no idea.

"I'll see you at work, Havanna," Aria says with a downhearted tone as she trots away. She started working with me a few years ago at an eatery I've worked in since I arrived in Ketra.

"Okay, see you there," I call after her.

Aria passes Darius, but not without nudging him on the shoulder. I can't help but smirk. To my surprise, Claeron notices her sad face, then turns to follow her. I'm a little envious of their romance. Instead of taking my own advice and admit my feelings, I stand here and wish I had the same attachment Aria and Claeron have.

"See, she's running away from you because you're an abusive teacher," Darius says, breaking me out of my trance and pissing me off again. Victor lowers the axe in his hand to watch the debacle before him.

My face doesn't lie when I give Darius a look of pure hatred. The lightning mark on my palm begs to show its electric power, buzzing with a vibration that I've come to know well over the years.

Then I remember the breathing techniques Jael taught me. Whenever I feel upset or angry, my hand warms up with the need to use electricity. She would stand in front of me, grab my hands with hers, and guide me through it, and it made all the difference in the world.

I do it on my own as I come up with a smart response to Darius. *Breathe in. Hold for five. Breathe out.* Then the words slip out before I can stop them. "At least I can fight better than you can act like a man."

The girls surrounding him giggle and I hear Victor sputtering out laughter. Darius's face falls in fury and it fills my heart with pride to know I've brought him down a few pegs. With that calm, resonant feeling, the vibration in my hand dissipates.

"You think you can do better?" Darius shouts. "Okay. How about a little friendly competition?"

He stomps onto the training grounds until a blonde girl loops her arms around his and stops him. "We're still walking at the beach later, right?"

"Sure thing, gorgeous." He winks at her and struts to the weapon rack with a macho expression plastered across his face. I roll my eyes so hard it hurts. I don't want to do this, but I know he won't let it go until I comply.

Darius grabs an axe and readies himself in front of a target. My stomach plummets. I don't have much experience in target practice. I'm screwed.

What makes this worse is that Victor has become utterly enamored with this scene. He stands next to Darius's girl group to see how it will play out. The pressure to perform perfectly and not look like a fool makes me sweat. Losing this fight might make him stop showing interest in me because he'll think I'm a wuss.

Hesitantly, I take a bow and an arrow from the weapon rack. I have some experience in archery, but not enough that I feel confident I will hit the bull's-eye.

"Say goodbye to your dignity." Darius sneers. He slowly lifts the axe above his head with both hands then throws it forward with all his might. Just as I expected, the blade cracks the bull's-eye dead-on. His cheerleaders squeal in excitement, jumping up and down. Victor remains stoic with no reaction. He studies me closely, waiting to see what I can do.

Darius perks his eyebrows at me in the cockiest of manners. "Good luck."

With my whole body shaking, I nock the arrow and pull back, sweaty palms affecting my grip. I make sure to keep the pulled arrow close to my face and do my best to aim at the target. Despair blurs my concentration when I release, and the arrow hits the ring just outside the bull's-eye—just as I suspected it would.

"Ha! I knew it!" Darius shouts in victory.

Victor's expression is one of pity—pursed lips and arms folded as he stares down at the grass. I know he thinks I'm a weakling, not a talented fighter.

I toss the bow to the ground as Darius creeps right up to my ear to say, "I knew you were a fraud."

Those six words spike my anger to an all-time high. So much so that I could cry, and the electricity tingles in my hand again.

Breathe in. Hold for five. Breathe out.

That has been my biggest insecurity my whole life. Hiding who I really am because *no one* can see my abilities. I'm the only one who can't leave the village because I have to stay in hiding from people that want to kill me. Not being able to find out the scope of my power because someone could be watching.

I feel like a fraud. Every single day. I'm tired of it.

I can't let Darius win this one.

He struts back to the girls, flowing with overconfidence with his head held high and swinging arms. As quietly as my boots will let me, I sneak up behind him and jump onto his back, then climb onto his shoulders.

"What—" Darius shouts. "What are you doing? Get off!"

He spins around and grips my legs so that I will unwrap them from around his neck. I clutch my knees as hard as I can then twist my body in a way that causes him to fall straight to the ground, taking me down with him. I hop to my feet, my dignity back intact and unharmed.

"Darius!" The girls whine and run to his aid. Despite being covered in girls, he remains on the ground, shocked and unblinking. Victor is laughing so hard he's on his knees. A confident smile spreads on my face and all the negative feelings melt into the grass below me.

"Well, that was fun. Off to work I go," I remark casually as I step over Darius's body and the girls shoot me dirty looks. I have zero tolerance for arrogance and anyone who has little regard for other people's feelings. If I can show them up, I will. And I'm thankful I received enough training to pull off that move.

Victor steps onto the low-cut grass once his laughter dies off and looms over Darius's body. He holds out his hand to help him get back on his feet. "You just got beat up by a girl," he remarks.

"Shut up, Victor." Darius pushes his shoulders and stomps away. Darius's childish demeanor puts an even bigger smile on my face and makes Victor laugh harder, a hearty and happy sound that causes me to forget how to breathe.

"Good job putting him in his place," Victor compliments with a chuckle. "That was fun to watch."

"Glad I could provide some entertainment." I lightly laugh and proceed to walk away from the training area. "I'll see you later, Victor."

He speeds up and keeps in step with me as I walk back to my hut. "Actually, I meant to ask you if you need your home cleaned by any chance."

"No, it's okay. Thank you, though."

"For you, I'll do it free of charge," he offers with his beaming smile.

I give him a questioning look. "Are you bored or something?"

"Nonsense. Just want to help you out."

These are the kinds of remarks that make me think Victor is attracted to me. Yet again, he hasn't openly admitted it. I fail to understand why the young men in this village are afraid to admit their feelings.

"I mean, if you really want to, sure." I shrug. "Just give me an hour or so and you can go in."

"Thank you," he replies excitedly and takes off in a dash. I watch him run away without another word, slightly offended that the conversation was seemingly cut off out of nowhere. It's moments like this that force my emotions into a tailspin of overthinking and not having concrete answers.

When I arrive at the eatery, there are only two people in the dining area, both drinking Corn Whiskey. Otherwise, it's empty and slow.

I remember when I started working at Ketra's eatery. I had only been in the village for a couple days. Jael thought it would be a good distraction while I waited for my parents to come get me. I was mad at her for putting me to work so quickly, but that anger didn't last long.

My parents never came for me and I had to learn to live with that.

Rose, the eatery's owner and Aria's mother, took me in and showed me everything there was to know about running the place. She taught me how to make Bakki, a pile of red rice with a thick, greenish gravy. It looked horrendous when I was young, but I made it anyway. I also learned how to make Loga, a chunky, white dish that reminds me of pudding with cubed meat. For dessert, people go crazy for Winterbulbs, a sweet, juicy, dark-blue fruit about the size of a melon found at the top of Montanha Peak, straight above the village. It tastes sweeter when cooked. I even added a dessert to the menu I used to eat in Cal-léa: Conna Mondaña. I didn't remember the exact recipe, but I knew it was honey-sweetened goat-milk yogurt with banana and mango, or sometimes with strawberries. People absolutely love it, and that makes me happy. We sell out within hours any time I make it.

Rose was the reason I learned to cook so well and how I came to love cooking. She was the reason I warmed up so quickly to being in Ketra. I was nervous about living with Jael, and she knew it. "She doesn't show it very well, but children are her soft spot," Rose told me. That sentence alone helped me to view Jael in a different light.

When Rose died a few years ago, the business was handed to me. Aria wasn't interested in owning it, but she knew enough about it to want to help me, so she volunteered. Rose wanted nothing more than for her "other daughter," as she used to call me, to pick up where she left off. Losing her left a big hole in my life, and in Aria's. During her funeral, when her body was covered in flowers and drifted into the ocean on a wooden plank, the only thing I could think about was how I didn't ever want to go through this again, at least for a very long time.

Aria is stirring a cast-iron pot of Bakki in the kitchen over a flame when I walk in to grab a wet cloth. "Darius is so infuriating," I announce, shaking my head. "After you nearly pushed him over, he challenged me to a target competition."

She cringes, well aware that my target skills are not advanced. "Oh no. I'm sorry."

"It worked out because I took him down with my favorite fool-proof move."

"The Twist and Drag? Good job!" Aria raises her hand and gives me a high five. "Leave it to us to show him who's boss."

I cackle as I step outside to the deck and wipe down the tables that are sprinkled with dead leaves and dirt. From here, one can get a good view of the potion shop run by the rainbow-haired Tetia and the training area on the other side of her. It's early afternoon and people are still shooting arrows and throwing axes.

When I lived in Cal-léa, my father taught me the basics of using a sword, but that was all I was allowed to learn. My parents may never have come for me, and waited a long time to tell me why

I couldn't use my abilities, but I give them credit for getting me started on being a fighter.

"Okay, let's do that one more time," Papa says, holding a sword in one hand and a metal shield on the other; the imprint of Cal-léa's olive branch neatly engraved on the front.

I focus on the blade in his hand. Bolt watches us from the branch of the thick, pale tree in our backyard. My best friends, Foss and Dahlia, sit at the base of the tree and watch us. Having Bolt in his enormous eagle form would raise a lot of questions, so it's best if he stays a mouse when my friends are around.

Foss and Dahlia always loved that my father was a guard and owned a sword and shield. Whenever he wanted to show me the ways of the sword, they would come over and watch just because the action of it all is so mesmerizing.

"Go, Havanna!" Dahlia cheers me on. Her flower-patterned dress is dirty from sitting on the ground, but she doesn't care. Her sleek, black hair complements and cups her light brown face. Foss takes on the appearance of a troublemaker with his shaggy dark hair and baby face, but he's very much the opposite. My parents love them both as their own children.

"Shh." Foss pats Dahlia's shoulder and focuses intensely on me and Papa. "She needs to concentrate."

Papa comes at me with his metal sword. I block it with my wooden one. He uses a different angle and swipes at me, which I block again.

"Okay, good," he says. "Now, I'm going to go faster, so keep up with blocking me. And use whatever spots of time that come up to attack."

His movements speed up, making my reactions and thoughts speed up too, increasing my focus and anxiety. His sword creates clunking sounds against the wood of my own, fencing back and forth for a lengthy amount of time. He recently began teaching me sword fighting because I wanted to be as good as him. Maybe one day I can be good enough to protect the town.

That is, until he pokes me in the stomach with his sword. He has a spot of time to attack and I miss it. I groan in frustration as my friends groan in supportive disappointment.

"It's okay, Havanna." Papa walks up to me and puts his hands on my shoulders, his face full of compassion. "You're only ten years old. You still have time to figure this one out."

"We practice all the time, though," I complain. "I should be good at it by now."

"Not necessarily," he disagrees. "You'll get older and it'll get stronger. Trust me."

Mama comes out the back door of our stone house and watches us regroup. A smile stretches on her face as she sees her husband train her daughter in the ways of the sword. I always loved seeing that warm smile on her. The one that says she is happy with this family of hers, and that she is proud of us.

"It's almost time for supper," she announces. "Foss, Dahlia, time to go home. You can come back tomorrow."

"Okay," Foss says, being the obedient boy he is. Dahlia stands with him, walking over the rocks that surround the tree, and exits from the side of our house. He takes Dahlia's hand and holds it, making sure she doesn't fall over. "See you later, Havanna."

"Bye." I wave sadly at them. I don't want them to go. I don't ever want them to leave when we're all together. But we see each other every day.

Papa pokes me again, pretending to kill me. I have completely forgotten that we aren't done with our session. "Distraction doesn't look good on you," he remarks with a devilish smirk.

Another frustrated groan emits from my throat and I angrily throw my sword and shield on the ground. "I want to practice using my powers, Mama," I whine.

"Warrioress, we talked about this," she tells me in a loving but admonishing way. "It's not safe. I have the same abilities but I don't use them for the same reason."

"I just want to do it once," I beg. "I want to know what it's like. I want to tell Foss and Dahlia why I wear gloves! I hate telling them I have a skin condition!"

"You heard your mother," Papa agrees. "It's not safe."

I take off my fingerless gloves and look at my palm. The mark of a thunderbolt on my skin greets me. In the clear sky above us, a small beam of light shows up, waiting for my call.

"No!" Mama shouts and closes my hand with both of hers. "You can't use that. You'll draw attention to yourself. Put your glove back on!"

"Why?" I whine again. "What's the big deal?"

"You need to hide that power," she demands. "And you need to learn to control it." Mama twists to face the house and says under her breath, "The sparks have been showing up more often lately . . ."

"Why can't I use lightning?" I shout at her. "What's going to happen? Are we going to be eaten by snakes?" I wiggle my hands in the air in mock fear. "Will cats take over the backyard?"

"Havanna, enough," Papa reprimands me.

"You'll learn in time," Mama adds, then grips my shoulders. "But you are not allowed to use your abilities and that's final. Do you hear me?"

That was what she always said when I asked. I'm tired of hearing that same answer. She's hiding something from me and I'm angry that she still won't tell me.

Shaking my shoulders from her grasp, I huff in frustration and stomp angrily to the house, tears stinging my eyes. I deserve an answer. I can handle the truth.

"I'm beginning to think if you don't tell her, she's going to rebel," I hear Papa mutter. Mama groans in equal frustration as I slam the door.

I release quick breaths to make myself not cry and instead punch my pillow over and over again. Once I spend all my energy doing that, I flop on the bed and sniff back the tears that want to fall.

I'm a warrior. Warriors don't cry.

"Havanna," Mama's sweet and calm voice calls on the other side of the doorway.

She sits on the edge of the bed next to me. I scoot up and lean my back against the stone wall behind me. Part of me has no desire to hear what she has to say. All I will hear is more excuses as to why she can't tell me everything.

"I think it's time I tell you the truth," she admits.

Her admission catches me off guard and I lean forward, ready to listen. "About my powers?"

Mama nods. "But you must promise me one thing." She points her finger at me. "That you will never, ever repeat this story. Not even to Foss and Dahlia."

My brows furrow in confusion. "Why?"

She sighs. "It's very important that you keep this story to your-self because . . ." She pauses and turns her focus elsewhere as she holds back her own tears. "If you use your powers . . . If anyone finds out who you are, bad people will want to hunt you down and kill you."

Mama sounds desperate and scared. She's never told me that I could die if I use my powers. I remember her always telling me to hide my palm with gloves and never to call down lightning. I wanted to please her, so I did as she told me.

"I don't believe that," I scoff, dismissing her.

"I'm serious, Havanna," Mama scolds. Her voice turns shaky. "There are people out there that want your powers and they've been looking for you and me for a long time."

My eyes go wide. She's not lying.

"And it's not just you they're after," she continues. "They're after three others with abilities too."

My jaw drops in shock. Then I grow excited because this means I'm not alone. I prop myself on my knees and lean into her face. "There are other people out there just like me?!"

"Yes, but they're hidden, just as we are," Mama explains.

Disappointed, I sit back. "Why?"

She sits up further in my bed, stretching out her legs and crossing her feet. "Many, many years ago," she begins, "when the kingdom of Petros came to be, five people were granted abilities and Bennarus by the entity Halivaara, called Ancestors. Each Ancestor repre-sented the elements as a means of protecting the land: Fire, Water, Lightning, Land, and Power. The Fire Ancestor could manipulate fire, called Blaze. The Water Ancestor could shape water and ice into anything they pleased, called Upsurge. The Land Ancestor could turn nature and animals into anything, called Transform."

I take my pillow and hug it as Mama weaves the tale.

"The Power Ancestor had Manipulation, the ability to control things with his mind. Then, there was the Lightning Ancestor, who could control thunder and lightning."

I blink incessantly at her. I find the excitement rising again.

"I'm related to the Lightning Ancestor?"

"Yes," she says solemnly, opening her right hand where she has the lightning bolt marked on her own right palm. "But there's more to the story."

I lean back to the wall, listening intently.

"It turns out the Power Ancestor didn't just have Manipulation. In an argument with the Land Ancestor, he found he could copy powers and use them as his own, called Usurp. He copied Transform from the Land Ancestor. With that power, he took various creatures and created awful, ugly, scary monsters called Dormants." Her tone turns soft and she reminisces about these monsters. "I have never seen one, but my parents told me what they look like. Four-legged black creatures with piercing red eyes. A mane of tentacles around their necks that throw fire and ice that could kill in one blow." Mama sighs. "They lived underground until summoned by the Power Ancestor. He wanted to be in control of the kingdom while the other Ancestors wanted to protect it. But he wanted to do things his way. That's how he became the Dormant King."

I gulp down the fear building in my throat. I have so many questions, but I can't think of what to ask first. My mouth is frozen.

"The Dormant King had summoned an army for anyone who supported him and dubbed them Backers. He promised them his abilities if they brought the other Ancestors to him. That way, he can copy their abilities and give them to the Backers. Because their

lives were at stake, the Ancestors separated to different parts of the kingdom to hide. They have remained hidden since, and their powers were passed on generation to generation. Their Descendants." Mama leans in and pokes me in the chest with her finger. "Because one day, those Descendants will have to reunite to finish off the Dormant King once and for all. But we don't know when that will happen." She then turns to face me. "And that is why no one can know who you are. Besides, most people believe the Descendants and Dormants are just legends. Which is good, because it means we've done well with staying in hiding."

With so many questions now answered by her storytelling, there's only one left to ask. And it's one that scares me. "Are the Dormants still around, Mama?"

She shrugs. "I don't know, Warrioress."

A sense of relief clouds my chest. I'm afraid I could be attacked or killed by one someday. They haven't been seen in many years; maybe I'll never see one. Maybe I'm safe.

"What about the Dormant King? Where is he?"

"I don't know that, either. He could be anywhere. Which is why you have to stay hidden from him and his power."

My fear is back. The Dormant King could be roaming Petros now, looking for me. He could find me in the middle of the night and take me away from Mama and Papa.

"Don't worry." She takes my head and kisses me on the forehead. "I won't let anything happen to you. We just have to be careful and hide from anyone that supports him, that's all. So promise me you will never use your abilities. It's the only way to keep you safe. Please."

All I want is to make her happy and not disappoint her. "I promise," I agree, snuggling into her embrace. She holds me, combing my hair with her fingers. I let the quiet air and her soothing touch calm me down. The Dormants and Dormant King sound terrifying. I don't know if I will ever be ready to fight them. Papa has taught me some sword skills, but not enough to take down a monster.

"Want me to read you that poem?" Mama asks.

With a dip of my head, I slip under the covers and get comfortable. Every night, Mama reads me a poem that she says her parents used to read to her. She tells me it might be about different gods from long ago or some legend that doesn't exist. I don't understand it, but I love the way she reads it. Her reading voice is so loving and comforting; I always feel safe when she recites it.

Mama pulls the looped knob on the top drawer of the nightstand and reaches for the piece of very old, brown, folded parchment paper. The light of the lantern in the room shows the poem's paragraphs forming a circle. Mama doesn't know why it was written that way, but she never thought anything of it.

She clears her throat to read.

"There is one who calls the storm,
Close to the ocean; a spark of hope is born.
There is one who disturbs the sea,
Who, near the hollow of a cliff, spares themselves to a degree.
There is one in mastery of nature,
Within the green, they blend in with great measure.
There is one who curbs the flame,
By a mound of stone, they dodge the eyes of fame.
Lastly, there is one with the greed of a thief,
Once gone, the world once again lived in relief."

By the last line, I'm asleep.

CHAPTER 2

The annual target competition is today, and I'm busily preparing the food in a buffet style. The eatery gets so full after it's over, I have to spend time setting everything up so people can scoop whatever they want and move on. I don't usually get home till the early hours of the morning the next day because people like to stay and drink Corn Whiskey and Winterbulb Wine in celebration.

The sound of clunking footsteps trails into the eating area as Vincent, the village gardener, walks in and sits at a table under the awning. "Two bowls of Loga, please, massy," he orders. "Then two more for me to take home."

Vincent, Thaeus the blacksmith, and Victor are close friends who often come in for alcohol in the evening. They drink themselves silly, then they go home laughing their heads off. I always find it entertaining to watch.

"Or I can just give you four bowls to have now," I suggest with a shrug.

Vincent eyes the ceiling in thought, then nods. "Yes, I should do that. Thanks, massy."

I go back to the kitchen and prepare his Loga. "You have the appetite of a ravenous horse."

"I'm a growing boy," he says, patting his stomach. "I work all day. I need my nutrients."

"Yes, you're 'growing,'" I say with air quotes while I set two bowls in front of him, then go back to get the other two. By the time I return, Vincent has eaten through half of one bowl.

"You make the best Loga," he says through a full mouth. He picks through his pockets for money and lays some coins on the table. "Crimey. This is all I have till tomorrow."

Vincent is a good, hardworking man. He's become an uncle of sorts to me. He was among the first people to make me feel comfortable when I arrived in Ketra.

I put the two other bowls of Loga in front of him. "It's okay. These are on me."

"Thank you, massy." He pats me appreciatively on the shoulder. "You're the best."

I walk back to the kitchen to grab large containers of Bakki, Loga, Conna Mondaña, and cooked Winterbulbs for tonight. From the open window in the kitchen, I can see Jael, Thaeus, and a couple other men are in the training area. The competition is in session with a line of soldiers readying their axes, bows, and arrows. My stomach sinks at the sight. These villagers can show their varied abilities without a care in the world. They don't have to hide who they are and what they can do. They *know* what they can do. It's the same feeling I had as a child in Cal-léa when Foss and Dahlia would ask me why I wore fingerless gloves all the time. I always had to use the excuse that I had a skin condition and I hated it. It still bothers me that our friendship was cut short when I had to leave. I have no clue where they are or if they survived the raid. I wonder how different things could have been if I stayed.

Questions about my history and my kind come to mind all the time as well. Did the other Descendants deal with similar false pretenses for their safety? Did they quietly oblige or did they put up a fight with their parents, as I did with my mother? Did they ever feel the need to rebel? Didn't they want to know who they were and what they were capable of, as I do?

Those questions remain to be seen. Questions that I hope to find the answers to one day.

Customers sitting outdoors strain to get a good view of the competition. I set down my tray by an empty table and lean over the railing to watch. The air is deafeningly silent. Ibarra, Jael's close friend and the other judge, stands next to her and closely watches the soldiers as they poise their bows, arrows, and axes, ready to shoot at some dummies. I've known Ibarra as long as I've known Jael. Both of them have serious countenances and have a businesslike attitude, but when they let loose and have fun, it's a comedic performance.

Jael holds a bell, ready to ring. Once she does, the arrows and axes fly. When they hit the dummies in the chest, cheers explode. Jael and Ibarra inspect the targets to see who was closest to the bull's-eye. The one who's closest moves on to the next round. If two people tie, they both qualify and compete until only one contestant remains. The competition usually lasts a couple hours.

I inspect Aria's stance as she holds up her bow and arrow, eyes aimed at the target, even though Darius is right next to her with an axe. Jael rings the bell. Weapons fly. Roars of encouragement sound throughout the area. I hold my cheer until they declare a winner for the next round. Ibarra holds up a green flag next to Aria's target and the crowd goes wild.

Darius completely missed his target; I suppose he's a fraud as well.

After a couple more hours and lots of rounds, Aria is declared the winner. This gives the whole village something to celebrate.

The eatery crowds faster than I can keep up with. Alcohol flows. Every seat is taken, so much so that some resort to standing against the back wall. The musicians who usually perform outside have made their way inside, dancing and playing their instruments around the tables. People clap to the rhythm, smiles and joy on all their faces. It's loud from all the chatter and music, the air stuffy from all the body heat—but everyone is having a good time.

"Massy, have a seat for a moment, you've worked so hard," Thaeus comments. "Your feet must be in terrible pain."

"Nothing I'm not already used to," I remark, holding a pitcher of Corn Whiskey as I'm about to walk past Jael and Ibarra's table. My feet do ache from working, although I don't mind this part of my job. A regular person who works my job would get a bin of steaming hot water to soak their feet in. Someone like me, who would be injured if dipped in water, has to resort to laying my feet by a roaring fire and letting the heat of the flames do the healing.

I hope Jael will show her loving side and rub them for me tomorrow.

"I'll take that, thank you," Ibarra says and snatches the pitcher out of my hand without reserve.

"Well, excuse me!" I lightheartedly swat at her.

"Hey, you're sharing that," Jael insists as she slides her glass for Ibarra to pour, which she ignores.

"Buzz off, it's been a long day," Ibarra slurs, the alcohol already making an appearance in her speech. She pours the whiskey in her glass in a sloppy manner, spilling some on the table. Her lips curl in a quirky manner. "Buzz, buzz, buzz . . ."

"Quit buzzing and hand it over, you sloppy slop." Jael drunkenly snatches the pitcher and pours some in her glass. Eyes glazed over, she looks up at me when she asks, "Do I still have to pay for this?"

"Yes, Jael, you do."

"I raised you for ten years and this is my thanks?" She grumbles and slaps a few coins on the table, then hands me the empty pitcher. "Fine. Refill for the old woman."

"You'll have water. And lots of it."

On my way back from the kitchen with a pitcher of water, I feel fingers pry at my elbow.

"Havanna! You dance now!" Paia, the ukulele player, forces me to join the line dance they started.

"Oh, uh—"

I have little choice when he drags me into the line. I march behind the musicians, holding the pitcher of water in my hand. I awkwardly raise it in the air, spilling water on the old wooden floor and on my clothes; but I decide to have fun with it. My dirty clothes will just be evidence of a fun night. Along the way, I grasp Aria's arm and drag her with me. Before I know it, people voluntarily join the line and it becomes a giant snake of dancing people slithering between the tables.

Eventually, I leave to refill empty water glasses around the room. My heart thumps against my ribs when I reach Victor's table and I feel heat rise to my cheeks when I display my shyness. "I didn't see you at the competition. I hope you were able to see some of it," he says.

I feel a sense of flattery when he says it. He noticed my absence and he was curious enough to wonder what happened to me. "I did get to watch. Everyone did well."

"You're probably glad Darius didn't win." He keeps his eyes trained on me, obviously watching for my expression regarding my distaste for Darius.

"Oh yes. That made my day."

He nods in agreement. "Same here."

"You fraud!" I hear a familiar, aggravating male voice yell. Darius stands from his seat and points a finger at Aria, who seems taken aback by this sudden outburst. "You don't know the first thing about archery! It was just by coincidence that you won!"

I know Aria. She won't stand there and tolerate his attitude. She stands up straighter and steps close enough until she's inches from his face. "And you're *not* a fraud?" she snaps. "You act like a man when you're just an immature, puny little boy."

"Oh please," he spits. "It gets me the ladies and you're just jealous that I won't let you have a piece of this." He motions to his slim, muscled body.

The crowd chatter simmers down as they observe the yelling match before them. The heat in my cheeks morphs from the nervous excitement of seeing Victor to pure embarrassment and sheer fury at Darius's behavior. Either he's good at acting sober when he's actually drunk or he's legitimately mad. He's not stumbling to stand or shuffling his feet to maintain his stance, but his eyes have difficulty focusing. No matter what's going through his head, I'm tired of his pompous attitude, and I'm not going to let him talk to my best friend that way.

I stomp over to him with purpose, my finger in his face. "Knock it off, Darius. Sit down and shut up, or leave my eatery."

His head slowly turns to look at me, lips curled into a snarl. "You," he growls. "You're always out to get me!" He motions around to the customers sitting and observing us. "But everyone knows the truth. You act like this tough warrior that can do anything, but in reality, you're *weak*. You're a fraud, just like her." He motions to Aria.

Even though I proved him wrong in the training grounds, I can't prove him wrong now. The more he says it, the more I begin to believe it. I have to pretend to be like everyone around me by not letting anyone see my abilities, or my hands.

My right hand warms with electricity. The sensation turns into a tingling, which sends panic right through me. I want to use Strike on this useless, waste of space of a man, more so than I did at the training area. I want him to know to never mess with me or my identity again.

"You walk around here acting like everyone likes you." He steps closer to me, the strong, alcoholic fumes of Corn Whiskey on his breath. "But they see you for who you really are."

"Darius, stop it," Aria scolds.

My breathing picks up speed as I try to maintain control of the sparks that beg to burst from my hand. Jael's breathing technique comes into play as my hurt feelings intensify. *Breathe in. Hold for five. Breathe out. Breathe in. Hold for five. Breathe out.*

The emotions about everything—feeling like an outsider, being tired of hiding, and frustrated that I can't use my abilities—are at their breaking point. Breathing isn't cutting it anymore. The tingles intensify.

Jael must see my hand emitting a soft, golden glow because she shoots up from her seat and takes me by the shoulders. She's back to being Ketra's chief as she somehow shakes off the effects of alcohol. "Darius, you need to leave." She points toward the door and punches out, *"Now."*

Darius moves to leave, forced to obey the chief's orders. I don't notice it because I'm distracted with my own thoughts and distracted with Jael dragging me to the back of the kitchen. Customer voices pick up, but this time it's more of a negative murmuring.

Once we're in a dark corner of the kitchen, Jael stands in front of me and takes my hands in hers. "Breathe in," she coaxes. *"Breathe in."*

My racing heart refuses to slow down, but I attempt to breathe in anyway. These techniques are easier done when Jael is in front of me, holding my hands, guiding me. Her low voice calms me, as it reminds me of my mother's voice when she would read the poem.

"Hold for five."

I hold it two of the five required seconds before I rapidly exhale. I don't feel any calmer, and that worries me even more.

"Breathe in." Jael urges me to follow along with her by holding my hands tighter, but we're not in sync yet. "Hold. Breathe out."

My heart slows as Jael doesn't let go of my hands; she doesn't stop moving me through the exercise until the golden glow dims and the brightness is completely gone. But it doesn't stop the flood of tears suddenly making an appearance. Exhaustion, anger, and feeling lost all convert into the waterworks going down my face.

"Shh." Jael takes me in her arms and hugs me. "Darius is a nobody. I'll make sure he's on strict watch immediately. You surely didn't deserve the things he said to you."

As I continue to cry against her chest, I shake my head. "That's not it."

She releases me and peers into my tear-stained eyes. "What is it, then?"

I break eye contact and sigh. "How long do I have to keep doing this?" I ask in despair. Jael's face falls. She knows, with that simple sentence, what this is all about. "How long do I have to keep hiding?" My voice cracks. "I'm tired of being so careful not to get caught using my abilities. I'm so tired of living in this sheltered life. When can I finally be *me*?"

Jael's eyes turn more empathetic, but her sigh tells me she's annoyed with my attitude. "We've talked about this before. The time will come."

"But when?"

She looks deep into my eyes. "Listen to me. I know you want to be free. I know you're tired of this life. Yes, the Descendants will unite one day. Yes, they will fight the Dormant King. And you will know when that time comes. But now is not the time, Havanna. Just because you *want* to use your abilities doesn't mean it's safe to, or in your best interest."

This was the same speech she used on me every time I had a moment of crisis like this. I hate it with every fiber of my being. It's the same answer my mother gave me when I wanted to use my abilities. *It isn't safe.*

Every time she answers my question, I hope for something that gives me a specific timeline. Telling me that I will know in time and that it's still not safe right now doesn't answer my questions or ease the agony.

"You will know. I promise."

Still somewhat angry, all I can do is nod and manage to get back to my shift. Jael stands there, arms falling limp at her sides and sadness in her eyes.

Plastering on a smile and grabbing a bottle of Winterbulb Wine, I return to the dining room where I see Aria turning and walking out of the kitchen herself. My heart drops to my stomach and my legs tense up enough to stop me from walking.

Did she hear everything? Does she know I'm a Descendant?

I watch her as she sits back at her table with a few other people, giving me a measly smile I know isn't genuine. Whatever high she was feeling for being the target competition winner has dissolved. My heart breaks that I'm seeing a new side to Aria right now.

I don't look forward to seeing what this new knowledge will do to our friendship.

***

Aria doesn't say anything to me the whole day when we work together. She's unusually quiet, and every time I ask her if everything is okay, she just says, "Yes, everything is fine. Don't worry." And she would conclude the statement with that shiny, white-toothed smile of hers.

She never hesitates to tell me when something is bothering her. There's a chance she didn't hear us last night if she's still being cheery and positive as she usually is. No point in bringing it up if she doesn't know.

As my best friend, I've wanted to tell her more than I've wanted to tell anyone else. But because Jael doesn't trust that Aria has the ability to keep it to herself, I am forbidden from saying anything. The risk of her telling her father, then her father telling the village is one Jael doesn't want to take. It's the biggest secret I've kept from her, and it eats me up every single day.

Whatever Bakki, Loga, and Conna Mondaña is left over from the eatery at the end of the day, I take in a burlap sack and make my way through a variety of huts. There are a few families in this village that have a hard time bringing food to their tables. It never seems fair for those people to go without eating. Rose hated it when I did this because I always gave it away for free, but I did it anyway. Everyone deserves to have enough food every day. Discretion is important, though, because everyone else might expect the same treatment.

With each door I knock on, the residents show me their gratitude by hugging me or giving me bread that they baked in return. Some offer to pay me, but I refuse it every time. I make enough at the eatery and I take pride in making sure my village is taken care of.

When I return to my hut, Jael is lying by the fireplace on the floor, relaxed and subdued with her hands clasped over her belly and feet crossed at the ankles. Since she's still in the all-black outfit and boots, she clearly came straight from the training grounds for supper.

"For the love of Halivaara!" she exclaims. "Took you long enough. I'm hungry."

"Glad to know you still expect me to cook for you." I smirk as I light the stove.

"I took care of you for ten years, Warrioress. It's your turn," she replies. "I'm growing old, you know."

When I was younger, I told her my parents called me Warrioress. As time went on and my parents never came for me, I wanted to feel like I was back home in Cal-léa. She calls me Warrioress as a way to reassure me that I am a strong, capable fighter. A warrior. Just the way I want to be.

"You're not even old, Jael," I respond. "But you have a point."

"Of course I do. I'm always right." Jael still comes across like a serious, unemotional, mean woman. This common assumption isn't helped by the fact that her hair is tied back so tightly it pulls her skin, creating a perpetually stern expression. But the people who know her, especially me, know she's actually a good person. She has a good heart and cares deeply. Otherwise, she never would have raised me.

The dancing flames of the fire reflect on the leather armband on her left bicep. It was one of the first things I noticed about her when I arrived in Ketra; it seemed fit for a warrior. A symbol of something grand.

"What?" she questions me.

I forget I'm staring at it and go back to making the fish and vegetable dinner. "Nothing," I say nonchalantly.

"I told you: you will only get it when I die." She nestles her head back on the floor.

She also said that to me when I first met her.

As I remove the Ocean Hake from the fire, I take a chunk and throw it on the floor for Bolt. He chomps it right up then points his beady eagle eyes at me, asking for more.

"Okay fine, here's some of Vincent's carrots, but that's it." I toss a few carrots at him and he immediately catches them with his beak. He saunters away on his bird feet, chewing in bliss.

When dinner is ready, Jael practically inhales the food when she doesn't take breaks between bites. "Wow. That bad?" I ask sarcastically.

"It's fine." She shrugs as if she's not impressed but it's accompanied by a sneaky side grin.

She always loves my cooking; she can't fool me.

"Well, I took care of you. I think a foot rub is well deserved," I hint, laying my foot on her lap against her will.

"Sore feet is evidence of hard work," she comments. "You need to learn to live with it sometimes."

"As if I don't already." Just to irritate her, I wiggle my toes next to her cheek. "I can do this all night."

"Sickening." Her lips curl in disgust. "Fine. If it will close that open hole in your mouth."

"Thank you," I singsong, lying back and letting her fingers smooth over my feet. Her strength proves she could flatten someone's body if she pressed hard enough. That bodes well for me when I need the knots worked out of my soles.

"Seems like Aria and Claeron are fond of each other," she mentions with a gagging motion. "I saw them sneak a hand-holding. Revolting."

I scoff. "I wish I knew what that felt like. Victor is hard to read. I don't know what to do."

Jael's hands slow down, her empathy making an appearance again. "Remember what I taught you."

"Let him initiate, I know. But, it's been a few months and he hasn't done anything."

"When he's more sure of himself, and of you, he will," she reassures me. "Besides, you're only twenty years old! Have some patience, child."

My lips lift deviously because I know she absolutely hates the question I'm about to ask. "What about you and Thaeus? Have you finally accepted that you have feelings for him that are more than just friendship? Are you just waiting for him to initiate?"

Jael glares at me, then playfully punches me in the stomach. I giggle when she says, "Don't make me throw your feet in the fireplace."

Her expression is irritated, but were she truly angry, her voice would match her face. I know her feelings for him are truly platonic, and he's secretly admitted to me the same about her—she's too intense for his gentle nature. Best friends suit them just fine. But I still can't stop from laughing at her response.

"We're best friends. And yes, he's the next chief of Ketra, but that's all," Jael declares in defense.

"Sure." I wink at her with a snicker as if she's overcompensating. She slaps the top of my foot but continues to massage my soles.

Drained from the day and relaxing to her massage, I'm nearly asleep by the time she finishes. "Off I go, I suppose," she says, dropping my foot like a sack of rocks. That perks me right up and gives me my cue to walk her out the door. With tenderness and love, she takes my face in her hands and kisses me on the side of my head, then departs as if she never showed a hint of affection. Jael isn't one to admit aloud she loves someone; she simply shows it in small doses. I learned to accept that at a young age.

Once I've cleaned up the kitchen, the last thing I want to do is bathe. At the same time, I loathe getting into bed dirty. While I groan in exhaustion and concede to my need to be clean, I set a pot of well water over the flames of the brick fireplace until it boils. It's a huge relief when I peel off my clothes and toss them by the steps leading up to the loft. With a large sponge and towel, I take my pot of water and bring it to the corner of the hut with a curtain for privacy. After rubbing a bar of soap with aloe and lavender on the wet sponge, I lightly dab myself, then squeeze out the excess water to scrub myself down.

Besides going to Ketra Falls at night, my way of bathing gives me time alone with my thoughts. People like Aria tell me repeatedly how relaxing a full bath is, especially after a hard day of work.

When Jael trained me, she covered me in wet cloths so I could get the relief of the cold for my muscles without the exposure to water. It was the same process when I needed heat. It was better than nothing, although I have craved to be submerged in hot water my whole life.

When I slip into my bed, the only thought that crosses my mind is that I'm not normal. I'm not what others would consider normal. I wonder what normal feels like. What being free feels like.

Despite the constant feelings I battle, I do appreciate Jael and all she's done for me. She truly became my mother when I needed her.

"Come on, come on," I hear a man's deep voice urging, and I feel someone repeatedly shaking my shoulders.

My eyes open into slits. The shaking stops and is followed by a womanly gasp, and someone sits. I open my eyes all the way. Nothing looks familiar. I'm not home. I'm not in my bedroom in Cal-léa. My parents are nowhere to be found. It's just me, two other people, and Bolt sitting patiently in the corner of what I think is someone's house.

Standing at the foot of the bed is a man with shoulder-length blond hair wearing a leather vest, linen shirt, and trousers. Next to him is a serious woman with hair tied tightly back, black V-neck shirt, black pants, and black boots. Her arms are folded, showing off a leather armband with a ruby on it wrapped around her left bicep. I shoot up straight in bed, breathing hard in rapid puffs.

"It's okay, it's okay," the woman says, calming me with her alto voice that breaks my attention away from her armband. She grips

me on the shoulder with a feather-light touch. "We're not going to hurt you. You're safe here."

I take in my surroundings. I'm in a wood and straw hut. The fireplace to my left has a roaring fire in it with a cast-iron pot hanging over the flames. I'm lying on the softest bed I have ever felt. There is some kind of loft above me that serves as a partial ceiling with stairs, although the bed I'm lying in is on the floor next to a window.

My breath doesn't slow and I shut my eyes tightly to think back to how I ended up here.

Mama taking me out of my room.

Her and Papa hugging me and crying.

Bolt carrying me as we galloped away from the chaos.

Cal-léa crumbling as we escaped.

The dread I felt when my parents sent me away comes back. They said they would find me. They should be looking for me now.

"Where are my parents?" I ask through oncoming sobs.

"We don't know," the man answers in some kind of accent and a deep voice. "You showed up to Ketra on a horse, and you weren't conscious. That's all we know."

Ketra. I'm in Ketra now. These people are from Ketra.

"They said they will come find me," I tell them. I want them to know I'm not going to stay here. "Mama and Papa said they will find me."

"Where are you from?" the woman asks directly.

"Cal-léa," I answer quietly.

They exchange a confused look for a moment, then turn back to me. "Why did your parents send you here?"

I swallow hard. I know Mama told me never to tell anyone who I am and what I can do, but they have to know what happened back in Cal-léa to explain why I'm here. "Backers," I squeak out.

They look at each other again, this time with very wide eyes. I don't know if it's because I said the word "Backers" or if it's something else.

"So it's true . . ." the big man whispers to the woman.

She adamantly waves her hand, dismissing whatever her friend is thinking. "Well, you're safe here," she says, clearing her throat. "This is my home. I'm Jael, the chief of Ketra. I'll be taking care of you. And this is Thaeus, Ketra's blacksmith."

"Hi." I wave at them both. Although I'm still scared for my life, I was still raised to be polite.

"What's your name, massy?" Thaeus questions.

Not blinking, I answer, "Havanna."

"Nice to meet you," his gruff voice responds.

My eyes dart back to Jael, who eyes me in return. With the way she's studying me, I'm some sort of journal with a secret code she's trying to crack. I feel myself sweating in nervousness.

"I suppose I should get out of your hair," Thaeus says as he steps toward the door. He's very tall and muscular—a giant, in my opinion. "Let me know if you need anything else."

"Thank you for your help, Thaeus," she calls as he exits the hut. Jael must notice my intimidated eyes following him because she leans in and says, "Don't worry. He's the only man in this village who's that big." I avoid eye contact with her. I'm not used to strangers asking me questions or staring at me. Jael hasn't smiled once since I woke up. "I noticed you looking at my armband." She points to it with her right hand. "You like it?"

This conversation went in a direction I didn't expect, but I feel myself growing more comfortable with her. I eye her armband again and nod.

"I got it as a reward after I finished training at Killios Training Camp," she explains. "A ruby means you're a trained warrior and an emerald means you're a novice. Once I was finished, Lieutenant Arthur sent me here." She peers down at it and fidgets with it. "It means a lot to me. I worked hard to get it." Looking back up at me, she adds, "Maybe you can have it someday. But only once I die."

I lightly chuckle at the idea. She seems a bit young to be talking about death. I don't see that happening to her any time soon.

"So, who are you, Havanna?" She changes the subject. She crosses her legs and arms with a grin. *I have difficulty understanding why she's asking this question. She and Thaeus saw Bolt carry me here.*

"What do you mean?"

"You have a lightning bolt on your hand and a tattoo on your arm." She points at my right arm. "None of those things can be washed off, which means you were either born with them or they were imprinted on you. Not to mention a horse brought you here and it changed into an eagle once we came in here."

In the corner of the room, Bolt ruffles his feathers at the mention of his eagle form.

Panic races through my veins. I didn't wear gloves when I left Cal-léa. I never wear my gloves to bed. It's the one time I can get away with it. My parents were in such a hurry to get me out they forgot about hiding my secret.

Jael furrows her brows at me and gives a hard stare. "Does the lightning bolt have anything to do with why your parents sent you here?"

I shake my head, denying anything she's trying to get me to say. Tears well up in my eyes, afraid that I'm going to end up dead soon. I scoot back to the head of the bed, as far as I can from her.

"It's okay, Havanna," Jael soothes me in her alto voice again. "It's okay to tell me. Since I will be the one taking care of you until your parents come for you, I need to know why you're here so I can make sure I do the right thing."

Out of nowhere, Bolt leaps onto the bed and caws angrily at her, and he's not quiet about it. She flinches, flustered at this sudden verbal attack, and pushes far away from him on her chair.

"I'll just tell her." I reach for him to calm him down. "I'll be fine." Bolt whips his head at me and tilts it to the side, like he's worried. "I'll be fine, bud," I repeat, petting him. He hops off the bed and back to the corner, satisfied with my answer, but never stops staring at Jael. When she explained it the way she did, it made sense. There should be no harm in telling her. I don't want to die, but I'm tired of hiding. I'm tired of not being able to use my powers.

"I'm the Lightning Descendant," I admit with a quiver in my voice. "I can control lightning, but I've never been allowed to use it. Mama told me it's because the Backers are looking for me and want to kill me. The Dormant King could be looking for me too, and I'm scared." Blubbering sobs escape me. "People have gotten hurt. And it's all my fault."

"Shh." Jael pats my hand consolingly. My tears soak into the pillow in my arms, but she doesn't seem to mind. Her initial cold persona has melted away. She lets me cry, softly shushing me and telling me everything is okay in a way a mother would.

Nothing feels okay. My life is falling apart.

Jael clears her throat. "You know, I grew up hearing the story about the Ancestors, the entity Halivaara, and the Descendants," she confesses. "It's a well-known legend in this land. When I was at the Training Camp, Lieutenant Arthur would send people to do research on the Dormant King and the Descendants. I didn't believe any of it was true, especially when Arthur wasn't getting any information on where they could be. But you proved me wrong, little girl." She takes my chin in her fingers and forces me to look her in the eye. "I will say this. I can assure you that none of this is your fault. None. This is the Dormant King's doing. Do you understand?"

I gulp down a lump in my throat, not sure what to do with myself. It's an unsettling, vicious circle that she knows who I am and my entire history, but I also feel better because I'm tired of hiding. She seems like she cares a lot about me, so I felt safe telling the truth.

Jael rises from the bed to stand in front of me. "With that said, I can guarantee that if you stay with me, you won't die."

I don't think she knows how to say things in a nicer way, but I also feel safer than I did when I first woke up. I still want to go home, though. I hope my parents are coming for me now. I miss them.

"Word of advice," she begins. "Next time someone asks who you are, don't cave so easily. Make them earn your trust first. If someone gives you what seems like a good reason for you to tell them who you are, hold back as long as humanly possible."

I feel disappointment sink in. From what she's saying, I'm not as free as I thought I would be. My parents tried giving me freedom by moving me, but that didn't change anything.

"Does this mean I have to keep hiding?" I ask, waiting for her to give me the answer I don't want.

"Without question," she states. "The Dormant King may still be at-large and we can't risk anything. Like I said, stay with me and you won't die." She moves to a dresser by the kitchen table. "You'll be kept on strict watch for a couple months."

"Why?"

Jael grabs a pair of fingerless gloves out of the dresser and turns back to me. "Standard process in this village. We don't want to risk it if you're a plant from someone else, like Backers. From what Arthur has told me, Backers are crafty in their search." She tosses me the gloves that plop onto my lap. "You will still need to cover up your hands."

I slide them on, though they could easily fall off with how big they are. The fingers in the gloves have gaps in them, but they'll do for now.

"I'll be sure to make you a pair that fits," she tells me. She puts her hands on her hips and grins again. "In the meantime, welcome to Ketra."

In the days to come, Jael shows me around, including where the compound is just in case the village is in danger or under attack. After that, I receive a full tour of Ketra. On the other side of the village, close to the vined entrance, a group of musicians play music for background noise. A flute, a ukulele, and a drum create a catchy melody that everyone passing by enjoys. It reminds me of the happiness of Cal-léa, and I grow homesick.

She brings me to the training grounds too. People use all sorts of weapons, whether to practice with someone else or against targets and dummies. Seeing everyone train reminds me of when Papa and I would practice in the backyard.

My parents still haven't come for me.

As Jael introduces me to more villagers, I run my fingers over each sword on one of the racks. Taking in the feel of the handles, the sharpness of the blades, the coolness of the different types of metal. I wish Papa were here to see this. I wish he were here to show me more techniques.

My hand stops at one particular sword, one that stands out in beauty and size among the others. A golden hilt with three rubies on it and a crown on the handle, engraved swirls on the blade. Something about it seems special, possibly because it's the only golden one on display, or there are rubies on it, just as Jael's armband has one.

Before I can grab it, she calls for me to follow her and I leave it behind.

Throughout the day and after supper, the training area calls my name. No, the sword calls my name. Since it's nighttime, I don't think anyone can see me.

I head straight for the sword, gleaming in the moonlight, illuminating its splendor. Slowly, I stretch out my hand, grab its handle, and raise it to the sky, watching the brightness of the moon scale the blade up and down as I swing it around me. The blade is lightweight, perfect for my body frame.

An idea gives me pause. No one is around. The alone time begs me to figure out at least one of my abilities.

I spread my legs and get into position to throw the sword at a target. Lifting it over my head, I thrust it forward, then immediately focus and attempt to use Gridlock with the aim of my hand. It stops for a split second before it bounces off the target and lands on the grass with a thud. Annoyed, I stomp over to the sword on the ground and back up again.

Instead of throwing it over my head this time, I use one arm and throw it. I lose the direction it goes and my focus slips. Three more times I try and don't catch it quick enough. No matter the amount of effort I exert, I can't seem to figure out how to make Gridlock work.

I wish Papa were here to teach me more sword techniques. I wish Mama was here to hold me. More than anything, I wish I didn't have to stay in this stupid village. I was happy in Cal–léa. Why are my parents not here yet?

All of these emotions swim around in my mind and all I can do is kneel to the ground and cry. I told myself that I wouldn't cry if I wanted to be a warrior, but this is too much. I feel lost, lonely, and homesick. Angry, I grab the sword and throw it across the grass as hard as I can.

"Be careful with that," a woman's alto voice speaks up behind me.

I spring to my feet and turn to find Jael standing below the incline that leads to the training area, arms crossed.

"I knew I'd find you here. You don't think I didn't notice you eyeing that sword?" She gives me a side smile. "That's the one I trained with years ago."

I examine her, trying to figure out if she's placating me with a smile but simmering with anger deep down, or if she's being genuinely kind. I don't know her well enough—at all, really—to know if she's about to do something scary or recall memories with her sword.

When I don't respond, she continues, "I take it you want to learn the ways of a sword." She gestures to the sword on the ground, a reminder of my pathetic attempt to use Gridlock. "I can teach you, if you wish. I don't have your abilities, but I may be able to help you with that too, away from watchful eyes. We can figure it out together." I stand enthusiastically as she steps closer to me, hands on her hips. "However, I must warn you, it's going to be tough. There are going to be times where you feel like you can't push yourself. It will be painful. Maybe even excruciating. You will have to learn to push past the pain. Do you think you can handle that?"

Pushing myself and being in pain should make me change my mind. I will probably cry and beg to stop. I will be extremely tired. And Jael is telling me it's going to be tough. To tell the truth, that doesn't stop me. I want to learn how to fight. If I'm going to battle the Dormant King and his Backers someday, then I need to be a trained warrior.

I puff out my chest and say with determination, "I want to be a good fighter. I want to be stronger."

Jael claps me on the shoulder, her brown eyes peering into mine. "Then I will help you with that."

CHAPTER 3

I can only assume my parents perished during the fall of Cal-léa. The pain of each day passing without seeing my parents eventually numbed, but I never stopped wondering what happened to them. The curiosity about their well-being haunts me every day, but I still can't leave Ketra, so that will remain an unsolved mystery burdening me forever.

By some miracle, Jael managed to keep my identity secret from everyone in the village, except Thaeus, who witnessed my Bennaru and the lightning bolt on my hand when I first arrived. It may have been easy for her, but it hasn't been easy for me to keep it from Aria. Sometimes, I feel intense anxiety over the possibility that I could blurt it out suddenly and get in trouble from Jael. Or get hunted down by Backers, if they still exist.

Over the years, Jael not only taught me the ways of swordsmanship, but also hand-to-hand combat. She told me if I ever lost my weapons or went without them, it's vital that I learn this method of self-defense. I now have full confidence I can fight the Backers and Dormants should they ever come my way.

I still use Jael's sword when we train together. I hope, one day, it will be mine to own instead of a weapon I borrow to practice.

The sword and her armband will be my way of carrying her legacy with me.

My bath leaves me feeling as refreshed and clean as one can be when submerging in a tub of water isn't an option. But I don't want to go to bed without my Twinkle Fireflies.

I go upstairs to grab my jar and make my way to the glorious Ketra Falls. Thick vines guard the waterfall and river, secluding it from the rest of the village like a bedroom in a hut. I move them to the side and it's as if a whole new world opens up. The small trickle of Ketra Falls creates a large puddle on a patch of sand. The Fireflies illuminate the space with their yellow light as they float gracefully. They make room for me when I enter, but still contain themselves in this small space. Palm trees and ferns provide leafy barriers from the rest of the village. The seclusion gives me a chance to be close enough to water to enjoy it without sparking questions from others as to why I don't get all the way in.

I open my jar and swoop it around, capturing the Fireflies to use as my night-light for later. I watch them dance in the jar for a moment after I close it, then I sit at the edge of the puddle, welcoming the ice-cold water that tickles my toes. That's as much exposure as my body can handle.

Though the flow from the waterfall is but a dribble, the sound of it echoes against the lush surroundings, creating a serene atmosphere in the otherwise still night that soothes my soul. I take a deep breath, close my eyes, and take it all in. The one place I can be alone with my thoughts.

Those thoughts go down a deep, dark hole as I reflect on how my friendship with Aria might be affected and how I felt when Darius taunted me. I appreciate that I have the skills to fight, but the disappointment I feel that I can't use Strike hasn't escaped me.

For many years, I've tried to accept that I may not be able to use it. The power itself tamped down when I willed it to, but my desire to use it never did. Besides, the Dormant King hasn't been seen in centuries and Backers have never made their way to Ketra. Using lightning just once shouldn't be a life-changing choice. I just want to *do* it.

Just once. Just to prove it's not unsafe. To prove I can live life.

The Ancestors were given their powers to protect their land. There's no point in being a protector of the land if I can't use the powers I was given. What good is Strike if I can't wield it? I'm tired of hiding who I am.

But who am I?

With a frustrated breath, I take my jar and head back to my hut. The irritated, negative thoughts further swirl in my mind. I want to do this. I've been obedient my whole life, and in this one instance, I'm done being obedient.

I turn in my path and look up at the tree-covered surface of Montanha Peak. If I'm going to do this, I need the lightning to be far enough away from the village so no one will get hurt. The peak is the perfect area to aim the bolts since no one lives up there.

I set the jar next to my feet and twist it into the dirt to keep it stable. I focus on the peak, raising my hand as sparks emit from it, tingling my skin. I keep my gaze on the sky as I take another moment to think twice about what I'm about to do.

It's a clear, warm night; this type of weather makes the occurrence of lightning unlikely and therefore, this may not be a good idea. This could change the dynamic of everything. After hiding my power my entire life, I'm finally going to bring it to light. This might be a life-or-death matter, and I'm dangerously toeing the line between the two.

Will this one chance be worth it?

I shake my head to erase my doubts. Yes. Yes, I can finally break free, find myself, and find out what I'm capable of. I no longer care if anyone outside Ketra sees it. I no longer care about hiding from Backers. I can fight them off if they find me.

A faint gold spot appears above the mountain, waiting for my signal with sparks poking out from it. I slowly stretch out my arm and focus on the peak, seeing if the lightning will follow the direction of my hand. The lightning mark on my palm lights up with the brightness of the sun, my palm hot to the touch but not so much as to do me harm. The glow begs me within the darkness of the clear night. I can't refuse it.

Now, I have to find the motion, or signal, to bring it down. No one told me what it was, so I'm left to my own imagination with this one.

First, I snap my fingers.

Nothing.

"Okay," I mumble to myself, then clap my hands together.

Still nothing. The bright spot in the sky still beckons me.

"This doesn't make sense." I examine my brightened palm. I just need to be creative in figuring out how it works.

Self-doubt clouds my mind when I flick my fingers at different paces and the magic still doesn't happen. Things seem to change, though, when I move my hand side to side. The spot in the sky shadows my motions. Gridlock works the same way. Once I freeze an object, it's a magnetic force attracting the two together.

Not all hope is lost. There's one more thing I can try.

On a deep breath, I swiftly bring down both my hands. In that moment, it became the most intense rush of emotions I've ever experienced.

Lightning crashes on Montanha Peak so hard that chunks of rock fly off and thunder booms through the night sky. The boulders roll down the mountainside, and I pray that there will be enough trees to stop them from moving into the village. I stare in amazement at what I just achieved. It was loud; there's no way it didn't wake up a few people.

The glow is still bright and alive. A soft vibration starts in the lightning bolt on my palm and scales up and down my arm. My left hand attracts the sparks stemming from my right, mending the power into a compact ball of energy. It gets bigger the longer I hold it, but the moment I constrict the space, it, too, shrinks in size. Maybe this is what my body has been aching to do—strike lightning and create it with my hands.

The smattering of palm trees behind me seems to be a good spot to throw this newly developed electric ball. Using the strength of my right arm, I throw the electricity toward the trees. The yellow ball speedily flies into the hanging leaves and explodes all the way down to the roots. It doesn't create any noticeable damage on the tree as much as lightning would have.

A shocked gasp escapes my lips as I examine my palms. The lightning bolt maintains its warmth. I feel liberated, but also exposed. It's been a few minutes, though nothing bad has happened, so maybe I truly don't have to stay hidden anymore. Jael's initial belief that the legend wasn't real might have some validity. Maybe the Backers and Dormant King don't exist anymore.

If that's truly the case, then the fact that my parents sent me to Ketra was completely meaningless. Which would mean my entire history was a complete lie. None of that is anything I want to believe.

"I knew it!" A loud whisper comes from nearby.

All the blood drains from my face and arms. Someone just witnessed *everything* I did. This may have been a terrible idea.

Aria marches at me, hugging herself tightly from the chill in the air. Her eyes blaze in anger and hurt. "I *knew* you were hiding something! I think I've known it all along, but this just confirmed everything!"

"Aria—"

"I'm your best friend, and not *once* did you tell me you had this . . . ability!"

"Aria, please," I whisper, holding a finger to my lips. "You need to be quiet!"

Her expression changes from hurt to realization when her gaze switches between me and Montanha Peak. "It all makes sense now. That's why you can't be in water."

Remorse runs through my veins and I don't know what to feel worse about: keeping my biggest secret from my best friend or disobeying Jael and blowing my cover. Both regrets fight for first place in my heart.

"Aria, come back to my hut and I'll explain everything," I reassure her. "I promise I have a good reason for this."

"You better," she says through clenched teeth. She grabs my arm tightly, nails digging into my skin. I resist her grasp as I bend to grab the jar from the ground and hold it close to my chest. Aria leading me to my hut reminds me of all the times I was in trouble and Jael wanted to discipline me out of the public eye.

She's about to give me a tongue-lashing.

"Havanna!" I hear Jael call in the darkness, her tone laced with fear and concern. "Havanna!"

Aria and I stop to watch as she storms over in our direction. She no doubt heard the thunder.

"We need to go." I push Aria toward my hut. My heart rate doubles as I turn her around and attempt to run from Jael's rage. "Go, go, go."

"Havanna, get back here!" Jael whispers as she catches up to me and twists me to face her. "Do you want to explain why I heard thunder just now?"

"Could be the weather." I shrug, masking my fear with nonchalance. "So what?"

"Havanna," she snaps, then points above her. "There are no clouds or rain, so either thunder happens when it feels like it or you just did something really stupid."

"So you think I did something stupid?"

Jael turns and sees Aria standing behind me. Aria folds her hands in front of her, twisting her body side to side and avoiding Jael's gaze. Her behavior tells Jael everything she needs to know.

Jael motions to her, holding back fury. "Does she know?"

My silence and guilty air answer her question. Years of secrecy and training wasted just because I wanted a few seconds of freedom. Those few seconds of freedom have only caused the two people I love most to be infuriated at me.

This was a very, very bad idea.

Jael steps closer to me in a fearsome way, a way that would scare the life out of a child. I know this tactic well. It used to scare me, but I became numb to it as I got older. Right now, though, that childlike fear is making a raging comeback.

"After all these years of protecting you," she seethes, finger pointed at my face, "you decide to put yourself at risk—"

"It's nighttime, Jael!" I shout. "I didn't hurt anyone!"

"The Backers could find you—"

"I haven't seen Backers in ten years!" I counter. "I'm *done* hiding. I've been hiding my whole life. You of all people know I've never had a chance to embrace who I am or what I can do. I'm done with this life. Besides, both you and my mother told me that one day the Descendants of the Ancestors will have to rise and fight the Dormant King. How can I do that if I'm hidden?"

Jael puts her hands on her hips and sighs heavily. She knows I have a point, but her expression is coated in worry. "I'm tired of having the same argument over and over again—"

"If the Backers happen to show up just because they saw me strike lightning, then I will fight them. I *can* fight, and it's because of you. I can protect you the way you've protected me all these years."

"This has nothing to do with your skills," Jael snaps through clenched teeth. "This is about making sure you don't end up being followed by these people. They're dangerous and they stop at nothing."

"How would you know that? From Arthur's research twenty or so years ago? We haven't seen Backers in years, and neither of us have ever seen the Dormant King! For all we know, the legend is fake! You said yourself you thought it was fake at one point. What if it really is?"

Jael's eyes don't hide the pure rage behind them. Huffing through her nostrils, she steps even closer to me until her nose is almost touching mine. "If you insist on doing something stupid like this," she replies, keeping her voice low, "then you'll pay the consequences. I never wanted that for you, but you don't seem to care. If you're done hiding, then I'm done having this argument with you." With a wave of her hand, she walks away, shaking her head. My stomach sinks knowing I let her down and that she thinks that I don't care.

She raised me and protected me, and I threw it back in her face with my impulsiveness, because I thought I knew better.

Once I'm finally able to move my legs, I turn around, where Aria stands with arms crossed, still angrier than I've ever seen her.

"I deserve answers," she states plainly.

"I know." I nod and motion to the direction of my hut. "But not here."

Aria is off before I can catch up to her. As I ponder all the questions she will most likely ask me, I peek at the sandy beach a few steps away lined with flaming tiki torches.

Two people stand by the shore. One claps the other on the shoulder with a magnetic smile. They're people I have never seen be friendly together, or have a civil conversation.

Victor and Darius.

My feet stop moving as I examine them. Last time I talked to Victor, he wasn't very fond of Darius because of his insufferable arrogance. I suppose it's possible they reached some kind of reconciliation.

"What are you looking at?" Aria barks.

Confused, I keep staring at the two boys, deciphering their facial expressions. It's too dark and they're too far away for me to hear what they're talking about. Victor made it sound like they weren't friends, yet they're behaving as such right now. Darius laughs at whatever Victor is saying, and something about the way he's laughing is . . . evil.

Something is very off here, but I have a more pressing issue to address.

"Nothing," I reply.

I catch up with Aria and enter my hut. She shoves me inside with a push on my back while she slams the door behind us. "Talk. *Now.*"

My heart pounds against my ribs and my hands turn clammy. "Okay. So, are you familiar with the legend of the Ancestors that were given elemental powers?"

She remains solid, glaring at me. "I've heard of it. But I thought it was just a legend, nothing that actually happened."

I sigh deeply before I continue. "It's not. For the most part any-way." For the first time in my life, I show her the lightning mark on my hand, no gloves present. "I'm a Descendant of the Lightning Ancestor. It's why I've been in hiding my whole life. It's why I was sent here from Cal-léa. It's why I have to wear gloves all the time. Backers were looking for me the night I left."

"And it's why you can't be in water," she repeats the fact to herself, still processing what she just saw. "You always told me you came here because your family wanted to relocate but your parents were killed on their journey."

"Yes," I whisper, ashamed of the lie I've let her live with. "But I don't actually know if my parents were killed."

"So, the legend is true," she says softly. "You're a Descendant who can control lightning—"

"And freeze things," I add.

Aria's hands go to her hips and she shifts her weight. "Excuse me?"

I point to the wooden ladle on the stove next to her. "Toss that ladle to me."

Brows knitted together, she cautiously moves to the stove and grabs it by the handle. Hesitant yet curious, she tosses it to me. I thrust my hand out and freeze it midair.

Aria's eyes go as wide as plates as she studies what's happening before her. My hand moves side to side, guiding the utensil.

"What the..." she whispers.

I break focus from the spoon and let it drop to the floor. She looks up at me in pure shock. I nervously shrug, uncomfortable with this entire situation.

"So, now you know." I take a seat at the dining room table.

She remains standing for a moment, still in a state of disbelief. All I can do is stare at my hands while giving her time to figure out how she wants to react.

"I get that you're mad at me," I add. "I'm sorry I hid it from you for so long."

Aria takes her time to sit at the table. "You had so many chances to tell me, yet you never did." Her voice is disheartened and hurt. "Why didn't you?"

"I was never allowed to!" I yell in deep frustration, holding out my arms in exasperation. "Jael didn't want me to tell anyone, *including* you! She was afraid that if I told you, you would tell someone else, and the whole village would find out, then it would get back to the Backers somehow and they would hunt me down."

"You should have known that you could trust me!" she yells back, pointing to herself. Then she slumps in the chair, deflated and even more hurt. "Especially with something that explains who you are, and that it's a life-and-death matter."

I choke back tears and lean in closer to her. "I wanted to. I wanted to *so* badly. You have no idea. But when a parent tells you to do something, and deep down you're truly worried you could die, then you just do what you're told."

"So, what was tonight? A rebellious move on your part?"

This is the other part of me I always wanted to talk to her about, but it was difficult to do without delving into the truth of my past. "I suppose you could say that. I'm so tired of hiding and being different from everyone else. I'm tired of being so cautious and careful with every move I make. I just wanted to do it once. Figure out what I *can* do."

Aria's tongue rolls over her teeth, arms folded in front of her, also trying to hold back tears. "I still wish you told me," she mumbles. "We're best friends. We tell each other everything."

"We are. And that will never change." I take her hand with my right. A tinge of electricity makes its way through my fingers and shocks her.

"Ow!" She jerks her hand away.

"Sorry." I cringe. "I'm still learning how this works."

Somehow, this gets her to giggle. Although a small one, it helps me feel better about our friendship. We might have a chance to still be friends. Go back to the way things were.

"Are we okay?" I ask, my face twisted in preparation for a negative answer.

Aria sighs and breaks eye contact. "I'm still mad, but I understand." She holds out her hand and motions for me to give her mine. I don't know what she's going to do, but I reach out again. She opens my palm and stares at the lightning mark that signifies who I am.

"It's actually incredible," she admits. "Being friends with a Descendant."

I wink in fake overconfidence. "Doesn't get better than that."

With another light laugh, she gets up from the table and walks around it to stand next to me. "Show me what you can do when you make electricity with your hands."

All the tension I felt about the possible sense of loss dissolves and my body relaxes. "Okay," I breathe out, standing and placing myself in front of her.

"From where I was standing, it looked like it threw you off," she notes.

"It did."

She motions to my hands with her chin. "Try it again."

Taking a deep breath, I bring my hands close together without them touching. I focus on the desire to create electricity and immediately, they warm up. My concentration intensifies and sparks come out of my right and meet my left. The electricity builds and melds into a small ball, just as it did the first time. Aria watches in wonder and awe, the shine of the sphere shimmering in her brown eyes.

"Your eyes," she whispers, leaning forward to take a closer look. "They change to a golden color."

Jael had pointed out the same thing when we first started training together. I never would have known it, as it never changed the color of the world around me.

I spread my hands apart until the ball is the size of a human head. Then as I close the gap, it's no bigger than a pearl.

"How do you get rid of it?"

"I don't know."

I play around with it, closing and opening my hands to change the size. Then I clap them together and the ball disappears. My hands are clear of volts and sparks, having been reabsorbed into my body.

"You . . . " Aria breathes out, stifling a dumbfounded laugh. "You're amazing!"

In astonishment, I can't help but respond, "I know."

✳✳✳

The next morning, I find myself deeply worried about Jael. Aria and I, on the other hand, are as close as we always were. It's the biggest burden off my shoulders that she now knows who I am. She ended up spending the night in my hut, sleeping on the sofa below my loft. She asked me to practice hand-to-hand combat with her again before starting her shift, so we headed to the training grounds and worked on some more techniques. Now that the target competition is over, it's not nearly as crowded as it was before.

It also means I won't have a chance to get sucked into Victor's charm as much.

At the eatery, Jael walks in and insists on talking to both of us in private. We glance knowingly at each other, presuming that this is about last night.

We lock ourselves in the tight quarters of the stockroom closet. Jael stands in front of us, and I can tell by the dark circles around her eyes that she got little sleep last night. For once, I finally had a peaceful night's sleep.

Jael keeps her voice as low as she can when she turns to Aria. "I'm assuming you know everything about Havanna."

Aria nods with confidence. "I do."

"Then I don't think I need to stress the importance of keeping her identity a secret from the rest of the village." Her voice is serious with the weight of this secret. "You. Must. Tell. No one."

"I know," Aria replies calmly. "She's my best friend. I would never do that to her. Or to you."

Jael breathes out a sigh of relief. "Okay. Thank you. If you see anything suspicious or worthy of note, come to me immediately."

"Yes, Chief."

"May I have a word with Havanna alone?" Aria gives my arm a quick squeeze of support, then leaves the closet. Jael eyes me again, annoyed but also regretful. "How are you feeling?"

I wring my hands together, slightly anxious about what she's going to say. "I'm fine."

She reveals a vulnerable side of herself when she releases a quavering breath, the uneasiness apparent in her stance. "I have to admit, Havanna, I'm afraid."

"Why? Nothing happened. We're fine."

"I'm just concerned that something *will* happen. I'm scared that all my years of protecting you will have gone to waste. If something were to happen to you . . ." She turns her back to me, hiding her emotions as she usually does. "I could never live with myself."

A part of me wishes she wouldn't worry. I imagine that if something were to happen, it would have happened by now. A delayed reaction to my disobedience wasn't something I pictured. At the same time, Jael being worried like this has me wondering if she has good reason to be.

I didn't tell her about Victor and Darius at the beach. It was a peculiar sight, but I can't imagine that whatever they were talking about was serious. There may be no point in drawing attention to it if they were making amends or something else of the sort.

"Just keep your eyes on everything around you," Jael tells me with warning laced in her voice. "It's possible that more people than just Aria saw what happened last night. It's best not to be too lax about this."

In the end, I still have to keep hiding. I still have to be careful of every move I make. In reality, using my powers made no difference in my search for freedom. But, as she said last night, she's done having that same argument, and so am I.

With a simple nod, we have an agreement.

***

Two days pass and life is back to the way it was. Although, it didn't stop Jael from having eyes on everyone and everything. All was well in my life, though. I trained, went to work, stopped at Tetia's potion shop for a bottle of Battle Elixir for sore muscles, dropped off leftovers at villager's homes, then I came home.

Nights in Ketra are typically quiet, but the unusual sounds of urgent shouting and overlapping commands wake me up from my sleep. Grogginess wants to put me back in a deep slumber until I hear a clear command that sends chills through my body.

"Jael! Get the Calling Conch!"

The Calling Conch is only for emergencies, and the last time it was blown, I was twelve years old. A pack of Winged Wolves and Swift Dingos had shown up looking for food. Swift Dingos are not to be dealt with lightly, due to their speed and sharp teeth. Fortunately, Bolt was able to turn into a gorilla to scare them off. The village chalked it up to some other predator chasing them away, but Jael and I knew the truth. I haven't heard the sound of the Calling Conch since. That was also the last time the village had to use Jael's underground compound.

Just as I get out of bed and peer through the window by the front door, I hear the drawn-out sound of the Conch. Soon after, yells, booms, and what sounds like a large, dying animal blend together in an awful noise.

I swing open the door. What I discover takes a moment for me to process.

Pieces of wood pollute the grass. Huts are up in flames. People are running amok for protection, or grabbing weapons to fight back whatever has invaded the village. I see a blur of people dressed in all white with masks that cover their entire head except the eyes, and what appears to be black ropes waving back and forth, sending fire and icicles everywhere. People are sent airborne and crash into already damaged homes.

This is what a nightmare looks like.

I grab the sword and shield that hangs on my weapon display beside the door and run toward the chaos.

"Havanna!" Jael shouts as she beelines to me with her bow and a quiver of arrows. A group of men in all white chase after her with two-foot blades that glow bright blue along the edges, the kind of weapons that appear innocent but are deadly in reality. These are blades of notoriety, of legend, of nightmares. Wasting no time, she equips three Pineapple Shell arrows simultaneously, and in a single movement, pulls back on the bowstring and shoots. The Shells explode on impact, emitting a yellow powder into the air. The nearby enemies lose their sight and stumble about with hands outstretched, trying to find their way among the smog.

Jael turns back to me. "You need to get to my compound, *now!*"

"Who are those people?" I ask in a panic. "What's happening?"

"Everything I feared." There's no mistaking the dread in her voice. "The Dormants and Backers have resurfaced."

My stomach drops. Guilt consumes every cell of my body, blood draining from my face down to my feet. The very thing my parents and Jael warned me about my whole life is coming to a head. The Backers likely saw the thunder I created and it aroused suspicion. How the Dormants came back to life, I have no idea.

This is all my fault.

I have to fight back.

I take off in a sprint, leaving Jael to call after me. As I run, I feel a nudge on my bum and I'm midair for a second before I land on the back of a horse that I know is my Bennaru.

"Thanks, Bolt!" I call out. He takes off in an all-out gallop while I ready my sword. "When I say 'now,' you buck."

Holding onto his mane, I steer Bolt toward the Dormants. There are too many of these horse-sized monsters, and specks of white are all over the place.

We're outnumbered.

The way my mother described the Dormants to me as a child is accurate. Black bodies, bright red eyes, a mane of tentacles around their neck, and razor-sharp fangs line their grotesque, evil mouths. And right before my eyes, they're destroying my home.

I'm going to kill every single one of them. No matter how much strength it takes.

"Now!" I give my cue to Bolt once we get close.

Bolt bucks me off and sends me high in the air. In flight, I take the hilt in both hands and aim the blade downward. I stab a Dormant in the back upon landing, killing it instantly. To my surprise, it turns to dust and coats my skin in an ashy, gray color, temporarily blurring my vision.

The other Dormants let out high-pitched screams and swing their tentacles toward me, icicles and fire flying in my direction. I flip and roll to avoid the projectiles. I parry an icicle with my shield and it bounces back at the Dormant, stabbing it in the chest and killing it. I deflect a ball of fire and it burns another. I swing my sword, shield still at the ready, cutting off tentacles and dealing killing blows between the eyes. Dust swirls around me as a sign of terminated Dormants.

A Backer appears in front of me with his sword. He swings at me, its shimmer leaving a streak of light in its path. With the way my collarbone immediately hurts and stings, I know he struck me. The warm trickle of blood streams down to my shirt.

Pain waits for no one.

From the corner of my eye, a Dormant whips a tentacle at me. I kick the Backer in the chest and backflip, just missing the tentacle's attack and sending the Backer to the ground.

Upon landing, I stretch out my hand and use Gridlock on the Backer. I shove him toward a hut, wood crashing on him as he falls. I turn and use Gridlock on two other Dormants. While maintaining eye contact with them, I spin and slash. They collapse as soon as I break focus, then they burst into clouds of dust. I spin my sword so it faces backward and thrust it behind me, stabbing another Dormant.

I run through the village searching for anyone needing rescuing. Pineapple Shells continue to detonate around me, just as they did the night I left Cal-léa. The ear-piercing, gruesome screams of those awful monsters blend in with the war zone the village has turned into. The traumatic noise of it all seems never-ending.

A cracking noise comes from my left and I see a palm tree falling in the direction of an encounter up ahead.

It's heading straight for Aria and a Backer she's fighting.

I dive and tackle her to the ground. The tree misses us, but not the Backer.

"Thank you," Aria breathes out.

"Go, get out of here!" I urge. "Get to the compound!"

"What about you? You need to get to the compound too!"

With everyone shouting around me, Backers invading the village, and Dormants attacking my people, I'm far from done here. I can't hide and let the few trained people we have fight an outnumbered battle. It doesn't sit well with me.

I spent half my life preparing to be a warrior, so I'm going to be a warrior.

"Not yet," I answer. "I'll be fine."

"Havanna—"

"Go!"

With incoming Dormants running in our direction, Aria takes off in a sprint. When I turn around, five Dormants encircle me, predators trapping their prey. They extend their tentacles, the tips opening like a blooming flower, ready to kill.

In a swift motion, I spin in a circle and use Gridlock on all of them. They freeze in place before they can use their tentacles. I spin again and slash at them. They break out of Gridlock and turn to dust.

"There she is! The Lightning Descendant!" I hear a familiar male voice announce, so familiar it has to be someone who lives in this village.

When I turn my head, I see a crowd of white with glowing swords at the ready; the one leading them to me brings me the ultimate shock and betrayal. Air and words get trapped in my throat, and an ache forms in my heart.

Victor, along with Darius, dressed in all white but no masks, charge at me with other Backers. His sparkling brown eyes—ones that, at one time, captured my heart—meet mine with a smidge of guilt. Darius is the epitome of a devious, sinister traitor when he smiles at me, opposite of Victor's behavior.

The betrayal hits me hard. In a place where I felt I knew everyone, I've been lied to by the only one I had romantic feelings for.

It all makes sense now. Why he came to this village and played the innocent traveler turned resident. Why he showed me attention and befriended me. He was searching for a Descendant and gradually observed everyone in the village for his target. He saw me use thunder, likely from the beach. Which explains why I saw him and Darius together, plotting my demise behind my back.

Those awful, despicable snakes. They deserve nothing but the worst of suffering, and I plan to inflict that on them.

Bolt saves me when he comes over in the form of a gigantic gorilla and sends them all into the air. He thumps his fists on the beaten earth and roars in triumph. I take that moment to get up and run.

I head to Jael's compound where most of the villagers are seeking shelter. Thaeus motions for stray villagers to get inside and guides them down the steps in a hurry. A villager trips and falls, crying with the fear of imminent death when the pounding of Dormant feet chase after her. I whip out my sword and cut off its tentacles, then finish it with a stab in the chest. The villager stumbles to get back on her feet and makes her way down the steps into the compound.

"Havanna, get in here!" Aria cries at the top of her lungs, the tears of fear evident in her voice.

"I need to help everyone get inside!" I scream back.

As I continue to guide people to safety, I see Jael up ahead on horseback, shooting arrows at Backers and Dormants, killing them on impact.

"Go help Jael, massy! I'm fine over here!" Thaeus commands.

Without responding, I make my way to her. As I run in her direction, a tentacle swipes her clean off her horse. She lands with a thud on the dirt, not failing to hide the pain as she lays a hand on her ribs.

I don't have much time before she gets attacked again. We're still swarmed.

Before the Dormant can do anything else, I thrust out my hand and use Gridlock. I know my focus on the frozen Dormant won't last long as the pain in my head grows. I narrow my eyes, keeping it in place until I get close enough to drop on the ground and slide toward it. I slash it in passing and the Dormant collapses before turning to dust.

"Good girl," Jael grunts out when she gets back on her feet.

Everything after that happens in a blur.

Jael, peering over my shoulder, sees something that makes her face go from war-ready to scared out of her soul.

"NO!"

She shoves me to the ground with such force that it knocks the air out of me. As I move to get back up, all I hear are the sound of footsteps and a pained grunt from Jael. That is, until I look up, and see a Backer standing in front of her, his glowing blade protruding from her torso.

I draw out in an agonizing scream.

I don't feel myself crying. I don't notice the tears streaming down my face. Bile rises in my throat while the rest of my body and emotions go numb.

My brain struggles to process what I'm seeing.

A Backer just killed Jael.

My confidant.

My mother figure.

My best friend.

I watch as the Backer pulls his weapon out of Jael and her body thumps to the ground.

I'm no longer numb. I'm angry. It grows in the pit of my stomach and converts into a boiling rage that climbs up my throat. I have never felt fury like this in my life, and it's about to be unleashed in a way I have never experienced.

First my parents, then Victor's betrayal, and now Jael. I've lost the most important people of my life because of the Backers.

Because of the Dormant King's goal.

The attacker turns to me, his weapon hanging by his side. His hungry eyes have one objective: get the Lightning Descendant.

Over my dead body.

The next moment is a blur. I release a scream, as much as my throat can muster before it feels ripped to shreds. The Backer hunches over and covers his ears from the bloodcurdling sound. My whole body tightens and looses all the energy I have, building enough tension in my temples that my head could explode. I don't know what's going on around me, and I don't care—I don't care if the whole world knows who I am now.

Still combining all the energy in my body to my vocal cords, I raise my hands to the sky. They're on fire from the sparks emitting from them, so hot it might burn my skin. I hear the crackling in the sky, ready for my cue. It's much, much noisier than it was the other night, but my eyes are closed, and I don't know what it looks like. Thaeus takes Jael's body and scrambles into the compound so they don't get hit with what's coming.

I swiftly bring down my hands and a huge lightning storm rains upon the entire village. The strong bolts punch holes in the ground, start more fires on the broken wood of homes, and kill every Backer and Dormant left. All I care about is knowing every enemy in this village has experienced my wrath, including Victor and Darius.

Finally, I open my eyes to blurred vision, my head still throbbing in pain. I smell the smoke from burning wood and grass, and the earthy scent of ash. The Backer that killed Jael is now dead. All is quiet with the exception of the hisses and sputters from the fires. Now I see I caused even more damage, though I'm too overwhelmed with grief to give attention to it.

Thaeus steps back out of the compound with Jael's limp body in his arms, eyes red and brimmed with tears. He lays her next to me, then kneels beside her. She's breathing, although strained. I can feel the vomit rising, despair and agony aching throughout. My body is depleted as if I were battling an illness, and the splitting, blinding headache behind my eyes begs me to go to sleep. I push my physical limits even more when I crawl to Jael's body with tears streaming down my face.

"Jael. No no no no no. I'm sorry, I'm so sorry . . ."

She weakly raises her arm and places her hand on my heart. "Go," she croaks. "It's . . . time. Find . . . the Dormant King . . ."

Her words sink in as I break down in a sob. She's giving me permission to stop hiding. She's giving me what I yearned to have my whole life.

"Find yourself . . ." she whispers, "Warrioress."

I haven't cried like this since my parents sent me to Ketra. I refuse to accept that Jael is dying in my arms. This can't be real. I have to be in a horrible nightmare. I'll wake up tomorrow and she'll be alive. She'll tell me everything is fine and she will still be Ketra's chief.

"I will," I finally manage to reply.

As I go back to repeatedly whispering my apologies, her hand slides off my chest and her light is extinguished. The one person that meant the world to me, that gave her life for me, is now gone.

The villagers emerge from the compound, surrounding Thaeus and me as I hold Jael's body in my arms. I feel Thaeus's big, strong arms wrap around me from behind, his body shaking with sobs. Everyone else watches, grieving in their own ways at the loss of their beloved chief.

My body slumps over hers, shaking with my own sobs. Warrior or not, I wail as much as my head and throat let me. I cry because I've lost my best friend. I cry because I will have the burden of grief and guilt hanging over my head for the rest of my life. I cry because life won't be the same without her. I cry because I've lost more important people in my life than I should have. And I have no one to blame but myself.

I close my eyes, and I remember nothing after that.

CHAPTER 4

I wake up lying on a cot covered by a tall, white canvas tent with two other cots and piles of clothes scattered about the area. My whole body feels drained of all energy. I'm still tired, my hair is stuck to my neck, and my body hurts all over, including my collarbone area where I was struck. I lift the bandage covering the cut and see the familiar pink hue of the Healing Salve made of crushed Pom Fruit, honey, and the strong, pungent smell of mint. The cut has already started to heal, which means the salve is doing its job. I recall having this treatment whenever I got hurt during training.

I press the bandage back into place and groan. The heavy humidity in the tent begs my eyes to shut and keep sleeping, but the urge to get up and see how the village is doing is stronger.

The tent flap opens as I rise out of the cot and Vincent stomps inside. His lips are a thin line, the expression that tells me he wishes I never woke up.

"How are you feeling?" he asks me flatly. His demeanor creates a nervous, nauseous feeling in the pit of my stomach.

"Exhausted." I groan as I rub my temples. My voice is raspy and squeaky from how much I put my throat through. "How long have I been sleeping?"

"Two days."

I thought I would wake up feeling more refreshed after two days. Maybe this is my body's way of processing grief along with muscle fatigue.

"How's everyone doing?" I ask.

Pressing his lips together with an expression of disappointment, he steps back and opens the flap. "See for yourself."

My arms are weak when I flip off the covers clumsily and step one foot at a time out of the cot. My legs are wobbly from lack of energy when I attempt to stand. Vincent waits for me with the tent flap still open, glaring and making no moves to help me. His current view of me is upsetting; it worries me that everyone else will glare at me in the same way.

I scan the state of the ruined village. What used to be a piece of flat, open land filled with beautifully designed huts and businesses is now an expanse of wood-covered grass with only a few huts that took little damage. The villagers drag their feet while picking up the remains of what used to be Ketra.

Disapproving looks are the only thing I am greeted with as I saunter through the ruins. Ibarra, with a stack of wood in her arms, stares me down with the anger of a thousand suns and uses more force than necessary to push me aside with her elbow. I watch her as she trudges away, shocked at the change in attitude of the people.

"Victor and Darius were found dead this morning," Vincent informs me under his breath. "They're quite bitter, along with the fact that you and Jael have been hiding your identity all these years. Me and Thaeus are the only ones that don't hate you right now."

"You certainly *seem* to hate me."

"I may be angry, but I don't hate you."

My stomach falls in despair. I didn't consider how everyone would figure out what I was capable of and how easily that could spread among travelers if given the chance. Jael spent years making sure that would never happen, and yet I cut it all down in the blink of an eye.

We stand side by side, staring out in the distance as everyone cleans up the mess. "So what keeps you from hating me?"

Vincent sighs and turns to face me, stoic and cold. "Because I understand why she hid it."

The moment he turns back around and walks away from me, I bring my selfish, defeated self back to the tent. And I don't hold back the tears that follow.

***

The villagers stand at the beach, surrounding a wooden plank that holds Jael's body; she's wrapped in canvas and draped with blue orchids and vines. I maintain my distance as Aria and the rest keep one eye on their beloved chief and the other on me. As Vincent delivers the eulogy through tears and a quivering voice, Aria shoots glares in my direction, ones that say, *"This is all your fault."*

Nothing I haven't already felt myself.

The hatred the villagers feel toward me is palpable despite the frequent sobs and sniffles. Vincent's words are drowned out by my wondering how I can make things right for the people I love. Little do they know that I'm just as angry with myself as they are with me regarding Jael. But I can't find it in me to regret striking down Victor and Darius. The only emotion I feel in that regard is pure numbness.

But here, right now, seeing the one I viewed as my mother lying dead on a plank, ready to be sent into the ocean as a final farewell, is an out-of-body experience. The last time we had a funeral, it was for Rose. Although that was awfully depressing, the hole left in my heart pales in comparison. Now I understand what Aria was feeling when she lost her only parent and how alone she felt.

"Loving leader, strong fighter, devoted mother," Vincent concludes his speech, wiping his face. "You will be missed. Rest with the sea, Chief. And may you give strength to our new chief, Thaeus."

Everyone forms the letter *K* with their fingers and places it on their hearts after Vincent's speech. Two men crouch on either side of the plank and push it over the wet sand into the water. We watch as it floats along the waves, drawing her farther and farther away from us.

I give way to tears again, watching Jael disappear forever. I'm not ready to say goodbye. I'm not ready to figure out the rest of my life on my own. I don't have a choice, though, and that's the reality that rips me apart. I knew that one day I would have to, but because of the curse of old age. I never thought I would say goodbye to her this early in my life. I still need her.

Most everyone disperses after the ceremony, talking about the next steps on rebuilding the village, completely ignoring my presence and need for support. I stay on the beach a little longer, watching the plank shrink on the horizon. Thaeus walks past me, but not without patting my shoulder in consolation. I touch his hand in silent thanks before his footsteps recede to the village up the hill. Aria remains far away from me, unmoving, with the waves as the sole background noise. My heart breaks as she avoids my gaze entirely, fury evident in the crease of her brow. The realization that I have lost absolutely everything crashes down on me like a lightning bolt. Aria's been mad at me before, but over little things like forgetting to clean something at the eatery.

This, though . . . might not be something I can come back from.

The thought of living in Ketra, living in this sea of animosity and hostility, feels just as awful and dangerous as if I were thrown into a literal ocean. I would rather trade places with Jael. I've fallen in the abyss of sorrow and I have nothing but vengeance and rage toward the Backers, which ultimately should be toward the Dormant King. Those are the only feelings that drive me not to completely sink in grief. I only want to live to accomplish what Jael wanted for me in her dying words.

I need to make things right. For Ketra, for Aria, for Jael . . . and for myself.

I have to leave. Tonight.

It may not fix everything, but everyone needs to know how much I want to repair what I have destroyed. It will be the biggest and scariest thing I ever do. One that puts my life on the line. I only hope they understand what doing this means.

Ultimately, even if they don't, it isn't enough to dissuade me.

I'm going to kill the Dormant King.

***

I made it my mission to pack what I could from the rubble that is my home. Once I have everything, I'm going to tell Aria that I've decided to leave Ketra and put her in charge of the eatery once the village is back on its feet. Jael's dying planted the idea for a quiet departure in my mind, but everyone's reproach made the decision a little easier.

Among my debris, I manage to find a bag and stuff it with blankets, a tent, and the two pieces of parchment paper in my toppled nightstand. I hoped to bring my glass jar with me for my nightly Fireflies, but I found it broken on the floor. As if I couldn't be angrier and more depressed.

Get it together, Havanna. You're a fighter. You have to be strong. You can find another jar later.

Thaeus and Vincent don't know I'm leaving and I don't plan on telling them. I know they will try to talk me into staying, regardless of everyone's view of me. As my loyal best friend, I feel I owe Aria a goodbye, despite her current feelings.

By the time I'm ready with my pack, it's dark outside and most of the villagers have retreated to tents set up for temporary housing. I blend in perfectly with the all-black outfit I wore during my days on the training grounds. Bolt, loyal as ever, props himself on my shoulder as a mouse.

I attach a small lantern to the waist of my pants and walk toward the training area. The sword I grew up with—Jael's sword—stands upright on the rack, waiting for me as it always does. I wanted to take her legacy with me someday, no matter what happened to either of us. This sword will be a reminder of why I'm risking my life and what I'm fighting for. I wrap the strap around my waist and sling the sword behind me.

I stare at the patch of low-cut grass, dummies, and weapons one last time. Jael spent countless hours with me here, turning me into a warrior and a fighter. Practicing till my body gave out. Concentrating with Gridlock till my head could split in half. Feeling soreness so extreme I was sure my whole body would crumble.

And now I'm carrying those moments of wisdom and knowledge with me.

Upon walking to Aria's tent behind Thaeus's shop, I glimpse at the damage his building incurred. A few windows are broken, a few holes in the walls, the door is missing, and tools and weapons are scattered on the floor, but other than that, it's in better shape than most of the huts around here. I remember when I played hide-and-seek with the other children in the village when I was younger, and we tried to hide in his shop more than once. Thaeus always got annoyed and kicked us out since he didn't want anyone to get burned from the coal fireplace or injured from flying pieces of metal. He always had tables full of scrap metal and tools, and the walls were lined with things like knives, pickaxes, and other axes meant for training or chopping wood. It was a danger zone for children.

I reach Aria's tent and quietly sneak inside. The shuffling around of my equipment and pack makes more of a ruckus than I care for as I approach her, but she doesn't stir. I crouch to gently shake her shoulder. She shoots up and grabs the spear next to her cot, alarmed and prepared for anything else that's going wrong.

"Holy Halivaara!" I whisper. "Didn't mean to scare you."

"Geez, Havanna," she groans. "What are you doing here?"

Giving her a moment to wake up gives me a spot of time to figure out how I'm going to tell her what I'm doing. As it turns out, there's no easy way to get into it.

"I just came to say goodbye."

She stares blankly at me, eyes blinking furiously. "What do you mean, 'goodbye'?"

"I'm leaving Ketra to find the Dormant King."

Suddenly, she's alert and wide awake. "Hold on, hold on, wait a second." She holds up her hand to pause my sentence, then stands from the cot and closes the flaps of the tent to make sure our conversation is private. "Have you lost your mind?" she snaps with a harsh whisper. "You're just going to leave us all behind? After everything you've put us through? "

"Yes." I stand and face her. "Look around, Aria! All of this happened because I was selfish and tired of hiding. Everyone hates me for it, including my best friend." I choke on my words, the absolute throbbing sensation of this situation gnawing at me. "It's the only way to truly apologize for everything. Even if I die doing it."

Aria's eyes glisten as soon as I mention the possibility of death. "We have a business to run." She struggles to get out the words as emotion wells inside of her. "You need to stay. Everyone will move on from this eventually."

"Will *you*?" I counter.

She shifts her weight, uncomfortable and flustered. "I don't know. Maybe? You lured monsters to our village and our chief was killed. It's hard not to blame you."

"So you see why I have to leave?"

"But I never said you should leave. No one is telling you to leave. Running away isn't going to fix anything. You need to deal with the ugly part of this, and it will get better in time."

"Do you really think it's that simple?" I step closer to her, eyes piercing hers. "It's not as if I accidentally broke someone's plate. Lives were taken and *destroyed*." I point a finger at my chest. "There's nothing else I can do that can come close to making this better. Telling everyone how sorry I am isn't going to undo the damage. But leaving, risking my life, and solving the core problem might."

Aria nods angrily, eyes ablaze. "Okay. Fine."

She marches past me to a corner of the tent where she riffles through her things before pulling out a burlap sack. She throws it on the cot and shoves clothes into it.

"What are you doing?"

"I'm going with you. I may be mad at you, but I never said I wanted you to risk your life."

"You're not going anywhere," I scold, tossing the bag off the cot.

"Says who?"

"Says the one who can freeze you in place," I threaten through clenched teeth.

"Threatening me with your powers? How mature!" She sets the sack back on the cot. "I'm going with you whether you like it or not."

"I have to do this alone!" I protest with a stomp of my foot. "Aria, I can't be responsible if something happens to you under my care. I wouldn't be able to live with myself." I turn away slightly and mumble, "I can barely live with myself now."

Aria folds her arms and exhales harshly. With no response from her, she knows I have a point. And the barrier she fiercely built between us is crumbling.

"I have *no one*, Aria."

This statement hits her like a stone to the head when she sits on the edge of the cot, attempting to hide her tears.

"I know whatever waits for me out there is life-threatening, but I don't care anymore. This is what's best for everyone." I lay a hand on her shoulder. "Besides, when the eatery is up and running again, I'll need you to run it."

She wipes stray tears on her long-sleeve sleep shirt. "And how long do you think you'll be gone?"

This question ran through my mind numerous times before now, but always with no answer. This could be a simple search that leads me right to the Dormant King or it might take more effort to find him. Either way, it will take time. "I don't know."

A sob escapes her as she buries her face in her hands. Tears fall down my cheeks as well, knowing that this is it. I'm leaving Ketra behind. Leaving Aria behind.

I may not live to see either one of them again.

"Take care of yourself," I whisper to her in a quivering voice.

When Aria says nothing in response and continues to hide her face from me, I know that's my cue to leave. I slowly back up till I hit the flaps of the tent, then open them to step outside, but not before I look back at her one more time. She does everything she can to avoid seeing me leave. I imagined this to play out differently. Maybe come to some sort of reconciliation and soften her heart. It's still guarded, although not as rigid as it started out. At the moment, I can't change that. With that realization, I release the rest of my sobs quietly on the way across my ruined home.

To avoid anyone catching me, I hide behind tents as I cut through the village on my way to the vined entrance of Ketra, eventually leading to the Dark Woods. Even though all the equipment I'm carrying is making noise, I seem to be able to make a smooth escape. The torches that normally illuminate the village are few and far between. Instead, the beaten earth pathways are littered with dim lanterns and makeshift tents.

I can't help but remember when Jael showed me around when I got here. I thought she was the meanest person I'd ever met, but she turned out to be just the opposite. The reminder causes tears to sting my eyes and takes everything in me not to succumb to them again.

"Where do you think you're going?" I hear a deep, commanding voice ask as a large hand grabs my arm and pulls me behind a tent.

Thaeus stands a few feet in front of me, eyes boring into mine when I turn to face him. He's normally a fun-loving, compassionate man, but right now he's mad. I don't see him like this very often, but it scares me a little when he is, just because of his overpowering size.

"I'm leaving."

"Over my dead body you're leaving," he growls.

"I have to go," I reply softly. "For Jael, and for Ketra."

"As the chief, I can't let you do that," he admonishes me, stepping forward.

"No one is going to stop me. Even you." My voice quivers when I point my finger at him, then gesture to the village around me. "All of this cost me the only family I had left. So I'm going to do what she told me to."

"The damage has been done, Havanna!" Thaeus raises his voice to a whispered shout. "There's nothing else we can do but to move forward. Leaving is not the answer. You've been hiding here for the last ten years for a reason. You may not make it out alive."

"Come on, Thaeus, have some faith in me."

"I do, but you need to understand how dangerous this is—"

"I don't care anymore. Jael is dead because of me. Aria is angry with me. The village hates me. There's no reason for me to stay."

Thaeus steps closer and grabs my arm again. "You can't go." His shoulders sink, crushed and downhearted. "I can't lose two good friends."

"At least I'll die knowing I tried to make things right." I turn away from him and head toward the vines. "I'm doing this."

Thaeus grabs my elbow and pulls me back. "Havanna—"

I unsheathe my sword and point the tip of the blade at his chest. "Don't make me fight you," I threaten him through clenched teeth.

Thaeus removes his own sword strapped to his back and aims it at my neck. "I'll fight right back, massy."

Unmoving, I watch how unsteady his grip is on his sword, then look back at him. His tough, manly stance does little to shield his trembling body and breath. The dilemma to take this further is written all over him. He has the strength to hold me back, no matter how skilled I am with and without weapons.

But I have to leave, no matter what he says.

"Thaeus," I say in a low voice as my hand vibrates and warms with electricity. I hold up my now-brightened palm. "You saw what I can do with just this. Don't make me use it on you."

His eyes shift between me and my hand. His throat lurches with a hard swallow as he holds back his own emotions. This vulnerable side of him awakens the vulnerability in myself again and my eyes well with tears once more.

"Please," I beg in a soft, quaking whisper.

Thaeus never takes his eyes off me when he wordlessly lowers his sword. His body relaxes while his breathing evens out, tongue rolling over his teeth in a silent protest. The glow in my hand reabsorbs into my body.

"Follow me," he grunts. "I have something for you."

He turns and expects me to follow his lead when he walks to his shop, but I stay in place. He may have a soft heart, but it doesn't mean he doesn't have another plan to stop me or an ulterior motive. When he sees I'm not following him, he turns and rolls his eyes. "It's not a trap, massy. Just follow me."

Sensing danger, Bolt emerges from my pocket. His mouse arms expand into wings in spastic motions; feathers pop out all over with a *poof*, his head and body fitfully fighting against itself to grow into an eagle body; muscles and bones bulging and fighting to find its rightful place under his skin. His mouse feet quiver before the bones and muscles grow bigger, talons springing out from scaly legs.

Fully converted, his feet waddle close to me, questioning Thaeus's motives with a tilt to his head. I don't know what Thaeus wants to give me, but he has me curious. Even if he has a plan to trap me, Bolt will hear my call and come to my rescue.

"Stay here, I'll be back," I command Bolt in a relenting tone as I follow Thaeus.

He leads me back to his tent, located close to his shop. It has tables set up inside and covered with a variety of scraps, but what he picks out from among the pile takes me by surprise. It was the first piece of jewelry that I noticed when I woke up in Ketra.

Jael's ruby armband.

"I kept it when her body was being prepared for the funeral," he tells me. "Given what it means and how much you wanted it, it seems natural to pass it down to you."

I take the band in my hands and examine it. The ruby, like all the gems we have in the village, came from a faraway city called Arythica, the gem capital of the kingdom and city of the wealthy. It was her reward, but it's also worth a lot of money.

The leather has many years of wear on it, but still intact. I smile at the memory of when I first laid my eyes on it, and how pretty I thought the ruby was. Plus, the way she wore it made her look like a true warrior, which is exactly what I wanted to be.

You can have it only when I die.

Her words, repeated over time, ring freshly in my mind. Little did I know I would lose her this early in my life.

"Here, I'll put it on for you," Thaeus offers, taking it from my hand. I offer my left arm and he ties it around my bicep, just tight enough that it doesn't slide down. "Perfect." He gives me a side grin. "Couldn't have found a better person to wear it."

I examine the new accessory that complements the rest of my outfit as it catches the light of the moon and dim lantern. "Thank you," I say gently.

My eyes lift up to an object on the table, igniting my mind with ideas.

An empty glass jar sits in the middle. A new home for my Fireflies. I already know I will crave having my jar next to me when I sleep, even if I will be in a tent in the woods. The jar is dirty, but it's in solid shape, and that's all I care about.

I step around Thaeus and grab it. It's the exact size of the one I had. I imagine the Fireflies floating around in their colorful splendor and I'm desperate to chase the feeling of security I used to feel when I watched them.

"Can I take this?"

A baffled Thaeus quirks a brow, but he doesn't ask questions. "Sure, I suppose," he says. "No one's claimed it so far."

I take my pack off my back and find room for the jar. I may be hesitant to believe I will find the Fireflies anywhere outside my usual space in Ketra Falls, but I want to be prepared just in case I do run into them.

Thaeus breathes out the burden of feelings consuming him. "Are you absolutely sure about this?"

My eyes rest on my pack after I close it up. "Yes. I'm sure."

He nods and veers his gaze elsewhere. His tough-guy outer shell is crumbling by the second, but his offer to give me an out is one I can't accept.

"At least allow me to walk you out," he says after clearing his throat and sniffling.

We leave his tent and walk in silence to the vined entrance. As we get closer, I realize how much of the world I haven't seen. I was able to get a glimpse of it every time I ran to the top of Montanha Peak, but I never truly knew what to expect if I ever left Ketra. All the creatures and Dormants that await me give me anxious nerves that claw at me with unrelenting strength, but I press onward.

Thaeus and I face each other once we arrive at the vines, both of us hesitating to say goodbye. This has been my home for ten years. It's the home that gave me what I needed when I needed it. Now, I'm leaving it to save Ketra and all of Petros. A daunting task.

"You're always welcome to come back, massy, you hear?" Thaeus says, patting me on the shoulder.

With pinched lips, I wrap my arms around his neck. He returns the hug and holds me tightly for a long time, years of history and the unknown future standing between us. I don't know when I will be back, and that scares us both. He was the second friend I ever made, just behind Jael. He always tried to make me feel I had a place in this village and I came to love him like an uncle.

I pull away from the embrace and take him in one last time: the scruff of his blond beard, his shoulder-length blond hair tied back into a ponytail, the musky smell of his leather vest that sits over a linen long-sleeved shirt, and dirty trousers with scuffed boots. He looks exactly the same from when I first met him when I was ten years old.

"Take care of Ketra, okay?" I pat his shoulder. "You're the chief now."

He lets out an apprehensive sigh. "I will."

Reluctantly, I turn around and move the vines to the side, ready to enter the tall trees and shade of the Dark Woods. Bolt scuttles to the other side and waits for me. Just before I step through, I regard

Thaeus one last time. Mouth turned up in a small smile, he forms a *K* with his right hand and lays it over his heart, topping it off with a curt nod of approval. The lump in my throat comes back, but I swallow it down when I repeat the gesture. This doesn't make it any easier for me to leave, but knowing I have to do this drives me to follow through.

The darkness of the woods is so thick, I can barely see a foot in front of me. The lantern on my waist and the moonlight shining in the open gaps of the tree canopy provide little assistance. Bolt's perfect night vision allows him to go on waddling ahead. He softly caws every minute to guide me through the gloom.

Stopping to look at my map, I take the lantern from my waist and hold it directly over the parchment paper. From what I can see, I need to go straight through the Dark Woods, then I'll hit Belt Canyon, with Alberi Jungle beyond that. Within the Alberi Jungle, Bena Lake feeds into Barto Lake below it. I'm curious what these places look like. The only reference I have is the flat drawings of the map.

All I cared about was leaving to find the Dormant King, but I didn't consider where my first destination would be simply because I don't know what to expect at each establishment. I'm not familiar with any other style of life except that of Ketra's. The Dormant King could be hiding within a town, a forest, or underground with the other Dormants. Or he's invisible and can evade anyone searching for him.

Perhaps I need to start with the next closest place that's considered civilization. Past the jungle, that place is Siro.

The deeper I go into the woods, the more nervous I become. My first time ever coming out of hiding and the first place I end up is the forest of no light. Excellent plan on my part.

Remember why you're doing this.

My breathing goes from even to shaky. I move further through the darkness; the crunching of branches and leaves beneath my feet the only sound piercing the quiet air.

Until I hear pattering footfalls accompanied by the unmistakable echo of a branch snapping in the near distance.

Immediately, I unsheathe my sword and hold it in front of me. Eyes as wide as an owl's, heart racing, my whole body sweating, I move forward, hyperaware of my surroundings. Up ahead, I see an opening—an entry of sorts to the other side of the forest.

The movement within the trees starts up again and has me trembling in fear. I make a run for it, straight to the opening, sword still in hand. Eventually, the sound stops, which makes me even more afraid because that means whatever it is is *close*. I speed up, my legs already cramping. With all the years of training, running up and down Montanha Peak, jumping through obstacle courses and rock climbing, I'm used to the gradual ache of exercise.

Once I reach the opening, I run through it and stop at a reddish-colored rock cliff above a narrow Belt Canyon, thick vines spread around the cliffside like veins. Alberi Jungle is littered with palm trees and ferns here and there among the tall grasses. In one of the trees across the canyon is a large Rainbow Hawk, adding beautiful colors to the large leaves surrounding it. Rushing water, heavier and larger than Ketra Falls, brings a calming ambience.

Attempting to jump across Belt Canyon will surely lead me to broken bones with its depth being extremely far below. Bolt stands in front of me and leans forward, offering a solution. I climb on his back and he lifts off the ground, gliding for a few seconds till we reach the greenery. I slide off him and step further into the jungle, taking in my surroundings. The cliffs below resemble a set of stairs, huge waterfalls feeding into the lakes on each step. The air is calm, clean, and relaxing. The kingdom of Petros opens up to me in a grassy expanse, stretching out for miles and miles.

A grayish-brown plot of dimly lit land—another village or city—stands out in the field. According to the map, it must be Siro.

Even further in the distance, a barely visible spot of illumination on the horizon catches my attention. It looks so tiny from where I stand, but I know that it's not.

It's Cal-léa.

I haven't been there since I left it while it was falling apart. My whole life, I've wondered how the people there have fared and if they were able to rebuild what the Backers tore down. I wonder how Foss and Dahlia are doing, if they're still around, still alive. In reality, I should have planned to go there first, but I don't feel ready. The back-and-forth feeling of fear and desperation of finding out what happened to my parents and friends prevents me from making a solid choice. Until I can choose what I wish to feel, I don't want to go there.

Bolt lands next to me and seems to enjoy the scenery. It's not his first time seeing this place, but he lets me have this experience. He lifts his head and watches me, waiting for my next move.

"I can't believe I waited so long to see this," I say, mainly to myself. "It's gorgeous." Meeting Bolt's eyes, I add, "Maybe I should've taken a risk and ran for it, you know?"

As much as I loved Jael and my mother, I'm resentful that they held me back for so long. It kept me from seeing what was out there and preparing for anything that may come my way. Growing up, Jael taught me about nature and animals, but not seeing it outside the bubble of my village makes me feel so inexperienced. I'm a baby being left out in the wild, forced to find my way by trial and error.

At least she taught me how to protect myself.

I wander over to the waterfall as the Rainbow Hawk spreads its vibrant-colored wings and flies away. The fallen yellow-green colored Spikefruit dots the grass below the trees, opened and pecked at from birds.

The waterfall beckons me to come closer. I could climb down the rock using the vines this time, but I don't know how old they are; they could snap from my weight.

"Can you float me down there?" I ask Bolt, pointing in the direction I want to go.

He waddles in front of me and leans forward again. I saddle on his back and wrap my arms around his feathered neck, careful not to choke him. Gracefully, he dives off the edge and glides down to the side of the waterfall, gently landing on the rock.

I approach the next cliff about fifty feet away and get a better view of Bena and Barto Lakes. It's too dark to see what the clarity of the water is like, but I'm drawn to how it ripples under the moonlight. It's such a cruel punishment to not enjoy the bliss of water. The irony of it leaves a hole in my heart. One day, I hope there will be a way for me to enjoy water without the risk of death. In a more positive light, I can make good use of cleaning the jar I grabbed from Thaeus's tent. I want to give the Fireflies a clean home for a night if I happen to find them.

I pop off the lid next to the river and shake water in the jar then dump it back out. The coloring of the glass is more of a copper tone than a clearer, transparent hue, but it's better than nothing.

Once I return the jar to the bag, I step back and examine the vines that loop from tree to tree. The odd-shaped plant growing on them is an olive-green color, a square pattern curved around it, with a green stem. I recognize them immediately from the markets in Ketra and from seeing them attached to arrows.

Pineapple Shells.

I remember Jael telling me that these only grow in tropical areas, but I had no idea just how close this place was.

I definitely need these.

I open my pack again and pluck the Shells off the vines, each one about the size of my hand. The exterior is tough but thin; knowing how they work on arrows, they can deal a lot of damage. I'm no archer, but throwing these while hunting will be effective. I just have to throw hard enough.

This gives me an idea.

Down below, I can see a little speck moving under the ripples in Bena Lake. In fact, there are a couple of things swimming in there.

Bolt assists me in floating to the edge of the lake so I can get a closer look. The fish are different shades of blue, about the length of my forearm. I'm guessing it's a Carpie, but I can't be sure until I open it up. I can only recognize types of fish when they're filleted and ready to eat as they are in Ketra.

One Pineapple Shell in my hand, I throw it as hard as I can at the surface, and wait for the result. When it bobs and floats on the surface with no detonation, I know that effort is a bust.

"Okay, Bolt," I say through a sigh. "Work your magic."

Bolt flies high up and glides in a circle while I step back under the protection of the palm trees and wait. The Shells I picked must have some use if I'm going to eat anything tonight. In order to cook, I need fire, and something to maintain it.

Shell in hand again, I throw it at the palm tree closest to me, yellow smoke erupting with the fire, and right away, the cracking of wood shows the result.

"Well, that was easier than I expected."

As I wait for the smoke to float into the air, the fire grows and roars among the wood. I sit next to it and let the flames heat my body. Bolt lands next to me and plops a couple of fish on the ground along with a few sprouts of Bluebloom, a light blue flower that mainly grows on cliffs and makes for extraordinary seasoning. It works well with most foods, but it's especially divine on meats.

"Thank you." I pat his feathered head before tearing up the Bluebloom to add to the fish. He quietly caws at me and bobs his head as if to make a point.

"Yes, yes, you can have some, Sir Needy." I work on gutting and cleaning the fish. I don't really know if I'm doing it right, since I don't specialize in fish at the eatery, but I'm just trying to make sure we're fed. "Can you grab a Spikefruit too, please?"

Bolt turns and launches from the ground as I set the fish on a stick over the flames. Clasped in his talons, he brings me two perfect, round, prickly Spikefruits. From what I understand, Spikefruit can be found just about anywhere, but they taste better from the jungle. I cut it open with a pocketknife and scrape out the seeds, then roast that too.

The roasted Carpie and Spikefruit is delicious. Bolt gulps down his fish in one swallow and licks the remaining yellow flesh of the Spikefruit while holding it down with his foot.

"Well, now I know how to be creative," I tell him. Upon standing, I wipe the dirt off my clothes then wash my hands in the lake. This cliff gives a good vantage point of where I need to go. Siro is still ten to fifteen miles away, which is a long way to walk from here in the middle of the night. Down below the rocky cliffs of the jungle is a copse of trees that could possibly provide temporary safe housing.

The rocky floor doesn't provide a comfortable sleep with all the bugs and critters everywhere.

"Let's head to those woods down there." I point far ahead so Bolt can see. He spreads his wings for me to get on his back again. "Just to the trees, then I'll need you to be a gorilla to stand guard." I rub his feathered head affectionately, which he soaks up with a happy nudge against my hand.

Sighing deeply, I contemplate the journey ahead. A lot of the unknown awaits me in Siro, and all I have to go off of is the dark spot among the field of grass and poor lighting.

Bolt floats me down to the field. As I start to settle in for the night, he works to shift into a gorilla. Within a few seconds, he's an intimidating primate, ready to guard his owner.

I raise a tent in a nearby tree. Years of campouts with Aria have prepared me to be able to set up camp wherever I need to. I grab the empty jar out of my pack, sad that there are no Fireflies around for me to catch. It won't be the same effect, but I can use my imagination and picture them floating with elegance in the jar.

I lay it next to my head on the makeshift pillow I formed with a blanket and stare at it. The imaginary bright yellow dots float in the captured space, carefree and at peace with themselves, reminding me once again to feel the same way.

The more I picture it, the heavier my eyes get, then I'm asleep.

✳✳✳

Surrounded by smoke, Ketra is in chaos. I'm recovering from being shoved to the ground, but I don't know why I was pushed with such force.

It isn't until I look back up that I see the reason.

The Backer standing in front of me. His glowing blade plunged through Jael's body. The blade that was supposed to be plunged into my body, but Jael shoved me aside to save my life.

I draw out in such an ear-piercing scream that it should tear my vocal cords. This time, though, there seems to be an emptiness to the word. The pain I felt when it first happened is absent. Emotions are hollow.

All of it is . . . empty.

My body shoots up and my hand automatically grabs for my sword. I fight for air as my breaths come out in gasps, a sheen of sweat across my neck.

Bolt pokes me in the side with his large ape finger, eyes blinking and head tilted.

"Did I wake you?" I mumble. "I'm sorry. It's fine. I'm fine. Just a bad dream."

He lays back down in the grass outside my tent, breathing out in relaxation. I feel bad for making him sleep out there. It's cold, even with the woven blanket on me.

"Get in here, buddy," I coax him. "I know you're cold."

The fur covering most of his body disappears as feathers poof out. Once the transformation is complete, he wastes no time in waddling into my tent.

"You could've just let me know you wanted in here," I mention.

He lets out a quick chirp and makes himself at home beside my head, then buries his beak under his wing, eyes blinking slowly as he falls back asleep.

I plop on my back, willing myself to sink back into a slumber with the sunrise lapping at the landscape. The effort is going to be in vain, though.

It always is after a nightmare.

There was a gaping hole in my life when I grew up without my parents. The idea of living the rest of my life without them seemed daunting.

Then came Jael.

She was able to fill the space when she took me in and raised me the rest of the way. Now that she's gone, the hole is back and there's no hope of anyone taking her place anytime soon. The feeling of despair and hopelessness is still raw, and now invading my dreams.

She was one of a kind.

My tired eyes watch the empty jar on the other side of my head, trying to imagine the Fireflies dancing and bouncing off the glass, and do everything I can to shut off my mind.

CHAPTER 5

S iro is disgusting.

The sourness of body odor and an outhouse fill my nose. There are broken barrels, crates, and paper all over the ground, covered in mud. The people are no different. They wear rags for clothes, no shoes, and they're just as dirty as the town around them. That alone is enough to unsettle me, but seeing they also have slits on their faces where their noses should be is enough to make my skin crawl. It's daytime, yet the depressing, dark ambience makes the place feel like night.

Now that I see it, sleeping in the woods was the right choice. The next closest place that's considered civilization was another ten miles from here. I'm not up for the journey, so I'll have to make do. As strange as these people appear, they might know something about the Dormant King.

Nerves clawing at my throat, I approach the entrance of the town, the mud squishing under my boots. The people roam around in a corpse-like way, giving me the sensation of a thousand spiders crawling up my body.

"Newbie!" I hear a gruff voice announce.

Before I can make my next move, a small group of people surrounds me and dances, waving their arms and hopping around.

Music plays off to the side, but the flute and drums are horribly out of tune and not in sync in any way. I appreciated the music in Ketra because it was pleasant background noise. This is anything but.

I slowly turn in a full circle, observing this fiasco unfold. I have no idea what's happening or what to do. The noises, the smells, the crowds of dirty individuals keeping their eyes focused on me while I try not to stare back at their nose-less faces, ash-gray skin, and sunken eyes, is overwhelming. All of it makes me even more nauseous. I didn't imagine that this pigsty would be home to insane people with no noses.

The music stops, the people still, and they return to wandering the streets as if nothing happened. I stand there for a moment, trying to understand what that was. Ten miles doesn't seem like such a bad journey now.

I realize as I stroll the muddy, wide walkway that this is the only main road in Siro, and it splits the city in half. Old, stone three-story buildings with gaping holes and caved roofs take up space on both sides with alleys slithering in between that all lead back to this main road. A couple of the buildings look like actual businesses with the citizens walking in and out of them. Broken, wooden stands set up in front of the stone buildings were meant to be places to buy household goods and food. It appears the people, for whatever reason, just gave up and let it all rot.

The townspeople stare intently at me as I examine the buildings for any indication of an inn. I imagine an innkeeper hears many stories from countless travelers, so maybe they could give me some clues on where the Dormant King is.

I approach a woman whose wispy, gray hair barely frames her grayish, wrinkled skin. She's perched behind one of the run-down stands. "Excuse me. Can you tell me where the inn is?"

She stares at me as if I spoke a foreign language. She stares at me for so long, it becomes awkward and I consider moving on.

"You like chowder, ma'am?" she finally asks, mouth lacking teeth. Her accent has a twang in it, but also indicative of a lower class. A savage.

I stare back at her, blinking repeatedly. I don't know how she heard "chowder" from anything I said. Maybe she didn't hear my question. "Can you tell me where I can find an inn? Better yet, someone in charge of this city? Perhaps a mayor?"

"Aye, missy, grab me them apples," she replies. Then she points to the building next to us, where people are stumbling inside. "Go to bar."

"I don't want to do that. I want to *find an inn*."

"Get me some wood too. Aye, me likes to chew on some good ol' wood."

What is going on? Does she not understand what I'm saying?

"Thanks, I guess," I grumble, stepping away from the strangest person I've ever met, aside from the sporadic dancers. I decide to take part of her advice, though, and make my way to the bar's door. Thaeus used to say the truth comes out after a pitcher of Corn Whiskey; I can see if anyone has insight while inebriated.

"You!" someone shouts off to the side.

A man charges with ferocious speed, a finger pointed directly at me. I wrap my fingers around the handle of my sword in case I need to act.

"I want a divorce!" His sour breath spreads over my face.

"I will happily arrange that for you," I deadpan as I make a prompt escape into the bar.

"You never loved me!" he bellows.

"At least we can agree on something."

The bar is bustling with laughing customers, and it smells worse in here than it does outside. Some are talking and clinking their glasses together. Others are so drunk they've fallen flat on the filthy, sticky floor and passed out with no one to help them up. The bartender has no system whatsoever. He pours random alcohol into foggy, unwashed glasses and hands it to people. No one pays; they just take their drinks and leave. No one says anything about it.

No one even notices that I'm the only normal person here.

I walk toward the bar made of rotting wood and sit on an empty stool. "Excuse me, sir?" I call out to the bartender while I shift my backside around as splinters from the seat poke me.

The greasy, dirty man turns and grins seductively while drunkenly trying not to fall over, much like the rest of the customers here. "'Ello, sweet toots. Want some chowder? It's our specialty."

"No, I'm looking for an inn—"

"Aye, you will have chowder," he insists, grabbing a bowl from under the bar. He takes a lid off a pot, spoons some gray, chunky slop into it, and hands it to me. The smell of decayed meat makes me gag.

There's no way I'm eating this.

"No thanks," I choke out, sliding the bowl to the side. He doesn't even acknowledge what I've just done and serves another customer alcohol. "Actually, maybe you can tell me if you've heard any interesting stories lately."

"I wanna go to the beach in the desert," he replies, lifting his chin with a smile and pouring another shot. "Warm sun, hot sand. Aye, that's the life."

"Oh, for the love of Halivaara," I groan loudly, planting my face in my hands. Clearly, no one in this town knows how to talk or understand how a conversation works. "I'm not going to find my answers here."

I twist on my splintered stool and examine the crowd. I need a new plan, and being among savages will not help me get there.

My thoughts are interrupted when a man with an eye patch stumbles to the stool next to me, his mouth lacking teeth as well. Missing teeth and missing knowledge seem to be the norm here.

"You're kinda purdy," he draws out with a slur, barely able to stand.

"Good for me," I reply, sliding off my stool to leave.

"Come 'ere, me love," he says, grabbing my elbow and yanking on it. My heart races, adrenaline zipping through me when he leans his face uncomfortably close to mine. His hand subtly slides farther up my arm and wraps around my bicep.

"Let go of me," I demand through clenched teeth.

He doesn't acquiesce. If anything, his grip gets tighter. Even when I try to yank it from his grasp, he doesn't let up. No one notices or pays any attention. Everyone here only cares for themselves, going on their merry ways.

"Let. Me. Go," I growl. "Last chance."

He returns a growl in protest, his tight grip bruising my arm. Little does he know I'm not a helpless, defenseless little girl who will comply with anything just to stay alive.

Swiftly, I whip my leg and kick him in the knee, which brings him tumbling to the floor. I add to his injury with a punch in the face that brings a shooting pain that scabs my gloved knuckles. He crashes to the ground, yelping in pain.

That prompts a group of men beside me to freeze dead in their tracks, and suddenly, the noise is nonexistent. All eyes are on me.

What did I just do?

"Monster! Attack!" someone screams.

The crowd goes on a rampage. And I'm their target.

The first thing I want to do is use Gridlock on everyone and give myself some time to escape. The raid from Ketra was a good warning for me to not use my abilities in front of other people. Right now, I don't have much of a choice. In a place where citizens don't know how to have a conversation, it's a risk worth taking.

I thrust my hand in front of me. I freeze about ten people at once, just inches before their attacks can hit their mark. Once they're frozen, I leap for the door. I can hear the clamor behind me as soon as I break concentration.

Once I do, though, I'm hit in the head with something, and everything goes black.

***

I don't want to open my eyes. Mainly because my head is killing me.

Footsteps ebb and flow close to me, keys clanging against one another with each movement. The closing of doors blends into the noise, followed by someone shaking their gate and screaming angrily. I attempt to blink my eyes open, coldness sending shivers through my body as I steadily wake up and remember how I got here.

The Siro bar, a man grabbing my arm, the bar fight . . . then everything turning black.

I'm in a small, dark stone room with water leaking through the walls, dripping from a run-down roof above me. The open holes in the roof give me a view of the night outside, which tells me I've been unconscious for a few hours. To my left is a barred gate keeping me locked in this room. I see the hallway dimly lit with torches on the wall. Another gate across from mine houses a dirty, ragged man sitting cross-legged on the damp floor who has seen better days. To my right is a stone bench and the bed I'm lying on is small with no blankets or pillows, similar to one I might lay on during a physician's examination. The only time I've seen a place similar to this was when Jael showed me drawings from books.

I'm in a jail cell.

I huff out a breath in anger. The people in Siro can't exchange helpful words, but they know how to throw someone in jail and take their stuff. They obviously have instincts and follow certain rules, as most places would. Somehow, they knew to confiscate my things and hit me hard enough to make me unconscious.

The rattling of the cell gate down the hall starts up again, worsening the throb in my head. A massage of my temples hardly eases the discomfort. I hear someone yelling next to me and find two guards on each side of a prisoner, holding his arms. He wriggles and thrashes about, screaming unintelligible words and crying hysterically. I roll out of bed and approach my gate, peeking my head between the bars as far as I can to see where they're taking him. At the end of the hallway, the guards open a door and throw the prisoner inside. He scrambles to get up and make an escape before the door closes, but he's too late.

The terror of it all makes my breathing pick up pace. I need to get out of here, immediately. They might throw me in there next, and I don't want to know what awaits me in that room.

Scooting back from the gate, I prop myself on the bench, fear clawing at every nerve in my body. Jael would be smacking my head to snap out of it if she were here.

A white mouse scurries on the floor and stops before me. I panic and lift my feet off the ground, but then I remember it's just Bolt. He gets on his hind legs and sniffs the air.

"Got any ideas?" I flap my arms, irritated at the ridiculousness of asking a mouse for advice. "Is this my life now?"

Bolt scampers away a couple feet and paces the length of the room. Then he flops his body on the ground and lays there on his back, completely still. Not even twitching. He stays that way for a few moments.

"Bolt." Anxiety obvious in my tone, I get down on my knees next to him and prod him with my finger. "Bolt. You're not dead, are you?"

Out of nowhere, he rolls back onto his feet and hurries to the other side of the cell. I lean back a little, my mind whirling with what he just did. Bolt pretended to be dead, just enough to make me worry, only to turn up completely fine. He stares at me intently, head tilted. He was trying to give me an idea.

Once I understood what he was doing, my head perked up. It's a genius, simple plan.

"Of course," I whisper with a mischievous smile. "Okay. I know what to do now. Thank you, bud."

I go to the stone bench in my cell and lay on it facing up, lounging my leg and arm off the edge of the bench, and opening my mouth to a slit. It wasn't too long ago that I heard footsteps thudding on the concrete hallway. It's a matter of time before they return and someone notices my dead body.

A couple minutes pass and the echo of footsteps returns, increasing in volume as they get closer to my cell. I use all the self-control I have to keep the anticipation to myself and remain still. My breathing is minimal to regulate the rise and fall of my chest and I keep my limbs as still as possible. I open one of my eyes just enough to spy on the oncoming guards.

The guard strolls onward, taking my hope of escape with them.

My arm and leg feel numb and achy. Keeping one eye open to a thin line, I watch for any passersby as I take a moment to adjust myself more comfortably.

This whole plan might take a while.

I hear someone walking by again. I stiffen my entire body once more and hold my breath. The footsteps keep going, then stop abruptly. All is silent.

Stay still. Little breaths at a time.

The silence lasts for what feels like an hour, but there are no continuing footsteps. Curious, I slowly—*very* slowly—open my eye to a slit again to see what's going on.

There is, indeed, someone staring straight at me. Although his facial expression is hard to read, he's as still as I am, studying this odd species of human before him. His eyes boring into me for this long is suffocating. My need to breathe is about to give me away if nothing else happens.

Keep it together. Keep it together. Just a little bit longer. You're almost there.

"Dead woman! Dead woman!" he finally hollers in a gravelly voice. The sudden burst replacing the silence in the hallway takes me by surprise and makes me jerk. He doesn't seem to notice, especially when I hear another set of feet padding down the hallway and stops in front of my cell.

"Bugga," one of them says. I hear the familiar rattling of keys, the signal to my near escape. In the meantime, I will the electricity to warm up my right hand, just enough that it could shock my victim to unconsciousness.

The gate slides open, a high-pitched screech on the tracks. I wait till they make a couple steps into the cell, then—

I sit up straight from the bench.

"Thanks. Now, freeze."

I use Gridlock on one of the men and concentrate on him to stay frozen. Moving my hand, I shove him to the side and slam his body against the wall of the cell, hard enough to knock him out. Once he falls to the floor, I shift my focus on the other man, who grabs a stick from his belt to hit me with. The buzzing and vibrating sensation runs strong in my hand when I grab his neck. The volts send his body into convulsions. I release him after a few seconds and he topples over, unmoving.

I turn out of my cell and curve left. All the doors in the hallway are exactly the same—color, shape, and design—with no way to tell one from the other, no way to figure out which one holds my equipment.

"Loosey loose!" An overly cheerful voice shouts from another hallway. I reckon that's their way of calling for help on a loose prisoner. Another round of anxiety rips through my body. Now that I'm being chased, my chances of getting out of here might be slimmer.

I keep running straight until I see another door on the other side of the prison. I use my body weight to shove it open and a staircase opens up, spiraling below me. I race down the steps to another door leading to the next floor.

Unfortunately, that leads me right into a group of guards bracing themselves with axes.

I focus intently on them, curling my fingers into fists and thinking up a quick plan. Either they will throw those weapons at me or they will think threatening me with an axe is enough to frighten me back to my cell.

This may be a moment where I need to use Strike. I need to do enough damage so they have no chance of getting back up and chasing me.

Eyes centered on them, I raise my hands to the ceiling. Although I don't feel the same warmth and vibration of electricity in my hand I did when I connected to the sky, I believe I can still harness lightning.

I grin with the anticipation of electrocuting them when I throw my hand back down.

Nothing happens.

I try it a couple more times. Raise my hands in the air, throw them back down, only harder this time. Still nothing. I know for a fact it worked when I used it in Ketra.

Self-doubt clouds my mind briefly. Why is it not working now? Was it just a coincidence that lightning struck that night?

The guards are looking at each other in confusion, wondering what I'm doing. Attacking me is the least of their worries.

"Is she deaf?" one of them quietly asks, thinking I'm trying to speak with my hands.

For the love of Halivaara.

I could use Gridlock, but I would lose concentration the moment I'm out of their sight. By the time they recover, I won't have much time to find my equipment.

However . . . I still have one more ability up my sleeve.

As quickly as I can, I force the electricity through my forearms and create sparks in my palms. I bring my left hand to meet my right and a ball forms. They fail to register what's happening as they see it get brighter.

Spreading my hands, the ball grows in size. Their faces fall and confusion is replaced with horror. They yell unintelligible words as they turn and run away from me. That doesn't stop me from throwing the electricity at their backs, though.

The ball hits one of the men and he convulses in shock, dropping his weapon on the ground. I build another and throw it, and keep throwing them until all the guards are stunned and all the weapons are on the ground. All of them collapse. I take that moment to squeeze past them and run around the corner to a quieter section of hallway that's all doors and no barred gates. My stuff could be anywhere in here. Opening every door will be daunting, but I don't have a choice at this point.

Until I see one with a big metal lock on it. There's no reason that only one door in this entire hallway should be locked, unless it contains something important.

"Bolt, I need to get in here!" I shout. I lost track of where my Bennaru went during this chaos.

He hops out of my shirt and plops onto the ground, then makes the smooth transition from mouse to gorilla in a matter of seconds. Beating his chest with his large hands, he roars and punches in the door, sending the wooden plank clear to the other side of the room.

Upon entering, it's very apparent that this is where guards store prisoner's items. Jackets, shirts, pants, belts, and bags full of personal effects take up most of the space. Through a gaping hole in the ceiling, the sun is rising, indicating that it's early morning now. The dim light proves to be useless in helping me find my things among the rest of the darkness.

Bolt shrinks back down to his eagle form. He waddles in, ruffling his feathers, and uses his perfect vision to help me.

After less than a minute, he's cawing.

"What? You found it?" I leap to my feet and clamber over to him, where he's sitting next to a bag.

My pack. And my equipment.

"You're the best, thank you!" I pat his head and throw the bag around my shoulders, but not without grabbing a couple Pineapple Shells first.

The men with axes have found me. The hallway is a dead-end. I have nowhere else to go and their sly smirks confirm it. With only two Pineapple Shells in my hand, my plan has to be executed just right.

I erase the smugness from their faces when I throw one Pineapple Shell at their feet. The impact of the explosion sends them soaring in different directions, with pieces of the wall collapsing on top of them and yellow powder billowing into the hallway. Then, I twist and throw the other Pineapple Shell at the wall behind me. The detonation creates a huge hole leading outside, just as I hoped.

The echoes of voices reverberate at the other end of the hall. Bag and weapons strapped on, I prepare to make a run for it through the hole. It's a risk I have to take, and I have to make that decision now. I don't know how far I am from the ground, and that fear makes my stomach launch to my throat.

Time is running out. Even more so when the guards recover themselves and a new group of men with weapons shows up and charges at me.

My feet move as fast as they can and I use all the power in my legs to jump. The three-story fall makes the landing on a broken wooden wagon much more painful than I expected. The dirty, damp tarp covering the wagon wraps around my body and tangles up my limbs. It takes extra effort, especially for my abdominals, to unravel myself from the mess.

I finally manage to roll off the wagon onto the muddy ground, followed by mold and dirt spilling off the tarp and seeping into my clothes and over my bare arms. The bruises forming on my back make it harder to run as fast as I want to out of this cesspool of a place.

Pain waits for no one.

Those five words ring continuously in my mind as I pick up the pace to the other side of the city.

A scuffle up ahead, just outside where the city border ends, slows me down.

Three Siro men surround a young brunette woman, tugging at her arms and forcing their hands into the pockets of her pants. She attempts to rip out of their grasp but they prove to be stronger than she is. The instinct to intervene clicks when she falls to the ground, the most vulnerable position a person can find themselves in. The men take advantage of this when they pull her bag off her back, tugging at it relentlessly.

My first thought is to use Gridlock on them and throw them off to the side to make this battle easier. I already took a risk when I used it in the bar, and that sent me right to jail. I have to be more careful to avoid other potential watchful eyes.

I approach them with speed and shove two of them away from her. They topple over easily. The one still standing comes at me, throwing punches, but I'm able to sneak in a punch of my own in his throat and a few kicks in the chest. He falls over, choking and grabbing at his neck.

The other two get back on their feet. I kick one of them swiftly in the stomach and head, then make a final spin and knock him to the ground. The other one comes at me with a thick stick, similar to the ones the guards carried in the jail. Pain radiates along my arms when I block his harsh blows. I then resort to the Twist and Drag where I jump up and wrap my legs around his neck. I use all the strength in my legs and torso when I swivel my body enough to bring us both to the ground. He groans until I grab him by the shirt and shove my fist in his face. That one punch is all it takes to knock him out.

The man I punched in the throat gets up while still holding onto his neck, now wide-eyed and afraid. He doesn't make a move to attack me, though. I don't know why he would try. I juke at him, and that's all it takes for him to shriek and take off running back into the slums of Siro.

"Pansy," I mumble.

The victim, still on the ground, groans as she rolls herself up. I quickly step over to her and grab her hand to pull her back to standing.

"Thank you," she says, making a futile attempt to wipe the mud off her clothes. "Ugh, that was a close one. I owe you."

"It's okay. I'm just grateful I'm not talking to anyone that actually lives in Siro."

"Not in a million years," she emphasizes, shuddering in disgust. "I was only here for research."

Research. Now maybe I finally found someone that might have helpful answers.

I eye the area around us and realize we're still standing just outside the city. "Come. Let's get away from here."

I lead her by the arm toward the open field with tall grass flowing back and forth with the wind. She follows closely behind me, wary of everything that could potentially attack her.

We stop in the middle of the field once we're far enough away that no one will come after us. "What are you researching?" I ask. "Maybe I can help you find what you're looking for."

"I honestly don't know if it's worth it, because I haven't found anything," she begins, "but I was sent from the Killios Training Camp to do some research on the Dormant King."

Every word in that sentence makes me freeze and forget to swallow. If she's from Killios, that means one particular person was responsible for sending her on this quest.

"Hang on." I hold out my hand. "Were you by any chance sent by a man named Arthur? Lieutenant Arthur?"

"Yes!" she exclaims. "How do you know Arthur?"

I laugh at the coincidence of all this. The odds of running into someone who also knows Arthur is slim, yet I found someone who's searching for the same thing I am. "I don't know him personally," I reply. "Just know someone who did. When I was younger, I was told he'd been researching the Dormant King for years but hadn't found very many answers."

"That's why I thought doing this research would be useless," she points out. "This Dormant King is really good at hiding. I thought Siro would be a good place to check because rumor has it that he knew people here, but that was a dead-end. "

For selfish reasons, I don't want her to give up her search. We're seeking the same thing at the same time. So far, she possesses more information than I do.

"You know, I just began looking for the Dormant King myself," I admit. "Maybe we can help each other. We both have the same goal, after all."

She hums to herself, face wrinkled in uncertainty. "I don't know. There was one other place I wanted to try, but it's quite a trek."

"What place is that?"

"Sabbia Town." She takes a folded paper from her back pocket and unravels it to show me a map. "I found that the town there may be home to some ancient tablets with paintings that could be traced back to the Ancestors. Arthur told me it's possible those tablets contain the answer to what happened to the Dormant King. By foot, it might take a day or so."

She isn't lying. From where we are standing, we would have to cross a large expanse of open land, climb down some cliffs, and walk through the sandy desert to get to the town. I remember whenever I reached the top of Montanha Peak, I got a panoramic view of the desert, although it was a pinhead size from that high up. While exploring the view, I wondered how people survived in the intense heat during the day and the bitter cold at night.

This might be the chance to find out.

"And it won't be easy to get in," she adds. "They don't typically let women inside." She rolls her eyes. "Men, on the other hand, are free-for-all. But it's the only place I haven't been to yet."

I quirk a brow. "No women allowed? Why?"

"From what I've found, they have what they call 'seeking parties' every night, where the men and women gather to meet potential suitors," she explains. "Allowing women inside who are not Sabbians gives the local women less of a chance of meeting a man. Supposedly, we nonlocal women pose a threat."

I fold my arms and examine the direction we have to go to Sabbia. Chances of getting in are slim, if that's their policy with women. However, we're not there to meet men. We're there to find clues about a common enemy. Surely, if I explain this to the locals, they would let us in.

My curiosity spikes. Artifacts that prove what happened to the Dormant King would be a major breakthrough in my search. Having someone to help me with the information she has gathered so far will be far more instrumental than anything I accomplish on my own.

I'm excited to go to Sabbia.

Bolt, now a mouse, sneakily crawls out of my pocket so the woman can't see him. He looks at me curiously, his beady eyes giving me the push to move forward with this plan.

"What if we go together?" I suggest. "If they know we're not looking for a man, they would probably let us in."

The woman shifts her feet, still uncertain. "I don't know if simply explaining it will do the trick, but we can try." She holds out her hand for me to shake. "I'm Lavi."

One of the first things Jael told me when I arrived in Ketra was to make someone earn the opportunity to learn my name, to not give it so easily, for safety reasons. Over the years, Jael also told me to be polite, which meant introducing myself when someone gave me their name.

This case calls for it.

"Havanna."

With a sly smile, she says, "Let's go, Havanna."

That smile—that calculating, mischievous expression—leaves me with an unsettling ball in my stomach as she gets a head start. The feeling is difficult to identify, as I have no obvious reason to feel this way, based on our conversation and everything she's told me.

Although Victor earned my trust, he betrayed me.

Stop. This is different. Lavi has been more open with me than Victor ever was.

With that thought in the back of my mind, I follow her to Sabbia Desert.

CHAPTER 6

"How long have you been looking for the Dormant King?"

During our extended journey to the desert, I take the time to ask all the questions I can about her research.

"Not very long," she answers tremulously. "I just happened to be crossing through the Training Camp when Arthur pulled me aside and asked if I could help him with something important and would pay me a lot of money to do it. I grew up in a family that thrived on treasure hunting for Arythica, since their wealth relies so heavily on selling gems, so I was perfect for the job. I'm a master at thinking outside the box when it comes to finding objects and artifacts."

"What have you found so far?" My breaths create misty clouds in the air.

"Nothing useful. Throughout history, people have claimed to have seen glimpses of him here and there. They were asked to make drawings of what they saw, but the drawings all looked so completely different from each other. Because that method proved to be a dead-end, nothing was confirmed. Then, more than one person told Arthur after hearing about his research efforts that they heard a creepy voice trying to talk to them. But it was all in their head."

"Do you know what the voice was saying?"

"Some people who came forward said they heard the voice say something along the lines of, 'I need your help. Come to me.'"

Those seven words are enough to send shivers down my spine.

"More than one person said this?" I inquire. "That's scary."

"You're telling me. But since the voice couldn't be identified, nor did anyone know what it meant or where it came from, the whole thing was put to rest with the conclusion that the people making these claims were mentally ill."

Something about that doesn't make sense. Why did I have to hide from him and the Backers for so long if no one even knew where he was? Did that mean Jael had no proof of his existence to keep me in hiding, and she kept me hidden simply because of a theory?

That wouldn't make sense either. The Backers and Dormants arose after I used Strike on a clear, cloudless night. So, with that fact, it's obvious that the Backers have a reason to keep working for the Dormant King, meaning he must be around somehow.

"So if no one has seen him, even after decades of looking," I reason, "then how are the Backers still working for him?"

Lavi stiffens, her lips forming a thin line. She hesitates to answer me as she avoids looking in my direction. "I don't really know. But I know the legend of the Ancestors says that the Backers were guaranteed to have the Descendants' powers if they help the Dormant King find them, therefore accomplishing their goal of acquiring power unlike any other ordinary person. Doing as they wish with said power. Maybe that's still the case."

My mouth forms into a frown at the thought that Backers could possibly "claim" the Descendants' powers. When my mother told me the story, she did say the Dormant King copied the Land Ancestor's Transform ability and promised to give the Ancestors' powers to the Backers if they found them. That begs the question: how can this be done if no one knows where the Dormant King is?

Unless the Backers know where he is.

"I wonder how that would work," I say more to myself than to Lavi.

"I don't know," she repeats in a quieter tone.

Her evasiveness is off-putting. The more I ask about the Dormant King and the Backers, the more she withdraws and holds back, confirming my suspicions. I'm positive she knows more than she's willing to divulge.

Maybe this is a sensitive topic for her.

Instead, to fill the silence, she asks me, "So which places have you seen so far?"

"So far, just Ketra and Siro. And Alberi Jungle."

"Oh, so not a lot. I suppose you haven't been traveling very long."

Her tone is knowing, and it flusters me. My mouth goes dry and my palms sweat under my gloves. She can probably see right through me, but is drawing me out in a calculated, sly manner. I hurriedly think of a way to twist the truth without telling her I lived in Ketra and never traveled outside of it. "Well, once I found Ketra, I loved it so much I decided to stay there a little longer. Everyone was telling me to explore the jungle, so I did, then I came upon Siro. I found it strange that everyone in Siro had slits for noses." I conclude the statement with a laugh, although it's more of a nervous one than genuine.

"Interesting."

I suppose we both have secrets.

We finally reach where the desert starts. According to Lavi, the town sells headbands with Ice Stones that come from the snowy Paluso Mountains to help deal with the heat of the desert. For the colder regions, they also have headbands with Fire Stones that are mined by the Mulhutna Tribe within Vulca Mountain.

My short-sleeved black shirt and black pants do little to keep me warm in the bitter cold of the evening. Even my boots barely provide enough warmth for my feet. My hands and arms are red and numb and I can't feel my cheeks.

"Once we get inside, you can take a dip in the Reddawn Oasis to warm back up," Lavi says. "I hear it's quite dreamy."

There's nothing I want more than to envelop my entire body in water that has been warmed up by the desert sun. I have to settle for the Fire Stone headbands, if those work as effectively as she claims.

Lavi's thick cloth jacket and heavy-duty pants seem to help her endure the cold, not nearly as fazed by it as I am. We don't have much further to go, thankfully. From here, Sabbia Town is about a mile or two away. The twinkles of the lanterns that hang around the stone borders with palm trees peeking over make it easy to spot in the darkness. The dull drone of bongos and a rattling instrument mixes with the *whoosh* of the breeze.

"Sounds like the seeking party has begun," Lavi remarks, then points up ahead as we get closer to the town. "There're two people blocking the entrance."

A man and a woman stand on either side of the wooden door. The bronzed female soldier has a hand on a scimitar strapped to her waist, a veil over her nose and mouth, bright blonde hair tied tightly back, eyes squinted in a serious and threatening manner. Her bottom half is covered by a paneled skirt with an exotic pattern, slits reaching her hips, an equally exotic-patterned sleeveless top that reveals the midriff and hugs the torso, and brown strapped sandals wrapped around her ankles and calves. The male soldier also has a scimitar attached to his waist, but no hand on the hilt as his eyes scan the area. A scarlet scarf hangs diagonally over his equally bronzed, chiseled torso. Linen pants and sandals cover the bottom half of his body, shoulder-length blond hair lapping behind him in the breeze. It's no hardship to take in the glory of his godlike body from muscled top to muscled bottom. He stares off in the distance, unlike the woman he's standing next to, whose eyes are boring into us.

"So, what's your plan?" Lavi asks, interrupting my gawking.

I shake my head to refocus. "I'm just going to tell them we're here for research only. If we show them evidence of our intentions, I would think that's reason enough to get us in."

"What kind of evidence?"

I reach in my pocket to pull out my map, being sure to hide the poem from her sight. She's already onto me for some reason; showing her the poem will only increase whatever notions she has. "Do you have some record of your findings?"

"Oh, yes." She reaches behind her for her bag and opens it to pull out a leather-bound notebook. Some pages have dark ink scribbles on them; others have yet to be touched. "I've been using this."

"That works."

"What if they still won't let us in?" she asks worriedly. "Should we have a backup plan?"

I give her a sideways grin. My backup plan is one I'm sure to win, if it comes to that.

"Yes. I'll challenge them to a fight. Once they're on the ground, we'll have time to run inside."

Lavi's eyes go wide in surprise. "They're holding weapons. They don't mess around."

"Neither do I."

She looks between me and Sabbia Town with uncertainty. I can understand her hesitation, but I'm more than confident in my fighting skills. I'm getting in, whether they like it or not.

"I suppose I should trust you," she relents.

"Good." I eye the two soldiers and take a deep breath to prepare myself. "Follow me."

Carefully, we walk along the sandy path, closer and closer to the Sabbian guards. They stand up straighter as we approach them with purpose. As we get within fifteen feet of the door, the female soldier wastes no time in whipping out her scimitar and pointing it at both of us. The man follows suit with his weapon at the ready.

"Halt!" the woman shouts at me, her voice deep and masculine. "State your purpose."

I hold up my hands in surrender. "We're here for research. That's all."

"Locals only," the man states plainly in a deep voice, thrusting his scimitar in my direction. Again, I find myself distracted with the indentations of his abs and the bulging biceps holding the curved blade. This physical attraction lights my insides on fire, a new sensation I haven't felt since Victor.

My gaze switches back to the woman. "We won't stay long," I grasp for a compromise. "We're just looking for someone."

"Who are you looking for?" she presses.

"I think they're really here for the seeking party," the man offers.

The woman scoffs, spitting at my feet. I have never felt such disrespect in my entire life. "Seeking parties are for Sabbian women," she says with scorn. "Are you a Sabbian woman?"

This seems like a rhetorical question, but since she's being so aggressive, I put my sarcasm to good use when I motion to my body. "What do you think?"

"Then buzz off."

"Look, we have proof that we're only here for research." I grab Lavi's notebook and open my map on top of it. "See, we're travelers." Then I shift to the notebook and file through the sporadically written pages. It may not even be used for research as Lavi claims, but I need something to work with.

"Who are you really looking for, then?" the woman asks.

I didn't expect this kind of interrogation, but I have to tread lightly when it comes to mentioning the Dormant King and why I'm looking for him. This admission will only confirm that I'm a Descendant, and the news of a Descendant arriving in a desert town will spread faster than I can stop it. Lavi remains silent, shifting her weight and offering no help.

I swallow hard. "An evil person that has caused a lot of destruction."

The woman's stance relaxes a little and I start to have a glimmer of hope that this plan worked, until the stupid male soldier loudly whispers to her, "I think she's lying."

The woman nods, her eyes saying more than her whole face ever could. "Locals. Only."

My annoyance has just about reached its limit with this conversation. I could take out my sword and challenge them to a fight right now, but I have one more tactic. Owning a business in Ketra has taught me that people like money, and will do almost anything for it.

"What if I paid you?" I offer, digging into my pack. Lavi scoffs and I see her shake her head from the corner of my eye.

"How much do you have?" the man asks, his attention drawn to my money pouch.

"Imbecile!" The woman slaps him upside the head. "Leave your greedy, pea-brained mind alone for a moment and focus!"

The woman, disdainful that I'm still here, turns her attention back to me. She steps closer with the tip of her scimitar poking my chest so hard that it already feels bruised. "No one in Sabbia would know anything about this *person* you seek. Now be gone."

My stomach sinks at the fact that my negotiating skills didn't work. There's one more tactic I didn't want to resort to, just to prevent it from escalating into a brawl.

"I really, really need to get inside," I beg her. As the words slip out of my mouth, I appear weak and desperate, two qualities I never wanted to show. "We came a long way—"

"Leave. Now," the man spits at me, now pointing his scimitar at my chest too. "You both are strangers and are not to be trusted."

"You can even follow us inside to make sure we're not a threat!" I shout, then motion to the inside of the town. "The men are all yours, I promise. I don't even want a man. Men disgust me."

"Hey!" the man yells defensively. Now angry, he moves his blade closer to my neck.

"Leave," the woman says firmly. "Or you'll have us to deal with."

There's the cue to my backup plan.

"Okay, well here's how this is going to go," I say in a more commandeering tone, pulling out my sword. "We're going to fight this out, and if you lose, you let me and Lavi in. If I lose, I'll walk away." I let my self-confidence shine when I swing the blade around. "But you might as well just let us in now because, let's face it, you're both not going to last long."

I hear Lavi's footsteps in the sand backing away from the scene to let me handle this battle, but I pay it no regard as I scrutinize the soldiers' next moves with caution.

"We'll see about that," the woman growls, then tries to strike me with her weapon. I dodge it with a side jump and get into a duel of blades with her, metal pinging together in succession. The man joins in when he leaps at me, holding the scimitar above his head and swinging down. I jump and spin midair, evading an attack that could have sliced me in half. As soon as I land, I feel a kick in the gut that knocks the wind out of me and another blow to the head that sends a throb across my skull. I fall flat onto the sand.

"Looks like you lose." The man cackles devilishly in my face. "You said you would leave. Now, leave."

With a crafty smile, I shift a little, then use the power in my legs to spring myself back to my feet. I twist and hit him in the stomach with the hilt of the sword, then finish him off with the edge of my shield to the chest.

The woman comes at me, weapon ready to kill, and I block it with my shield as she slashes. She pushes her body weight into me and tries to send me to my feet again. Loudly grunting, I put all my strength into my left arm, shove her away from me, and cut her on the leg with a swipe of my sword. I could have done way more damage, or even killed her, but that's the last thing I want to do to these people.

"Are you done yet?" I ask with confidence and a hint of arrogance, seeing she's breathing heavily from exertion. She doesn't have much fight left in her.

"I will be when you're on the ground begging for your life," she responds as she leaps at me. I hop to the side just in time as she lands in the sand. Right after, I jump and spin again, but she dodges my blade and comes at me again, slashing in different directions. I drop to the ground and trip her with my foot, and she lands back flat on the ground. Both soldiers lay there, groaning in pain as I get upright.

"Well, that was fun." I clap my hands together as if to rid them of dust. "Now, if you'll excuse me, we have some research to do."

My intense confidence dies down when I notice Lavi is nowhere around. I assume she must have made her way inside and now she's just waiting for me. Maybe she's getting a head start on finding clues on the Dormant King, which would bode well for me, but odd that she didn't wait.

I open the door to the town and keep my eyes open for signs of her. There are people paired off all over, whether they're eating, dancing to the beat of the music, or flirting with other men.

Sabbia Town knows how to throw a party.

Reddawn Oasis is the center of the valley, taking up a large part of the land, yet so clear and free of debris that I can see the depth of the enormous sandstone pool. The deeper the water goes, the more the stone narrows in an upside-down cone. It draws me in, but the sadness of never knowing what it's like to be in water overtakes me.

Men and women submerge themselves in the oasis, drinks in hand, enjoying themselves. Around the edge of the water, men and women have paired off, dancing much too close together than I would be comfortable with, spilling their drinks and laughing at themselves about it. All the women wear veils and traipse along the sandstone pathways. Some are in brown strapped sandals while others are in high-heeled shoes that accentuate their backsides. That technique appears to be working because the men gawk at them.

Why these women are so desperate for a man is a concept I no longer care to explore. I never want to attract a man ever again. I may appreciate the chiseled physique of a gorgeous male, but that's as far as it will ever get. I refuse to live through another betrayal of someone I trusted. Romance only leads to disaster.

Structures lining the pathway and oasis are also sandstone, beige and smooth. Each business has a symbol carved in the stone above the door. A glass with a straw sticking out is the bar, where people are being handed drinks like presents. A half moon above the inn, a shirt over the clothing market, a potion bottle over the apothecary, and a fish over the eatery. I will be stopping there soon. I'm starving.

In a nearby corner of the town is a tall set of stairs that lead to the opening of a throne room. The lack of doors gives me a chance to see the long, dark purple rug leading to the throne and a crown symbol resembling the squiggly rays of sun sits above the entrance. An extravagant home with uncovered windows sits on the top floor. My imagination delves into what it would be like to live up there, to see the beige stretch of desert from a higher point of view. I can imagine the bedroom is big enough to fit everyone in the entire desert.

What makes being among this crowd unbearable, though, is how intensely the Sabbian women are staring at me. Veils may cover their faces, but their eyes speak horrible insults. For some, those insults come out in murmurs.

"How did *she* get in here? She's not Sabbian!"

"I bet she's here to take a man for herself."

"She reeks of desperation, coming in here with filthy clothes like that."

"She's not even pretty."

I am definitely not welcome here.

"It's fine," I say to passersby, giggling uneasily and waving. "The guards let me in."

That does little to help. The murmurs get louder until the entire town is aware of a strange girl in their midst who deserves a tongue-lashing. Within seconds, I'm swarmed by angry women.

"You don't belong here. Go back to where you came from!"

"Seeking parties are for *Sabbian* women!"

"There's no possible way the soldiers let you in!"

Everyone ends up chiming in, and all the hurtful words blend into each other. The men just stand by and watch, neither contributing nor stopping the situation.

I shouldn't have come here. The level of criticism and careful eyes is out of control. I was wrong to think that fighting my way in would prevent anyone from asking questions.

The murmurs, the insults, the judgments . . . It reminds me of everything I felt about myself before I left Ketra.

Darius was right. I'm a fraud. I didn't belong there, and of course I don't belong here.

Beneath my glove, my hand tingles and vibrates. My heart races in anxiety and distress while my breathing picks up. Tears prick at my eyes as I cover my ears and hunch over, wanting to disappear as the people hurl more insults. Running away from it wouldn't do me much good; I have nowhere else to go.

I'm angry that I have to deal with this alone, just when I thought I had someone on my side after everything I've lost. Lavi is still nowhere to be found, and as far as I know, she's made no effort to find me. The feeling I had when I watched Jael's body float out to sea claws its way back to my chest.

I should have let the Buckers kill me.

The stress of this encounter is becoming too much, sending me to my knees. My vocal cords itch to scream at the top of my lungs while I do everything I can to control the sensations rolling in my hand, begging to launch electricity. The vibrations are harsh against my palm, the sparks unable to be contained.

I'm at my breaking point, about to let out a bloodcurdling scream and let the thunder fall, then—

"Shaanti!" A deep but female and authoritative voice bellows louder than those of all the Sabbian women combined.

Immediately, everyone goes silent and we all turn our heads toward the direction the voice came from. The crowd splits in the middle to make room for their superior. One by one, heads bow to who I can confidently say is the most elegant, immaculately dressed, unbelievably stunning woman I've ever seen.

A bronze-colored leader walks gracefully along the sandstone pathway with a golden spear taller than her held upright, the butt of it clacking on the ground in time with her shiny, golden high heels. Her flowing red-paneled skirt curtains her bottom half with the slits reaching her hips and a snug white top tightly wraps around her chest, showing off her muscular arms. Enormous golden hoop earrings dangle next to her neck above a golden necklace of the sun that sits just below her throat. Golden bangles clang around her wrists as she walks and a golden crown that mirrors the symbol above her throne sits tall on her head. She has no veil over her face, which gives me a full view of her almond-shaped eyes and full lips. Her very presence shines royalty, power, and strength.

"I will be the one to question her. Let her be," she says in such a comforting, soothing, yet commanding tone that reminds me of my mother and Jael. She turns to her people with eyes that could ignite

a fire, then lets go the growl of a ferocious beast as she slams her spear to the ground. "Now, *passé*. Go."

The women scurry away in deference to their leader. I remain on my knees, looking up at her with what I know is childlike eyes, my face wet with tears I didn't realize were there until now.

"Now, my child." She bends down to meet my gaze, still clutching her spear. Her compassionate smile reaches her chocolate-brown eyes when she takes her long, perfectly manicured finger and wipes the tears from my cheeks, bangles nearly making contact with my face. "How did you get in?"

I swallow before I come up with the words to say. I stare at her smooth, perfect face, wondering if it's just a dream that Sabbia's leader is the only one being so kind to me. I don't want to tell her I beat up her soldiers, even if that *was* the only way I could get in. "I made a deal with the guards," I squeak out in a rasp.

She presses a button on her spear and it collapses into a short stick so quickly that I flinch. "Are you looking for a mate?" she asks, as if that didn't just happen.

"No."

"Do you dance well enough for a man to notice?"

I squint at her, wondering how that question is relevant to this situation. "No."

"Then why did you want to come in so badly?"

I suppose I can see why she's wondering what my plan is here. Any other woman desperate for a mate would find a way to fight their way inside, but my reason for doing so has absolutely nothing to do with that. I keep my answer as basic as I can. "I have questions I need answers to."

She lets out a throaty chuckle. "Is it really that simple, child?"

I shake my head in response. It really isn't. I'd bet my entire pouch that the soldiers guarding the entrance are still shocked from my victory over them.

The chief—this angelic, goddess of a woman—chuckles again, this time showing me her full, bright-white smile. She's shockingly calm for someone who discovered a random girl in her land. It's worrisome, to say the least.

Despite the fact that I'm not sure what to expect from her, my hand finally stops begging me to use Strike and I feel the sensations subside.

"Here, come to my palace and you can tell me what you're looking for. Maybe I can be of assistance," she says, standing back up and giving me her hand. The condition of her pristine nails causes me to hesitate in taking her up on her offer. "I wouldn't offer you my hand if I was worried about my nails," she remarks when she sees me studying her nails. "Besides, nails grow back. Nothing that can't be fixed." I take her hand and she yanks me back to my feet as if I were as light as a feather. "What is your name, child?"

"H-Havanna."

"Havanna," she repeats to herself. "I'm Calista."

Quite the goddesslike name if there ever was one.

I follow her back to her home, the one in the corner of the town deemed fit for royalty. We cross the open-concept purple-and-beige throne room, and I see two thrones on the dais about a foot above the ground. The seats are covered with velvet and the armrests and legs have an engraved swirled pattern. I picture Calista sitting on these, addressing her subjects as they bow to her and whoever sits next to her.

We go up the spiral staircase in the back that leads to her living and dining quarters, her bedroom located on the third floor. The rugs, furniture, and bar in the living area are so impeccably clean that I feel out of place with the current state of my clothes. Off to the side down a short hallway are two extra bedrooms, one of those acting as a study or library. In the washroom are two women, one shorter and slightly chubbier than the other but still athletically built, walking in and out with fresh linens to replace the dirty ones. Like typical Sabbians, they have the same garments and wrapped sandals, but their blonde hair is pulled back with wide headbands with Ice Stones in the middle.

"I'll get some fresh clothes for you," Calista announces and motions to my filthy black outfit. "And have these ones washed."

Being treated as a superior doesn't sit well with me. I never had things done for me; I always did it myself. Except when Victor offered to clean my hut.

"Oh, you don't have to—"

"Shaanti." She holds up her finger to make me stop talking. "I insist." She snaps her fingers and within seconds, the women drop everything and hasten to stand before her at her service.

"Yes, our queen?" the chubbier one asks while eyeing me with a dubious expression.

Queen. Calista is a *queen*. That explains why she lives above the throne room. But I haven't seen a king since I've been here.

"Freya, will you please grab clean clothes for our visitor here from my bedroom? And wash the ones she's wearing promptly," Calista orders. As someone who wields as much power and control as she does, she shows kindness and respect to her subordinates.

"Of course, our queen," Freya answers softly.

"Havanna will be staying here for the night," Calista informs them. "I ask that you please treat her as you would any other

Sabbian." Her polite tone shifts to serious and authoritative again when she adds in a low voice, "That is an order."

I pinch my lips together to hold my composure. The only way to explain why I'm being treated so well is that an unknown deity has blessed me with the opportunity to sleep in the queen's home. Although, she only said for the night. That doesn't give me much time to investigate the Dormant King, or where Lavi ran off to. Even so, I won't reject such hospitality.

"Yes, of course, our queen," the skinnier servant responds with a tremulous voice. Her fidgety demeanor tells me Calista doesn't have guests from outside Sabbia very often. "I'll make sure her bedroom is ready."

"Thank you. When you're done, please help yourself to the bar. You both have worked very hard today."

If the queen isn't the definition of perfection, then I don't know who is.

Calista saunters over to the bar to grab a glass and sets her compact spear on top. The counter and shelves holding liquor bottles and glasses are made of some sort of good quality black stone with unevenly cut edges, smooth and cool to the touch. I take a seat on a tall, black-painted wooden stool that is just the right height for me to reach the bar. The entire space emanates a sophisticated, neat vibe.

"So, is there a *King* Calista?" I ask her with a giggle.

"Why yes," she answers with a happy sigh. "King Malik. He's keeping an eye on the party from our bedroom. You noticed I was without a veil, correct?"

"You're the only one not wearing one."

"Sabbian women only wear a veil when they're not currently attached to a male companion," she explains. "A woman only takes it off when she has found a man worthy of seeing her beauty."

I should have had similar values when I knew Victor. Had I been more watchful and guarded, my trust never would have been broken and maybe I wouldn't be so leery of other future love interests. My heart was too openly accepting of his charm when I needed to keep up my walls until I knew more about him.

"Here. You must be hungry. I can have Freya or Zena cook some Dewey Fruit, Chill Grapes, Petros Rice—whatever suits your fancy."

"Why are you being so nice to me?" I blurt out as soon as she stops talking.

She flinches, somewhat taken aback. "I beg your pardon?"

"Calista—I mean, *Queen* Calista," I correct myself. "You have a strict rule for your people to not allow non–Sabbian women in here. You have every reason to ban me from Sabbia. Not that I want you to, but—"

She smirks. "I saw you with the guards. Usually, women accept that they're not allowed inside and go on their way. But you didn't."

"Wait. Then you must have seen Lavi sneak in. Where is she?" I ask. I slide off the stool and round the bar in a threatening manner. "What did you do to her?"

Calista raises her hands in surrender. "I didn't see anyone with you. All I saw was you dueling with my soldiers from the bedroom. I get a decent view of the desert from there."

Lavi snuck in and avoided being caught by the queen herself. And no one else saw her. Something about that is strange and disturbing. I swallow hard, waiting for whatever punishment she has in mind for me, whether that involves killing me in my weakest moment or sweetening me up so I fall into her trap. I return to my seat and listen intently.

"My soldiers can hold their own in almost all circumstances," she explains, maintaining her smirk. "But you bested them. And you didn't kill them, even when you had the chance to. I was intrigued."

She reaches into a cubby below the bar and grasps the neck of a liquor bottle that I know is Winterbulb Wine. "I thought, 'for her to go so far as to fight my most skilled people, but to not kill them, there must be something she wants. Desperately.'"

She pours herself a glass. "Had you *badly* hurt my people, or killed them, I would never have shown kindness to you. Not in the slightest." Thoughtfully, she sips her drink. "With the way that battle ended, I knew that wasn't your intent, but simply that you wouldn't give up until you got what you wanted. Because, for whatever reason, what you're looking for is that important to you."

It boggles my mind that Queen Calista gathered all of these assumptions by just watching from her bedroom. I say nothing as she continues.

"And the way you reacted to everyone taunting you," she adds, "you weren't some entitled traveler." She gestures to me with her glass. "You've been hurting. You have been through unspeakable things that have brought you a lot of heartbreak. And that intrigued me even more. I needed to know the reason behind your desperation since your lack of interest in the seeking party was made evident."

My chest wells with a mixture of emotions. Comfort, and also heartache and grief. And there's only one reason I can think of as to why.

Calista is a replica of Jael.

Her genuine kindness, hospitality, and warmth toward me sums up everything that Jael was. How she comforted me when I arrived in Ketra, how she took me under her wing and taught me everything she knew. Calista is taking me under her wing, helping me more than anyone else has, even though I'm an outsider.

Freya comes down the stairs and hands me a fresh set of clothes. Sabbian skirt, shoes, and tight top.

"Thank you so much," I breathe out with relief. Freya gives me a silent dip of her head and moves back down the hallway.

"Change your clothes and come back here," Calista says and gulps the rest of her wine. "We have a lot to talk about."

I feel so exposed.

The skirt and shirt given to me shows more skin than I'm used to. Thankfully, my body has been sculpted by years of training and I have decent curves, so I don't have to be self-conscious in that regard. I leave on my armband and gloves, though. Those won't be going anywhere.

The sandals, on the other hand, are excruciatingly awkward. The straps pinch the tops of my feet and squeeze my calves hard enough to leave red imprints. Out of respect for the queen, I leave them on. She giggles when I walk down the hallway, my gait similar to a newborn colt. Bolt stays hiding behind the sofa so Calista won't notice him and try to kill him.

"You've had quite the journey for someone so young," Calista says after I give her the basics of how I ended up in Sabbia. "I learned about the Ancestors from my school teacher. But it's all legend. No one has proof that there's even such a thing as the Dormant King."

My hand clenches into a fist, restraining myself from spouting out everything I know. There is so much proof of the legend's validity, yet I can't tell or show her. All I would have to do is take off my gloves. Telling her that I struck lightning, which led the Backers and Dormants to my village, which led to Jael's death and everyone hating me, hence leading to my decision to leave Ketra, is a story I can't tell her. At least, not yet.

"Although, when I was young," she reminisces, "my teacher talked about the Backers and how they destroyed homes and towns for the sake of the Dormant King, looking for the Descendants and their abilities. I recall telling myself 'if this was a true story, and those horrible nobodies went after my people, I would show those Backers with all the strength I had who was stronger.' After all these years, that feeling has never changed."

"That's why you fit the role of a queen," I reassure her.

"This place means everything to me and Malik. We always make sure the people in it are safe."

"Oh good, so you won't kill me in my sleep?" I ask her. I'm half joking, but I'm also not. I've had too much wine.

Calista flinches in surprise from my random question. She swerves in a way that indicates the alcohol has made its impact on her as well. "What? Why would you say such a thing? I don't kill people!" She takes another drink from her glass, then admits in a low voice, "Unless I have to."

I shrug. "I'm still a stranger."

"Rest assured, I have no valid reason to kill you." Calista gives me a comforting side smile and perks her eyebrows. "Again, had you killed my guards, you and I would not be drinking together."

"Understood. Thank you." I feel the nagging fear of death slowly crumble and be replaced with calmness. That might also be from the alcohol.

"But there's something I need to understand." She leans in closer to my face, her eyes glazed over and the odor of fermented fruit on her breath. "Why did you decide to leave Ketra? If no one else has found him, what makes you think you can?"

For someone who doesn't know everything about my backstory, I understand her reasoning. I have all the proof backing up the decisions I'm making.

All of which I still can't tell her yet.

"As much as I want you to trust me, Queen Calista," I begin, "that might have to be a story for another time."

"Deep-seated reasons, I see. I can respect that." She rises from her chair. "Maybe in time, when I've earned your trust."

Suddenly, the glass in my hand shatters, liquid and glass spilling on the bar. My body seizes up in shock and horror. My heart stops and blood drains from my face.

I find the culprit sticking out of the wall next to us, and my stomach drops.

An arrow.

My head whips to Calista's open window in the living area. I scramble to my feet to look outside, and there I see it.

Lavi, holding a bow, surrounded by a crowd of men dressed in white.

Backers.

CHAPTER 7

"What was that?" Calista asks in bewilderment.

As the Backers equip their bows with arrows, I use all the strength in my legs to leap from my seat and pin Calista to the ground, just in time to miss the onslaught that ruins her living room furniture. I may not be able to protect Jael now, but I *will* do what it takes to protect Calista.

"Who are those people?" Calista shouts over the noise of destruction happening next to us. Glass bottles break, alcohol trickling onto the floor and seeping into our skin.

"Don't worry about that right now!" I shout back irritably. "You need to get to somewhere safe. I can take care of this myself."

"You most certainly will not." Calista crawls across the alcohol-covered floor, careful to avoid the broken glass, and grabs her spear that fell from the bar. "You wait here."

"Calista!" I attempt to grab her foot to hold her back, but she's on the move quicker than I can get her to stop. She bravely races downstairs toward the line of fire, resolute and ready.

"Keeley!" I hear her scream, her deep voice booming. "Round up your army! We have an invasion!"

I crawl to the window and see Calista below approaching the Backers with purpose. She holds up her spear and presses the button, both ends shooting out into a full-length weapon. I watch in complete mesmerization when she spins the spear around her neck and hits a Backer across the face. She flips it and thrusts it behind her, hitting another Backer hard enough for him to double over. She trips one with her spear and kicks him with her heel, then stabs another in the foot before picking it back up and hitting him across the face. Then she stabs the ground and uses it to propel herself in the air and kick over another Backer. Her attacks are fluid, her precision near perfect as she takes down one Backer at a time, all before they can even fight back.

A small army of soldiers in exotic-patterned breastplates and gold pleated skirts seem to be holding their own against the other Backers by the oasis who are determined to make their way toward me. Keeley uses two scimitars to hold off a Backer, then spins and swings her blades down on him. The other Sabbians are running toward the inn screaming in terror. Some take cover in nearby shops and hide behind the counters. The men are doing what they can to protect the women while also staying hidden.

I was walking among a crowd of Backers and I had no clue. Neither did anyone else.

Once I believe Calista can hold her own, a Backer slashes her across the torso. She grunts and doubles over, holding onto her bleeding wound with her free arm.

"Oh no," I whisper. "No no no no."

I need to intervene. Now.

As soon as I rise from the floor, I'm immediately reminded of how uncomfortable these sandals are. I rip them off my feet and throw them across the now-destroyed living room, then race to the sofa to grab my sword and shield.

Once I make it to the throne room, I hide behind a life-sized vase where I get a clear view of the chaos between the Backers and Calista. One has her in a choke hold with their weapon and another is holding her arms behind her back. The woman who cut her torso stands in front of her with her blade. Calista's face is twisted in pain. Jael held her ribs the same way when she fell off her horse. The next thing I knew, I was on the ground and she let the Backer kill her instead of me.

Calista is about to die because of me. Just like Jael did.

And there's only one way I can help from this distance.

Barefoot, I exit the throne room and take one step at a time down the stairs with my hand raised. A bright, golden spot in the clear sky opens, my hand tingling more and more as I rev up my power. The Backer lifts her weapon over Calista, my cue to act.

With a grunt, I throw down my hands with force. In a split second, lightning crashes down on all three Backers and they thump to the ground. One hit was all it took.

Calista stares at me, completely stunned and still holding onto her torso. I rush to her side and fall to my knees next to her, fighting for breath and ignoring the oncoming headache.

"You..." she gasps breathlessly. "You're a Descendant? The legend is true?"

"Yes, but we don't have time for that right now." I try to lift her up, but she yelps in pain and I immediately drop her.

"No need to worry about me." She waves me away, her breathing labored. "I'll be fine. Save my people. Please."

I'm about to protest when a few Sabbian soldiers run to Calista's aid. "We need to get her to the emergency shelter," they tell each other. One soldier proceeds to lift her up by the shoulders and another grabs her by the feet, and they work in unison to get her away from danger.

Feet clapping against the sandstone, I run as fast as I can across the now-empty town to aid Keeley's army in their fight, until my path is cut off by two Backers. I whip out my sword, my hand still tingling. They narrow their eyes at me, proud and cunning.

Then I notice something incredible.

The electricity from my hand travels up my sword, from the hilt to the tip of the blade. The Backers watch in awe as it has become an electric weapon. Unfortunately, that doesn't deter them when they come at me with their blades.

I block them with my shield and swing at them with my now-electrified blade. Metal clashes together in quick bursts until I slash with my sword, then immediately swipe my shield and hit them both with the edge. I use this opportunity to see if I can try something new. I raise my sword in the air, where it attracts the lightning in the sky, buzzing and vibrating in my hand and along my arm.

Holding the hilt with both hands, I hop and stab the ground. Bolts of electricity emerge from the blade and shoot straight to the Backers. Their lifeless, unmoving bodies tell me the lightning did its job.

I keep running toward the battle between Keeley's army and the Backers. They're outnumbered, with one Sabbian soldier fighting two or three Backers at the same time. Those good-for-nothing scums are here and causing distress to these innocent people because of me.

The only way to take them all down at once is to use Strike again.

I ready myself by sheathing my sword and shield behind me. My hand still revved up, I raise it above me and focus on all the

Backers the Sabbians are holding back, and throw down my hand. The lightning hits every single Backer that I can find, and they each drop with a thud. All is quiet now, save the booming echo of thunder hanging in the air.

Keeley and her army freeze at the sight, wondering what just happened. Slowly, they turn their heads, equal parts amazed and puzzled. The ache in my head becomes more prominent at that point and I close my eyes to calm it down.

Until I hear footsteps making a run for it.

I turn and see Lavi attempting to escape through the entrance. Finally, I can pay her back for what she's done to me.

"Halt!" Keeley shouts at her, readying her scimitar.

Lavi's disobedience motivates Keeley to chase her down. Narrowing my eyes at Lavi, I thrust out my hand and use Gridlock. She freezes in place just as she reaches the wooden door that would lead her back to the desert. I step closer to her frozen form, focusing on keeping her in place and making sure that she doesn't have an easy getaway once I break concentration.

I toss her to the side with a quick motion of my hand. She skids along the stone pathway with a grunt, groaning in pain. The adrenaline, fueled by hurt and anger, makes it easy for me to lift Lavi off the ground by her shirt and hold her close to my face as if she weighs nothing. The look in her eyes is beyond petrified. The Sabbian army stays in close proximity to us, weapons ready in case they need to act. Lavi writhes in pain as the electricity softly coursing through my hand shocks her.

"I'm sorry," she pleads. "I'm sorry. I'm so, so sorry."

"You tell me that *now*?"

"I was blackmailed!" she cries. "I swear, I was blackmailed! They took my son and said they would kill him if I didn't find you!"

"How did you even know who I was?"

"Back in Siro," she answers in a quaky voice. "At the bar."

When I used Gridlock on all the men who were about to attack me. Just before I was knocked unconscious and sent to jail.

This has to be some kind of sick joke.

In a place full of savages, it didn't occur to me the moment I used Gridlock that there may have been a more civilized person watching me. The only option I had for that situation—one that I put myself in—has brought me here, in conflict with a traitor.

Then there's Lavi's son. Anything involving child endangerment should soften my heart to her. Jael's heart certainly would be. She would drop everything in a heartbeat if she knew someone's child was in grave danger.

But I'm not Jael. She's never been betrayed. Twice.

My heart remains a cold, hardened shell of what it once was. Lavi is as good to me as the dirt on my feet. Nothing she's told me can be a reliable source of information. It will be a wasted effort to ask her which facts she told me were actually true. And that puts me back at the beginning of my search.

"That's a nice story, but I don't believe you."

"It's the truth! These Backers have no mercy! I only did it for my Finnegan. You have to believe me. Please. Please don't kill me. He needs me!"

Angry breaths huff through my nose as I grip her even tighter and force more electricity onto her. She begs and pleads to be released; I stop believing anything she says as my hand creates burns on her pale skin.

On the off chance she's telling the truth, I don't want to be responsible for killing the mother of a child that desperately needs her to save him. I waited for my parents to save me, and they never did.

Jael is gone; I don't have her to save me anymore, or to erase any doubts in my mind about every single move I make.

That child probably feels alone, just as I do.

I spare no injury when I shove Lavi to the ground. She lands on her back and peers at me, deathly afraid that I will end up killing her. I may regret what I'm about to do, but I need to follow in Jael's footsteps.

"If you were anyone else, I would have killed you a while ago," I inform her. "And I could easily do that now. But, because it's possible that you're telling the truth, I'll spare your life." I bend down to her level, being as intimidating as I can. She breathes out a quick breath of relief, but that doesn't stop me from instilling fear. "So I hope I make myself perfectly clear when I tell you that I never want to see you again. Go back to wherever you came from and stay there. If I find out you told anyone about what occurred today, that you found a Descendant, I won't think twice about hunting you down and striking you dead. Do you understand?"

Lavi nods, her body shuddering in sheer fright.

"Get out of my face before I change my mind."

Flustered, she stumbles as she gets back to her feet. She mumbles a measly "thank you," then runs for her life to the door, exiting Sabbia Town.

Keeley's army surrounds me with absolute astonishment, but at the same time, just as afraid of me as Lavi was just now. I'm still angry beyond my wildest dreams, but I make certain they know I'm on their side. "Are you okay?" I ask in a feeble endeavor to diffuse their tension.

They all nod silently. Keeley, on the other hand, steps forward while sheathing her scimitar.

"Who are you?" she asks softly. Her question isn't accusatory or suspicious, but surprised and curious.

"Sergeant! Sergeant!" two people shout at the top of their lungs.

The two soldiers from outside the town race toward Keeley at top speed. They stop in front of her and catch their breaths.

"Monster . . . in the desert," the terrified woman informs Keeley. "Too big . . . for all of us . . . to take on."

A mighty roar in the distance interrupts us and freezes everyone in their tracks. Dread courses through me. I've heard it once before, and it was a noise I hoped to never hear again.

The question of how it popped up out of nowhere crosses my mind, but I don't have time to dwell on it. Sabbia, and Calista, still need saving. My head hasn't crossed the *excruciating* threshold yet. One use of Strike on the creature should be an instant kill.

Keeley mutters something I can't decipher; I can only assume it's some kind of curse word. "Emergency shelter! *Passé!*"

Instead of following her orders, I run to the entrance and throw open the door to find the monster.

Not too far in the distance, a large lump swims under the sand searching for an opening. It's huge, at least three to four times bigger than the Dormants that raided Ketra. I can only hope Strike will be powerful enough to take it down. Otherwise, no one in Sabbia will live through the night.

Sand erupts in the air as the monster breaks through and it crashes back down with a boom as loud as my thunder, the earth quaking under my feet. It's no doubt a Dormant, but it's a very abnormally shaped one. It possesses no legs, but the usual ring of tentacles around its neck is present. Its black body coils itself and raises its head. Its red, piercing eyes bore into me, and it lets out an ear-shattering roar. It displays its long, sharp fangs and split tongue, tentacles waving about from its neck. Its immense size has me shaking to the bone and my head is beginning to hurt. But for the sake of Sabbia and Queen Calista, I'll do whatever it takes to kill this thing.

"Bolt!" I call out at the top of my voice. "I need your help!"

Within seconds, Bolt answers my call in gorilla form and scales over the town walls. He lands in the sand next to me with a loud *boom*. He stands up straight and pounds his chest with his ape hands, roaring and baring his teeth right back at the Dormant.

The Dormant shoots icicles at me from its tentacles; I'm quick to use my shield and parry, running back and forth in the cool sand with my bare feet. It hits the Dormant, but incurs little damage. Bolt charges it at full speed, heading for its tail. Icicles and fire keep coming my way, all of which I deflect with my shield. Suddenly, it appears as if the Dormant is being yanked by something when Bolt takes hold of its tail and lifts it up. As the frightful monster roars in protest, Bolt slams it down, then lifts and throws it on the ground again. Grains of sand permeate the air and blur my vision. The impact of its head slamming in the sand reaches the Dormant when it lifts itself up in a wobbly state.

"Bolt! Horse!"

Bolt races toward me while shifting into horse form. Still galloping, I leap onto his back and he runs at the Dormant's head.

"You know what to do, right?" I ask, to which he neighs in response.

The Dormant watches us as we get closer to its face, red eyes rolling and dizzy. I unsheathe my sword and hold it beside me, charging it with electricity with one hand while holding onto Bolt's mane with the other.

"Now!"

He bucks me off and sends me in the air. I grab the hilt with both hands and aim the blade down, my Sabbian skirt billowing and flapping against my legs as I fall straight onto the Dormant's head, plunging my sword right between the eyes.

I lose balance and fall back onto the sand just as the Dormant thrashes about with my sword stuck in its head. Covering my ears with my hands while running does little to soften the sound of its high-pitched roar. It doesn't seem to die, though, as it continues flailing its tail and tentacles, kicking sand in the air. Due to its size, I might have to use what energy I have left on my abilities. I've never used both of them at the same time, but I feel that's the only choice I have now.

I extend my hand and focus entirely on the Dormant, harnessing all the energy I can muster to use Gridlock. From tail to head it freezes, one body part at a time. The pressure behind my eyes is worsening by the second. I use one hand to keep it frozen, then the other to ignite lightning. Using every last bit of focus and energy I have, I throw down my hand with a triumphant yell. Lightning crashes on the Dormant in one powerful blow, so powerful that the boom of thunder reverberates through my body in a single rush.

The Dormant slumps over into the sand, then bursts into a cloud of dust. My sword hangs in the air for a split second before it falls with a metallic *clang*.

My legs give out from under me and I sag to the desert floor, my body making an indentation in the sand. My head throbs in an intense ache that forces my eyes closed. I have no more energy left to move from my spot, let alone the ability to get myself to safety. The night brings a chill that sends goose bumps along my arms, but I don't have it in me to care.

The wind of flapping wings blows right by my face and sends grains of sand up my nostrils. A metal *clang* drops in front of me, then a beak nudges my shoulder. My eyes are barely open in slits when I see what the source of the sounds are.

A worried Bolt has fetched my sword for me and wants to make sure his owner is still alive.

"Good boy," I whisper to him.

The faint sound of shouting commands from the town is the last thing I hear before I fully pass out.

***

The Dormants and Backers have raided Ketra. Smoke, fire, and debris are all I see as I'm laying on the ground.

Jael stands with her back to me, facing a Backer, as I lay flat on the ground. My gut knows what is about to happen. This is my chance to save her; to protect her as she protected me.

"Jael! Move!" I yell at her in desperation. I curl up to reach forward and grab at her. I end up fisting the leg of her black pants she always wears. I tug at what little I can grasp to get her attention, hard enough that she should have fallen over and dodged the Backer's sword.

But she stays standing. When she twists to look at me, it's not Jael's face that I see.

It's Calista's.

"Avenge me, Havanna," her voice echoes, just as the Backer gets ready to stab her from behind.

I wake up with a gasp. My eyes are heavy and my body feels drained of all energy. Whatever I'm laying in feels like a pile of clouds instead of the stiff cot I woke up on in Siro's jail. My hands skate over the covers, which feel like velvet.

My eyes slowly blink open. The bedroom is unfamiliar, but the stone walls and open windows give me a stronger reminder. I have a view of the town, sun shining brightly, and people milling about close to the oasis.

The last thing I remember is collapsing in the sand from overexertion after fighting a Dormant, pouring every drop of power into killing it. Someone must have noticed my limp body and carried me to this room.

Groaning, I sit up and wipe my eyes with my bare hands where I can see the lightning bolt clear as day. I stop mid-rub and gasp.

My gloves are gone.

I get apprehensive for a second before I realize almost everyone in Sabbia already knows who I am. I used Strike right in front of them. It was the only way I could save everyone. I spent my whole life wearing gloves, a habit that's tough to break now.

Next to the bed is a table with my gloves neatly folded. With a sigh, I snatch them up and slip them on, curling and extending my fingers to adjust.

From this vantage point, glancing at the open window in front of me, I'm guessing I'm in one of the guest bedrooms in Queen Calista's house.

Queen Calista.

She was hurt.

I need to find her.

Just as I hurriedly swing my legs out of bed, Freya enters with a potion bottle. From the shimmer swirling around inside, I recognize it right away from Tetia's potion shop in Ketra: the Battle Elixir. The recipe is meant to heal muscle fatigue and regain energy, especially for soldiers in training.

"Oh good, you're awake," she says politely. "I was just about to give you your second dose."

I climb onto my feet. "Where's Calista? Is she okay?"

"She's okay, she's okay," Freya consoles me. "She's resting in her bedroom right now."

"How is she doing?"

"In moderate pain. It hurts where she was struck, but she's stable. She has the Healing Salve on, so she should be up on her feet in no time. I'm very surprised it wasn't worse."

I sit back down on the bed. I'm surprised as well. From experience, I know the Healing Salve works wonders, as it helped heal the cut I got on my collarbone from Ketra's raid, reducing it to a faint scar.

As glad as I am that the queen is okay, a storm of emotions floods my mind and I don't know what to feel first.

Guilty. Furious. Depressed.

Calista never would have needed to fight if the Backers didn't have a reason to be in Sabbia. Had they not been there, she never would have been hurt. My being a Descendant just hurts everyone around me. Jael, Aria, Ketra . . . and now Calista and her people.

"Is there anything else I can get you?" Freya asks with a sweet tone.

Swallowing down my current emotions, I shake my head. "No, I'm fine. Thank you."

"When you're ready, there's someone who wants to talk to you in the throne room," she informs me with an excited smile. "He would like to thank you for everything you did a couple nights ago."

A couple nights ago. That means I've done nothing but sleep this whole time. When Jael was killed in front of me, I poured all my despair into Strike and killed all the Backers and Dormants in the village. That also put me out for two days.

But who else besides Calista wants to thank me?

"Okay, I'll be out in a second."

Freya leaves the potion bottle on the nightstand. "Calista wants to make sure you take this consistently. You're going to need it."

Without hesitation, I swallow the potion in one gulp. The bitter, floral aftertaste slips down my throat and leaves a cooling sensation throughout my body. I exit the bedroom and follow Freya into the living area. The sofa has been replaced with straw chairs and cushions, and the rug that covered the floor is missing and is now bare sandstone. The bar and the floor around it is swept clean, free of glass shards.

I head down the stairs that lead to the throne room where I see a young man sitting on one of the thrones, listening intently to someone who is sitting prostrate in front of him. His golden crown, the same design Calista has with the rays of the sun emanating around it, is set on his neatly combed black hair. Just like the Sabbian men, he has a scarlet scarf wrapped diagonally around his bare torso and purple linen pants, setting him apart from the other men in white. His skin is the same pale but tan complexion as mine, a sign that he is not from Sabbia.

"Our king," Freya addresses the man, bowing to him. His mud-brown eyes almost twinkle when he sees me, his smile whiter than the linen pants of Sabbian men.

"Thank you, Freya. One moment, Havanna," he says in a deep but loving tone. Freya turns and leaves me with King Malik, who dismisses the person he was talking to. He shows his warm smile again as he rises from his throne and approaches me. The thick silver necklace with an Ice Stone on it hangs heavily from his neck, different from the one his wife wears.

"King Malik," I address him with a clumsy bow. "It's an honor to meet you."

"The honor is mine, Havanna." He holds out his hand to shake with a firm grip, dismissing my bow. "I want to thank you for saving my wife while I was trying to guide everyone to the emergency shelter. I owe you for that."

"It was the least I could do after she's treated me so well."

King Malik stays silent, but his face says more than words ever could. There's a measure of sorrow behind them, maybe even regret. I can only imagine he's angry that his wife is hurt because of me. I presume Calista brought him up to speed on who I am and what I was doing in his town.

"I'm so sorry that she was hurt because of me, though," I swallow through my words. "And that the town was in danger because of me."

"You have nothing to apologize for." Malik pats my shoulder consolingly. "Whether you came or not, we still would have had Backers in our midst, and we still would have had to fight them off."

"Even so, they were here looking for me." I beg the tears to not pool in my eyes, so I stare at my clasped hands to at least show him my sincerity. "It bothers me. And I want to make it right, if you will let me. Whatever you need. Queen Calista was so kind to me, it's the least I can do to show my appreciation."

My words don't seem to erase Malik's sorrowful expression. His lips curve into a sad smile when he says, "I see what Calista sees in you."

"What do you mean?"

With a half-hearted chuckle, King Malik wanders back to the throne and sits on the edge of the platform in front of his chair. "You're young. A child in her eyes," he says, avoiding eye contact with me. "It makes perfect sense why she came to your aid."

I move to sit next to him to respect his place as king. "Why would that matter?"

"She always wanted a child," he begins. "We almost had one a few years ago. I was elated to pass on our name and royalty to him." His eyes sparkle as he reminisces, but he doesn't hide whatever pain he's feeling. "Then she woke up one morning . . . and we lost him."

My jaw drops slightly at the horror of this news, and I place my hand over my heart. Calista, a natural mother, lost a child, before she and Malik even had a chance at parenthood. Something they both wanted, and deserved.

I know how it feels to have one's heart split in half.

"It was the worst day of our lives," Malik continues. "She wasn't very far along. But the excited expectation of having your dreams come true then crushed is not something I would wish on my worst enemy."

"You both would have been incredible parents," I reassure him through heavy emotion that wants to show itself in the form of empathetic tears, but I swallow it down.

"Ever since then, Calista's been scared to try again. So she seeks opportunities to be a figurative mother to whoever needs it." Finally, Malik turns to face me. "Like you."

Thinking back to how Calista comforted me and listened to everything I had to say, I can piece it all together. I've been missing the feeling of having a mother, even if Jael wasn't my biological one.

She was my mother in every sense of the word. Calista has a hole in her life, just like I do. She wishes she had a child, just as I wish I had a mother. I may not be a child, but I'm still young.

"Well, I'm happy to reciprocate," I tell him. "Freya told me she's doing okay, but I still feel horrible. It's my fault."

"Far from it, child," Malik assures me with another pat on the shoulder. "Come. She would be delighted to see you."

He gets up and makes his way to the stairs, signaling for me to follow. "Did you meet Calista at a seeking party?" I ask.

"Yes indeed. A few of my friends from Arythica wanted to make the trip. They wanted to see if they would meet someone on the first night. They invited me to join, even though I was far from interested in meeting a woman."

"Why did you go, then?"

"I thought it would be funny to watch my friends fail at their task." Malik chuckles to himself. "Turns out, I was the one who met someone on my first night. She was the only one that was disinterested in the whole thing, and that caught my attention." He shrugs and smiles sheepishly. "And the rest is history." We reach the top of the stairs and enter the bedroom. "My love, you have a visitor," Malik calls.

Calista lays in a bed that has enough room for five people. Behind the bed is a washroom and large closet, and straight ahead from the foot of the bed is a huge open window that gives the perfect three-hundred-sixty-degree view of the desert, the sun shining strong enough to make the heat waves in the distance visible. There is a divider with garments draped over the top and a wooden dresser beside it. Opposite it is a full-sized mirror framed in gold. On the wall above everything is a painting of what I believe is Malik and Calista on their wedding day. The artist did an impeccable job of bringing out the love and happiness in their beaming smiles.

"Havanna!" Calista exclaims, shifting to sit up straighter in the bed. "I'm so glad you're well!"

"Same to you." I motion to her laying in bed.

"I'm going out of my mind," she groans. "My limbs want to have a mind of their own and run across the desert."

Malik moves to her side and adjusts her pillow. "You're still healing, my love. Here, let me help you." As carefully as he can, he grabs her shoulders and gently lifts her so she's positioned upright, and she muffles her cry of pain.

"My apologies!" Malik exclaims as his hand goes straight to her belly where the pink hue of the Healing Salve is seeping through the bandage wrapped around her entire torso.

"Don't trouble yourself, my love." Calista smooths her palm on her husband's cheek in reassurance. "It's getting better. The physician says I need to wear this bandage with the Healing Salve for a couple more days and I should be back to normal."

"My amazing warrior." Malik leans in and kisses her on the forehead. He turns back to me and winks. "I'll leave you two be."

I nod as he walks past me to the stairs, and it takes everything in me to not burst into a fit of sobs. I tell myself it's just the guilt I feel for Calista's current state, even though Malik reassured me neither one of them have ill will toward me. Seeing their love for each other has instilled emotions that are foreign to me. An emotional conflict that I've never experienced.

The way Malik talks about his wife, the way she makes him react, how deeply he loves her . . . I wanted someone to react that way to me. I wanted someone to love me the way Malik loves Calista. I wanted to make someone smile and reminisce about how our story began. That was all something I, at one time, wanted for myself, but that changed when Victor betrayed me. I don't ever want a man to seek me out. I'm absolutely sure of that.

So why am I crying?

"Havanna? Are you all right?" Calista's concerned voice breaks through my conflicting feelings.

Suddenly embarrassed, I wipe my tears with the heel of my hand. "Yes, I'm sorry. I just feel awful that you have to deal with this."

"No need to worry, child," she consoles me and pats the edge of the bed. "Injury is inevitable in battle."

I hold back the sob that begs to burst from my throat as I position myself beside her on the mattress. "I know. But it's my fault you were hurt."

"No." Calista shakes her head with conviction. "Those Backers were hunting for you. They've caused you to go into hiding your whole life, and that is *not* because of anything you did. You did nothing to warrant their actions. Do you understand?"

That's essentially the same line of reasoning Jael told me when I first arrived in Ketra. I believed it was my fault that the Backers tore through Cal-léa. They were looking for me, after all. Hard to believe that wasn't my fault.

As if that were not enough, the Backers set up camp in Sabbia because they were looking for me, then caused chaos when I walked into their trap. Again, hard to believe none of that is because of me.

Leaving Ketra was a mistake. Coming to Sabbia was a mistake. I should have listened to Aria and done what I could to make amends to Ketra for my poor decisions and let time dissipate their disgust and hatred for me. All my leaving did was prove that anyone who knows me or has an affiliation with me is in danger.

I don't belong anywhere. I have no place I can call home.

"I think leaving Ketra was a mistake," I mumble to myself, wiping the tears from my cheeks. "I should have stayed there. Stayed in hiding. Everything was fine then."

"Why would you say that?" Calista tugs my arm so I can turn and face her. "I disagree, but I'd much rather hear it from you."

I heave a sigh. I'd practically have to give her my life story in order for her to see where I'm coming from. "There's a lot to tell."

"If you haven't already noticed, I'm going to be immobile for quite some time." She motions to her body laying in the large bed. Then she leans back against the headboard and folds her arms over her chest. "Speak your heart, child."

And I do.

I fill in the gaps of the story I left out when we first met. I tell her how I was sent to Ketra from Cal-léa when I was ten years old. I tell her how my life in Ketra was wonderful, but I was tired of hiding myself and constantly being careful not to draw attention. I tell her that my using Strike caused the Backers and Dormants to raid Ketra and kill Jael. I tell her that everyone's rejection of me, along with my desire to redeem myself, are the major reasons I left. But my leaving has seemed to make things worse for everyone I've run into, including her.

When I'm finished, Calista's thoughtful hum is her only initial response. Her thumb and forefinger lay on her chin as she thinks.

"That is certainly a lot to take in," she finally says. "Give me a moment to think about the right way to say what I need to say." She groans as she sits up just a little bit more; a stance that tells me she's going to be serious and honest with me. "First, I must say that staying in hiding would solve nothing. The Dormant King and the Backers would still be looking to find you, whether you stayed in Ketra or not." She emphasizes her point with her intricately painted fingernail. "The second thing I will say is that I've never known anyone who succeeded in something without hitting a few obstacles. You've already come this far. I say you see this through."

I let her words sink in. Staying in hiding would indeed solve nothing. That solution just allows the Dormant King to win. So far, I'm the only Descendant brave enough to break out of hiding to find him. None of the other Descendants have. The Ancestors never fought back, and it's about time someone does.

Calista prods me with her finger. "The question to ponder is: is it still important to you to avenge Jael and the people you love?"

This gives me two options: go back to Ketra, humiliated that I gave up on my mission and risk living among villagers who will hate me for the rest of my life, or remember that I want to redeem myself for Jael's and Aria's sakes and not give up in my search for the Dormant King, even if it takes longer than expected to find him.

Only one of those choices is the right one. The one I know, deep in my bones, that I have to do.

"Yes," I whisper. "It is."

Calista pats my hand. "Then you just solved your own problem."

Something about her encouragement ignites a flame in me. The same flame I had when I first left Ketra. That desire—that motivation—had dimmed with Lavi's betrayal. Now, it's a roaring fire.

"But before you do anything else, you must stay here and rest," she advises. "Everyone thought you died the other night."

I shake my head vigorously. "No. I've slept for two days. That's long enough."

"Havanna," she reprimands, "you will accomplish nothing if you're not at full strength. You can't take care of others if you haven't taken care of yourself first."

My first instinct is to argue with her that I'll be fine if I leave now. That my well-being isn't as important as everyone else's. But my body is still physically weak from the events of the last couple days.

When Jael died, one of the first things that gave me a sense of dread was how I would go through life without her. I never imagined having to live without her mentorship and wisdom this early. Somehow, by coincidence, Calista has taken over that role. Jael must have been looking out for me and knew I still needed someone to rely on.

"Okay," I concede. "You're right."

"Besides," she adds, "it will give you some time to thoroughly plan your next move without kissing death again." She winks at me playfully before she asks, "Where did you plan on going after this?"

"Killios."

Her eyebrows knit together. "What are you hoping to find there?"

The memory of Lavi betraying me comes rushing back and I take a deep breath to tamp down the emotions tied to that moment. "Growing up, Jael talked about someone named Arthur from Killios Training Camp that she trained with. I suppose he's been doing research on the Dormant King's whereabouts for a long time. When I met Lavi, she told me Arthur sent her to do some research on him too. She said she was coming to Sabbia because she heard that there may be some ancient tablets that could be tied to the Ancestors and the Dormant King. I thought it made sense to come here with her, only to walk into her trap." I scoff. "I can't believe I fell for that one."

"I beg your pardon. Lavi tricked you?"

"She was the one that tried to kill us," I answer through clenched teeth with a shake to my voice. "She was working with the Buckers the whole time. Said she only did it because they held her son hostage."

Calista mutters a string of angry sentences under her breath that I don't understand, then shakes her head and releases a deep exhale. "Was she telling the truth about her son?"

"I don't know. I chose not to take on the guilt of her death if she happened to be telling the truth."

She studies me with understanding. "I can't say I wouldn't have done the same thing." She shifts her focus to her hands, bunching her brows and squinting her eyes as she thinks. "You know, even though she was deceitful, I think she may have been on the right path with the ancient tablets."

I look at her with skepticism. "She may not have lied about her son, but she definitely could have lied about the tablets to lure me to her trap."

Calista holds up her hand to silence my arguments. "True, but that doesn't mean her claim about the tablets has no value."

"How so?"

Calista shifts herself under the covers and lets out a slight groan. "When I was younger, I remember coming across a stone slab my parents confiscated from a thief that our soldiers caught trying to escape with a handful of Ice Stone headbands. It looked like some-one cut it out of the wall of a cave. The artwork was so beautiful and fascinating that I decided to keep it. Now, I wonder if it's a clue tied to the Ancestors somehow. Maybe Lavi heard about it from a gossipmonger or something."

Excitement brews in my chest. Physical evidence tied to the An-cestors is exactly what I need. Even better, I can bring it to Arthur and he could determine if it's a valid clue. Anything that can help me get closer to the Dormant King, the better.

"Do you still have it?" I ask eagerly, leaning to jump off the bed.

She reacts to my question and eagerness with a sideways smile. "I have it on display in the library downstairs." She grumbles, "If it's still there after the Backers ruined the rest of my home."

It takes a great deal of self-control to not run straight to the library. Instead, I calmly rise from the mattress and wander over to the stairs.

"Ah, ah! *Ruken!*" she barks, which stops me in my tracks and makes my eyes go wide. Calista puts on her mothering tone when she points at me and demands, "Rest first. Research later."

I spread out my hands and shift my weight to one leg. "Can I at least look at it? Then I can rest and think about the drawing. I can do both things at once."

She shoots me a disbelieving look in response to my alternative. Eventually, she sighs in exasperation and flaps her hands. "Fine. But just *look*, then go back to your bedroom. In fact, I'll have Zena go with you."

"Decided you don't trust me?" I ask with a playful lilt.

"I will neither confirm nor deny," she responds before calling, "Zena!" She winces in pain, the use of her diaphragm aggravating the wound.

"Will she even hear you?"

"Yes, our queen!" Zena calls back from the floor below.

Calista winks at me. "All open windows. Voices carry."

Zena appears in the bedroom in what feels like seconds, shimmering with a sheen of sweat from the exertion it takes to clean this palace of a home.

"Please escort Havanna to the library at your earliest convenience. And *please*, make sure she goes straight to her guest bedroom when she's done. She's not quite finished getting her rest."

"Yes, our queen." Zena turns to me, seemingly still unsure about treating me as equally as the rest of the Sabbians. "Whenever you're ready, *mahina.*"

"I'm ready," I say politely.

My eagerness to see the closest connection to the Dormant King I have can't wait any longer.

CHAPTER 8

"**R**ight this way, *mahina.*"

Zena leads me down the hallway to the very last room. A desk with an unlit lantern sits in front of me with a chair. The seat of the chair is designed with pieces of straw woven together while the rest of it is wood. Bookshelves line the walls on either side of me, reaching all the way to the ceiling.

In a glass case on the desk is a flat chunk of reddish stone, over a foot long and about six inches wide. I sit, never taking my eyes off the slab. I'm so heavily focused on it that I forget that Zena is standing behind me.

On the right side of the tablet, the painting shows four people dressed in white gathered together with an elemental symbol above each of their heads: a water droplet, a lightning bolt, a flame, and a leaf. On the left side is one person dressed in dark purple with a large black circle behind him with the symbol of a tree above his head. Based on the symbols alone, I conclude that these people must be the Ancestors. Without the symbols, this artwork could easily be interpreted as something involving the Backers.

The one with the water symbol has their arm outstretched toward, who I presume, is the Power Ancestor. The Water Ancestor is doing something to Power, but I can't figure out what it is. The way their hand is positioned reminds me of the way I use my own powers. The only mystery here is if the Water Ancestor is using their abilities in this painting, it's not a water-related one. On top of that, considering that the Power Ancestor turned himself into the Dormant King, it's hard to discern if this event displayed in the artwork happened before or after he transformed. In that case, these people can't possibly be the Backers. They *live* for the Dormant King.

When my mother told me about the Ancestors, she said the Dormant King had two abilities, Usurp and Manipulation. With Usurp, he could copy the Ancestors' abilities once the Backers found them. She acknowledged that I had more than one ability.

Does that mean the other Ancestors had more abilities too? If not, then what exactly is this depicting? Is this even about the Ancestors? Is this something else entirely that still tells the story of Petros's history?

I only have one person in mind who might be able to read this tablet, and he's all the way at the Killios Training Camp. Arthur might be able to use this to draw conclusions from his own research over the years. It will be a triumphant moment when I show this to him and help him reach the goal of success.

Maybe Arthur is the key I need to find the Dormant King.

"Is there any way Queen Calista would let me take this when I leave?" I twist around to ask Zena.

She shrugs with a polite smile. "I'm sure she wouldn't mind, seeing how much she trusts you."

I'm already planning out how to carry this with me when I leave. I wish there was a way for me to leave right now—sneak out the door and avoid the soldiers' eyes and head to Killios. But Calista wants me to rest. And she's right; I need it.

Standing from the chair, I turn back to the stone slab, thoughts swirling through my head. "Do you think I can at least take this to my room? Study it while I rest?"

"Let me ask the queen for you," Zena offers politely with a bow.

Once she is out of sight, I examine the tablet again. My instinct tells me the Ancestors had more powers than I know about, but the question of what powers the Water Ancestor possessed in this tablet hangs in the balance. What the black hole is behind the Power Ancestor is a much bigger question.

I run my fingers over the edges, taking in the slab's rough curves, the smooth surface of the stone, the fading and chipping of the paint. My mind reels with even more questions than I started with.

"She said it is fine to take it to your room." Zena's voice breaks my silent reverie. "She also said you can take it with you when you have to leave."

"Thank you, Zena."

"But she wants you to make sure to let your brain rest at some point." She raises her eyebrows to emphasize Calista's order.

I chuckle. "Okay, it's a deal."

Grabbing the case off the desk, I follow Zena back to my temporary bedroom. A pitcher of water, an empty glass, another bottle of Battle Elixir, and a small plate of cut up Dewey Fruit wait for me on the bedside table.

"Our queen requested that we leave you with all the necessities for your recovery," Zena points out, fascinated with this offer. "It's unusual for our queen to treat her guests this way." Shrugging with a grin, she turns and saunters down the hall.

I pick up the potion bottle and watch the swirls dance in the light. A smile spreads on my face from the endearing gesture, warm affection coating my heart and touching me in a way I haven't felt since Jael was alive. More for Calista's sake than my own, I drink the potion in a couple gulps and put the empty bottle back on the table. With the way my knees shake and my eyes want to close, I wonder if I just drank Sleeper's Brew instead of Battle Elixir to force me into a slumber.

Before I can think about anything else, I crawl into the velvety-smooth sheets and place the stone tablet on the table next to the water and fruit. Before I can focus on it and think some more, I succumb to the bliss of sleep.

***

When I wake up next, it's nighttime. I don't know if I slept for a few hours or for a few more days.

Echoes of laughter, chatter, the bangles of a tambourine, and beating of a drum outside makes it clear the Sabbians have resumed their regular seeking party routine. They celebrate as if they never had a Backers invasion or had a Dormant just outside their town. I briefly wonder if the events of the other night scared off most of the men so the women wouldn't have many options for a suitor during seeking parties. That thought is a fleeting one when I remind myself that I don't really care.

A warm breeze squeezes through the open window of the bedroom and sweeps over my face. The welcome relief tells me I've been sweating under these sheets. I drink some water from the pitcher left on the table, gulping down the whole glass in a couple swallows. My body feels much more energized, my mind is clearer, and my head doesn't hurt nearly as much as it did a few nights ago.

Bolt makes an appearance on the floor as a mouse, sniffing the air on his hind legs as I put on my now-clean black outfit and gloves.

"I'm going to get something to eat," I tell him. I stoop down to pick him up with my hands, then place him on the windowsill. "Just stay here and watch over the place. I'll call for you if I need you."

He squeaks in response and I make my way downstairs across the throne room to join the throng of partying Sabbians.

The further into town I go, the more people stop what they're doing and fixate on me. This time, the looks are of respect and admiration instead of pure disdain. Appreciative smiles and nods of approval surround me; a vast difference from the attitude and negativity that prevailed when I arrived. I take it as an unspoken agreement that I will be treated without contempt from now on.

"Havanna," a woman calls out from behind me. The music stops and so does everyone's talking. I turn and find Keeley approaching me, dressed in regular Sabbian garb, no weapons or armor present. "We, Sabbia Town, are forever indebted to you," she announces loud enough for everyone to hear. "For not only saving this beautiful place from peril, but for saving our beloved queen. Without your assistance, strength, and bravery, most of us would not have survived. For that, we thank you."

The sudden humility is astounding, and I find myself patting my cheeks with my gloved hands to hide the pink hue of my blushing. I've never received recognition or attention in this way, considering I spent my whole life in hiding. The last time I had a whole crowd's worth of attention was in Ketra, and it was the worst kind of attention one could receive.

"From this day forward, we vow to do our best to assist you in your efforts to destroy the Dormant King and his allies, and to keep your identity as the Lightning Descendant strictly within the walls of this town."

Keeley concludes her statement with a slight bow. Before I can protest, everyone, including the men, do the same, bending forward in submission. Behind the crowd, I see Malik and Calista, holding hands with proud smiles, observing their people showing gratitude for their savior. Calista wears a longer shirt with her paneled skirt, most likely to hide the bandage from her injury. Malik then snakes his arm around her waist to make sure she's stable and safe. They obviously put forth effort to make sure the town shows its gratitude.

Thank you, King and Queen.

A smile begs to break out on my face, but I hold it back as I turn in a circle and observe the crowd of about three hundred bowing, earning each and every person's favor and praise along the way.

Saving Sabbia wasn't a second thought. Even if I was treated poorly at first, I didn't want to be responsible for anyone who died at the hands of people who were on the hunt for me. Protecting everyone is my duty. More importantly, I owed it to Calista. She thought only of the well-being of the town when she was injured, which speaks volumes.

I lay a hand over my heart. "Thank you. Truly, thank you."

As everyone straightens up, the music starts again and blends in with the chatter. Calista makes her way through the crowd and points at the eatery behind me. "Order whatever you want, free of charge."

She has been too kind to me and I start to feel guilty for accepting it. "I don't mind paying for it."

"Consider it an apology gift from the town," she remarks with a nudge to my arm. "They owe it to you."

I smirk at her. "Thank you."

"Enjoy." With a wink, Calista turns and squeezes through the crowd, back to her beloved husband. Seeing them together returns an unwelcome ache to my chest for reasons I refuse to identify.

I enter the open-concept eatery, a similar setup to the one I owned in Ketra. As I take a seat at an empty, polished-wood table and peruse the menu, I'm reminded of home.

Of Aria.

My thoughts take a deep, dark turn. I left Ketra not that long ago, but I can't help but wonder how she's doing. How Thaeus is doing as the new chief. How the village is faring while they restore their home to what it once was.

Deep regret surfaces over how I left things with Aria. Just when I thought I had her on my side, the village goes up in flames, and knowing the reason behind it forces her to turn her back on me. There was nothing I could say that would make her understand my side of the situation, or about me being a Descendant. I hope she understands I'm not taking this responsibility lightly; I'm willing to sacrifice everything to make things right.

More than anything, I hope she hasn't already forgotten about me.

"Some Chill Grapes to snack on, *mahina*," a Sabbian waitress says when she sets a plate of the pale blue pearls in front of me.

"Thank you." I smile appreciatively at her, my stomach grumbling in response to seeing the snack. My thoughts took my attention away from the menu, so my intense hunger forces me to order the first thing I see. "Can I get the Midnight Pig with fire-roasted cactus leaf and Petros Rice?"

"Of course."

Once the waitress walks away, I pick the Grapes off their shoots and eat one, letting their ice cold and sugary sweet juice fill my mouth. I suppose there's one perk to having left Ketra: trying different types of food. Growing up with Jael, she gave me all the books she had on the different fruits and vegetables from around the country that Ketra didn't carry. After I finished a book, she gave me a test based on what I read. Remembering those days, I wonder if she was testing me because she knew I would venture out of Ketra at some point and she wanted to be sure I had enough knowledge to survive on my own. She's the reason why I know only Sabbia sells Chill Grapes, that Sabbians rely on it as a temporary relief from the desert heat, and that they're even used as ice to preserve food.

The Chill Grape juice slithers down my throat as I swallow the rest of it, the icy sensation traveling through my body. Now that I'm cold, I wish more than ever to swim in the Reddawn Oasis to warm back up.

As I eat my dinner in peace, mixing the cuts of deep purple meat with the light blue grains of rice, I plan out what I'm going to do next. Based on my newly acquired piece of potential evidence, the most logical thing to do is let Arthur decide if the tablet means anything. I feel more energized and healed, and I don't want to waste any more time on doing nothing. I need to leave first thing in the morning before the searing heat makes the trip unbearable.

Even if that means I have to leave Calista behind.

Just when I feel like I've found a mother figure again, I have to leave her. Part of me doesn't want to. I feel safe and comforted here in her care. I'm in a place where people actually see my value and care about me and my mission.

Safe and comfortable is the trap, though. Those feelings can prevent one from being productive. It won't eliminate the Dormant King.

You've already come this far. I say you see this through.

Calista's words come back to mind. I'm so close to making a breakthrough; I can feel it.

Once I finish my supper, I walk back to Malik and Calista's house and head up to my bedroom. Bolt, still sitting at the window, peers at me with his beady eyes as I stand next to him, observing the party for the last time. Men and women standing around with drinks in hand, dancing to the music, and flirting their hearts out. Malik and Calista, hand in hand, slither in between pairs of people, then he spins her around, dancing to the beat of the drum and tambourine. Her happiness shines all the way over here.

I already dread my departure, but having these people as my support somehow makes it that much more endurable.

I wait until the beginning of dawn to pack my things.

I safely bury Calista's stone tablet among the other items in my bag and make sure the map and poem are secured in my pocket. The purple and pink hues of the sunrise shine their rays over the edge of the desert. The darker shades around the luminescent sunrise indicate that it's very early morning, making this the perfect time to travel before the heat of the day gets worse.

To be a kind guest, I fixed up the bed that was so lovingly provided for me. Bolt, still a mouse, crawls up my leg and squeezes into my pocket as I take one last look around the room. I don't know when I'll be back—if I do come back—so I make a point to take in everything I can.

I try to be quiet as I tiptoe down the hall, pack slung over my shoulder and shuffling around with each step. In the living area, I scan every surface for something to write a note on. Writing a goodbye note to someone who has taken me in is a better option than dealing with the emotions of saying goodbye face-to-face, no matter how immature this choice seems.

"Leaving without saying goodbye, are we?"

The sudden voice frightens me out of my skin and I jump. Calista stays frozen on the stairs, barefoot in a white silken nightgown that reaches her knees and hugs her curves. Her eyes show something akin to rejection.

I cringe. "I didn't want to wake you."

Calista steps off the staircase and stands in front of me. "I believe we crossed the threshold of such boundaries a while ago," she responds.

I shift my weight, uncomfortable that she caught me, but more uncomfortable that I have to say goodbye to her regardless. I chew my bottom lip. "You're up early," I bring out lamely.

"I enjoy watching the sunrise." She shrugs. "Besides, being a queen is a hefty responsibility that robs me of sleep sometimes. I'm surprised Malik can sleep through his troubles the way he does." She steps past me and stands in front of the open window in the living area. "I may have lived here my whole life, but the glory of a desert sunrise is unmatched." She eyes me with a side smile, crossing her arms. "It never ceases to amaze me."

I stand next to her, watching the beauty of nature out in the distance. The pink and purple slowly convert to orange and yellow to indicate the passing of time. I make sure to commit the scenery to memory, as I want to come back to it someday.

"Are you still going to Killios?" Calista's soothing voice breaks the silence, preventing eye contact.

"Yes."

"Do you have the tablet?"

"I made sure to not forget to pack it," I answer with a shy grin.

"I figured as much." Calista's shoulders sink as she turns to face me. Instead of playing the part of a respected authoritarian but caring queen, she has the demeanor of any other subject—a person with raw, human feelings. Underneath the confident exterior, she's still her own person. "Listen to me," she begins after clearing her throat, "don't be a stranger. Visit anytime. Come back whenever you need us." Sniffling, she lifts her eyes to the side. "Whenever you need *me*."

Now she makes me want to cry, and that was exactly what I didn't want to do. My throat wouldn't be sore with the sign of oncoming tears if I had simply found a pen and paper.

I swallow down the signs of my aching heart and nod, my eyes glossy. "I will."

Calista launches forward and throws her arms around my neck, holding me tight. The hug takes me by surprise, but I find myself warming up to it, and I slowly wrap my arms around her.

The last time I was hugged was when my parents sent me to Ketra.

Jael wasn't an affectionate person. I know she loved me, but she never said it, and she did little to show it in physical ways. She occasionally gave me a kiss on the head, but she wasn't one to give hugs. I learned to accept that over time, even though I yearned to remember what it felt like to have loving arms wrapped snugly around my body. Deep down, I hoped for a chance to hug Victor, if things had blossomed romantically between us.

Calista holds me tightly for a while, then lets me go and grabs my shoulders. "I know you're going to win. I believe in you."

Her words mean more to me than she knows, but I suppress those feelings. "I hope so," I whisper with a tremor in my voice.

She holds up a finger that tells me to wait and turns to head back to the stairs. "Let me give you something before you go."

She's already given me so much; I can't imagine needing anything else.

She comes back a few seconds later with a small, thin gold necklace, just long enough to wrap around my neck. An emblem of the sun, Sabbia's symbol, sits in the middle of the chain, with a dark blue Ice Stone attached inside the core.

"I think you'll need this," she says, clipping it around my neck for me, her nails lightly scraping against my skin. "The Ice Stone will help you keep cool from the desert heat. The stone is detachable, so you can wear the necklace on its own if you wish." She peers down at her feet shyly. "And something to remember me by."

The necklace fits the circumference of my neck perfectly, the emblem sitting right at the bottom of my throat. The coolness of the Ice Stone surrounds my entire body, sending goose bumps along my skin. The chain is just long enough to stay out of the way during battle. I grasp the cold emblem and squeeze. From now on, I have this as a reminder of who is on my side during this journey, and any battle I come across.

"Thank you," I tell her softly.

Calista cups my face with her hands for a second before they slide down to my shoulders again. "Go. Save Petros."

Pursing my lips, I pat her hand affectionately, then head to the staircase. As I go down the steps outside her palace, farther and farther away from her house, I tell myself to not turn around and look at her one last time, but I do anyway. From the window, Calista doesn't take her eyes off me; but instead of being sad, she seems proud of my bravery in taking on this mission.

With a final wave, I make my way to the doors of the town, on to my next destination.

I know the heat of the day is intense, but thanks to Calista's Ice Stone necklace, I barely feel it. And for that, I'm grateful.

Sabbia grows smaller and smaller as I ride horseback on Bolt and cross the expanse of sandy desert, leaving my heart right along with it. Now there are two things I miss dearly.

Calista, and my Twinkle Fireflies.

Bolt trots along the path leading back to greener fields while I take in the surroundings of the landscape. Snapping Pelicans and Lime Geese swim along the surface of a pond surrounded by long grass. Snapping Pelicans got their names from how they snap their beaks if someone intrudes in their personal space. The Lime Goose, on the other hand, got its name because its feathers resemble the color of the citrus fruit. Their meat has been said to have the citrusy aftertaste of lime, but I have no sure testimony to rely on. Oddly enough, they're common birds in the wilderness, yet I never saw them around Ketra. The theory about the Lime Goose meat has me curious enough to try it sometime. I wonder if it really tastes of lime. The only problem is I don't enjoy hunting animals and preparing them as meals. I can kill a fish with a Pineapple Shell, and I can gut it, but that's as far as my skills go.

The only exception to this is the Swift Dingo. It was a serious danger when they invaded our village with the Winged Wolves, as they never hide their vicious, gnarling teeth. One would be smart to kill it before it attacks. Winged Wolves are much less fierce. Even though they have wings, they can't fly. Much like the Clucks.

Bolt continues trotting at a steady pace as we cross the rocky terrain between Stoneland Hills and the base of Vulca Mountain. The heat from the river of lava above me coats the air in its humidity and reddens my cheeks despite the Ice Stone wrapped around my neck. Weeds and bushes are spotted in various spaces between rocks with Mulhutna Peppers growing on some of the twigs.

"Let's take a break for a minute. My bum hurts." I tug gently on the hairs of his mane to make him stop, then hop off to pick a couple Peppers off a bush and take a huge bite from one. The hot steam rises from the open Pepper and hits me in the face. Eating the pepper in this condition is similar to eating something as soon as it's been taken off a fire. Crunchy on the outside, soft on the inside. Spicy with a charred flavor.

"Okay, I think we can keep going now," I say as I sloppily wipe my mouth with my bare arm.

I'm not prepared when Bolt gets behind me and lifts me off the ground with his muzzle. I find myself giggling as I tumble over his body ungracefully with my legs in the air and end up draped across his back. He whinnies again and shakes his head as if to laugh at me.

It's been much too long since I've had a good laugh.

I lift myself up and turn around in a seated position. In my own way, I thank him for making my day a little better with a rub of his head, which he returns with a nudge to my hand. Once I gently kick his sides, we're moving again.

The setting sun dims the world around us when we finally pass Stoneland Hills. The moonlight glimmers in the grass and billows with the soft, chilly breeze. While I think about it, I take off the necklace and open the casing to remove the Ice Stone. It's cold to the touch, even colder than the Chill Grapes. I slip it in the front pocket in my pack before it freezes my entire hand and put the necklace back on. Just like Jael's armband, this necklace has become a part of me now.

We enter a patch of monstrous, leafy trees that create a natural roof over us. The white dots of the stars paint the sky, twinkling in the open spaces of the trees, just as the waters of Ketra Falls did in the moonlight at night. The homesickness makes a vigorous appearance as I remember the memory of catching my Twinkle Fireflies and bringing them back to my hut. The yellow specks floating in my jar as I fell asleep helped me relax. Imagining them with an empty jar, as hard as I try, doesn't quite have the same effect.

Just then, a sight in front of me among the trees has me halting Bolt to a stop, and smiling ear-to-ear.

Yellow specks of light float around the space, minding their business, being content with the solace of night.

Twinkle Fireflies.

I found my Fireflies.

As I scramble to remove the glass jar from my pack, my heart fills with joy with an unfaltering smile. I can't move quickly enough as I nearly fall off Bolt's back. Just when I thought I would never see them again, they appear out of nowhere in my travels. Fits of cheer and blissful hysterics blurt out and echo under the canopy of trees.

"Thank you, Jael!" I yell. This must be Jael's way of watching over me, giving me yet another way to ease my grief over losing her. As much as I want to believe this all happened by coincidence, I still have to know she's still with me, no matter what form that comes in.

I swoop the jar back and forth to capture nature's lantern, crouched and stepping about stealthily to prevent scaring them away. I shut the lid when I'm satisfied with the number of Fireflies I've collected.

There they are, searching for escape in the glass, gliding as pieces of cotton in the wind. I watch in admiration, and still in disbelief, that I even found them.

Bolt's hooves clopping in the grass grabs my attention when he comes closer to me. His head tilts inquisitively as if he wants to know my next steps.

"Let's camp here for the night," I tell him with much more animation than usual when I have to set up my tent.

I hang a canvas over a thick branch, hang another one over the "door" to keep the light out, then I unfurl my blankets. Bolt shifts into his gorilla form and sits outside my tent for my protection while I sleep. I set the jar right next to my head along with my sword. The Fireflies' light is so bright it illuminates the entire space and could prevent me from shutting my eyes. The effect will be just the opposite, though. Tonight, I can sleep in peace.

Finally, nighttime doesn't feel so lonely.

CHAPTER 9

"I think it's only a couple miles to walk to Killios from here," I inform Bolt.

Once I pack up my tent and hesitantly release my Fireflies, I reexamine where we are on the map. Killios is a couple miles away on flat, open, grassy land once we exit the forest. The pathway makes for easy travel but still provides a hiding place for dangerous wildlife.

"See that dark spot out there?" I point past the trees to a dark area straight ahead. "That's where we're heading. You should probably stay a gorilla for now, in case there are lurking creatures."

He huffs a breath of confirmation and walks on all fours next to me as we head for the dark spot that is Killios.

The tall grass crunches beneath my boots as I traverse through the woods, then the world seems to open up when I get past the trees and come across the wide-open field. The walled area that I know is Killios Training Camp gets bigger and bigger the closer I get. The pieces of grass get sticky and attach themselves to my pants, all while my aching legs get exercise from making high steps instead of regular ones.

A faint but vicious snarl stops me in my tracks. It's a noise of having its prey trapped and about to pounce. My hand rushes to the hilt of my sword, my leather gloves crunching in response to the tight grip. The air is quiet now except for the grass softly moving in sync with the subtle breeze. Maybe it was just the wind. After a few seconds, I press onward.

The snarl comes back, more prominent this time. I unsheathe my sword and turn in a slow circle, vigilant and on high alert. The creature might mistake me for prey if I were to run, and would probably catch up to me with ease.

The grass moves back and forth in the distance, indicating that something is approaching, but doing well to hide its identity.

It all happens in a blur, so fast that I wonder if it's a nightmare.

A large gray canine pounces from the grass at tremendous speed. All I see are legs stretched out and teeth bared, eager to tear me to pieces. Bolt slams it down with his muscled arm. The canine flops on the grass, but Bolt doesn't stop there. The earth thumps under me as he punches the creature over and over. Once Bolt is sure the creature has stopped moving, the ground is still again.

"What was that?" I exclaim as I run over to where the creature lies. There, surrounded by tall grass, is the carcass of a Swift Dingo. Its mouth agape and needle-sharp teeth bared as if the goal of killing its prey still lives on in its soul. I gasp at its unsightly, distorted face from Bolt pulverizing it to oblivion.

That beast could have killed me.

I kneel and sit back until I'm seated on the ground. Bolt appears next to me and emits an apelike huff of air.

"I'm okay," I whisper. "Just recovering from my heart attack."

Bolt switches back to a mouse and scurries up to my shoulder, waiting for me to be ready to move on from the trauma. I take the time to recover from the shock of the last few minutes. My brain struggles to wrap around the fact that I just had a near-death experience. Had that Dingo killed me, then everything I worked so hard for would have been for nothing. The Dormant King would still be looking for the Descendants. The Descendants would still be in hiding. My purpose for making things right for Jael, Aria, and Ketra would lie flat.

I can't let that happen. I will crush any opportunity that could get me killed as I make my way to fight the Dormant King.

"Okay. I'm okay." I stumble to get back on my feet and shake the feeling into my limbs. One more look at the dead Dingo has me shuddering and just a bit afraid that it will come to life and attack again. That gets me running the remaining distance to Killios.

The camp is surrounded by brick walls with a twenty-foot iron-clad gate, fronted by two guards and the roaring fire of torches burning above them on either side. The guards have metal-plated armor, including a metal helmet and a black panache springing from the top of it. They stand completely immobile, holding their spears upright at their sides, not even acknowledging me as I approach them.

My hands tremble with nervous energy as I bend to reach into my pack for the encased stone tablet. My legs feel weak when I come back to standing. I study the camp in disbelief.

After all these years—hearing stories about this man, his connection to Jael, the information he possesses about the Dormant King—I'm here, at last, getting closer to meeting him and uncovering the muck of confusion I've experienced. My hand reaches for Calista's necklace and my eyes avert to Jael's armband on my left bicep; I'm in need of their support.

"Young lady," one of the guards finally greets me with an accent, bowing his head.

I walk toward them with a salute. "I need to speak with Arthur," I pronounce confidently.

"What business do you have with him?" he asks. The accent is dignified with tall-sounding words. The Rs in the words sound more like "uh" and the vowels are elongated.

With a grin, I lift the tablet in the air. "I have something I think he'll want to see. It might be tied to the Ancestors."

That perks him right up. "Oh yes! Of course!" He steps back to his position, then he and the other guard slam the ground twice with the heels of their spears. The gate splits in half and opens inward, slowly granting me access to the camp.

One-story, dark-wood buildings line both sides of the gray brick walkway, the small glass windows flicker with dim candlelight, although the early morning sun shines brighter now. The red roofs of the buildings are angled at a sharp peak. The path veers to the right or left, a building with at least three floors with the same peaked roof set straight ahead.

To the left are chants and stomps from what seems like hundreds of soldiers. After a moment of silence, it happens again. It entices me to follow the path to the center of the camp, where the source of the noise is.

Soldiers, both men and women, line up in five rows with ten people in each, standing straight and stepping forward in perfect alignment at the exact same time. The same one-story buildings surround the training grounds, I suppose to act as sleeping quarters for the trainees. Breastplates, combat boots, and brown trousers are the common outfit. Leather armbands with an emerald wrap around their biceps to signal the beginner level of training they're stationed in.

Soldiers stop and crouch and release a triumphant yell. I spot one of the women who has the serious countenance and battle-ready stance that Jael once had. It feels as though I've gone back in time to watch her in the beginning stages of her journey as a warrior. I imagine her being among the trainees, marching and chanting, sword sheathed and equipped around her waist, learning the skills that she passed down to me.

A longing ache blossoms within me.

I miss her.

The ache dissipates when I spot a man in front of the marching crowd, a touch of salt-and-pepper color in his black beard and hair who shouts something unintelligible. Soldiers pair off and practice sparring with each other with their various weapons. My eyes stay glued on the bearded man, his thick brows knitted together in concentration, hands held behind his back. He carries himself with authority as he steps away from the training camp and up the stairs to a large building behind him with a giant bell within the roof.

This must be Arthur.

The stone tablet still in my hand, I walk the perimeter of the training grounds toward the stairs, making sure to dodge any swinging weapons. I take two steps at a time until I reach the double doors and yank one of them open.

Weapons and knights' armor border the walls of the room, the floor covered in gold and red area rugs. In front of me is an area closed off by a sheet of thin red curtains with the murmur of a candle flickering behind it, a small table with teacups and a kettle of boiling water, and large, red velvet pillows set on each side of the table.

The man I presume to be Arthur stands just outside the curtain. Words are lodged in my throat as I take him in. The fact that I'm now seeing him in front of me still seems surreal.

He quirks a bushy brow and regards my appearance. "Can . . . I help you?" he asks in the same accent as the guards.

"Are you Arthur?"

He crosses his bulging, muscled arms over his chest, eyeing me in defense. "Who wants to know?"

I don't think I should mention I know Jael. He has most likely met thousands of people in his life; the odds are low that he remembers her. "I heard that you have been doing research on the Ancestors and the Dormant King."

My statement doesn't change his stance. "And who told you that?"

Doubt clouds my vision. His stance and skepticism indicate I may not be talking to the right person. Maybe there will be value in giving him a name as a reference. And mine, when the moment calls for it. "Jael. She used to train here. Many years ago."

"Jael," he says thoughtfully. "I remember her well. Unique name. Never met a woman with such a tough exterior yet such a soft heart." His arms begin to relax, his shoulders dropping. "How do you know Jael?"

The longing I just felt for her while watching the other soldiers is fresh in my mind and it takes all the self-control I have to not let it show in my voice or the tears stinging my eyes. "She was a mother when I needed one," I answer with my face turned away from him. "She told me about someone named Arthur that had been doing research on the Dormant King and the Ancestors." I hold out the tablet for him to see. "I wanted to show him something that I think might help in his research."

"I see." He nods, uncrossing his arms. "Then I am the Arthur you seek. And you are?"

As he is now a trusted confidant, I can give him my name without reserve, as Jael taught me. He earned it. "Havanna."

"Pleasure," he replies with a low dip of his head. He steps over to the curtained area and opens it. "Join me for tea. Show me what you have."

I set my things by the door and settle myself on the pillow across from him. Arthur takes the iron tea kettle between us and pours it into small ceramic cups.

"I got this from Sabbia," I say when I hand him the tablet. "The queen thought it might have something to do with the Ancestors, but I can't be sure."

Arthur sets the kettle back down, then reaches for the item. He examines it in amazement, lifting up the case protecting it to further see its details. "Well, I'll be."

"Does it mean anything?"

He skims his pudgy fingers over the aged stone with a feather-light touch. "I'd say so. This might bring me one step closer in my research."

I will myself not to clap my hands in glee, but manage to smile instead while picking up my own teacup. The heat of the water sears my lips before I even take a sip of the bitter, unsweetened herbal water. The burning sensation makes me wince and I promptly set my cup back down, the ceramic clinking against the saucer.

"What does it mean, then?"

Arthur covers his mouth with his hand, in deep thought. "Looking at this," he mumbles, "I'm positive this is depicting the Ancestors, based on the symbols above them."

"That's what I thought too!" I shout excitedly, making him flinch in surprise. I knew in my heart that this tablet might be a breakthrough for both of us, and I'm relieved to be one step closer to finding the Dormant King too. I calm myself down with a breath before I ask eagerly, "So, what do you think this is depicting?"

"Well, if I'm reading this correctly," he says more to himself than me, "the Water Ancestor is in the process of banishing the Power Ancestor. Or as we know him, the Dormant King."

"But the Ancestors only had one ability, not two."

"That's debatable," he argues after taking another sip of tea, his statement taking me aback. "If the Water Ancestor had the ability to banish the Dormant King, then it would make sense to conclude that the other Ancestors were granted two different abilities too. It's the only way to answer the question of how he ended up with both Manipulation and Usurp."

The Dormant King was able to copy abilities and make them his own, and did so when he made contact with the Land Ancestor. Which means the Land Ancestor had more than one ability for the Dormant King to copy. The Water Ancestor banished the Dormant King, also proof that they had more than one ability.

Then there's me. The Descendant of the Lightning Ancestor with two abilities. It wouldn't make sense that the remaining Ancestor—Fire—wouldn't have two abilities also.

I motion to the tablet. "Unbelievable. All the Ancestors had multiple abilities."

"Unless you have reason to believe that only particular Ancestors had one ability and others had more, then yes."

A gasp escapes me as I ask myself why I never used my brain to figure this out. This is eye-opening. "What ability is the Water Ancestor using here?"

"That's the big question. We know the Dormant King was banished, but it is unknown as to where."

Great. Right back where I started when I arrived.

"I will say, though, wherever he is, he's making an impact."

I want to declare at the top of my voice how well aware I am of his impact on our land, but I feel the need to play dumb so he can reveal more secrets and I won't accidentally reveal my identity.

"You said the queen of Sabbia had this?" Arthur asks with surprise. "Of all people, I never would have expected someone of royal status to have it."

"She said her parents confiscated it from a thief when she was younger," I respond with a shrug. "She liked the artwork."

"It's quite remarkable, indeed." He puts the case back on it with a grin.

"Like you, I'm also looking for the Dormant King. Anything you can tell me from what you've found would be greatly appreciated."

The double doors bursting open interrupts us. "Lieutenant!" a soldier calls. "A moment."

"Pardon me." Arthur leaps from his seat and addresses the soldier. I examine them both, talking and whispering in deep conversation. I watch Arthur's body language and how he reacts to what is being said. The way his back is to me and his hands are on his hips, it's hard to tell what their conversation is about.

Then, he turns to face me with a thoughtful expression, as if he's deliberating a decision. He stays that way for a moment, grinding his jaw, then turns back to the soldier and nods at him.

Something about that has me shivering. If I didn't know any better, I would conclude that something in Arthur's eyes was . . . cunning.

Perhaps I should've waited longer to give him my name.

I stare at my teacup in deep thought. I could very well be misreading that exchange. It must be in my head. Any evil intentions he has, he would have followed through with them by now. That's my hope at least.

"My apologies." Arthur brings me back to the present and sits across from me again. "Where were we?"

I clear my throat and blink a few times to refocus. "I asked you to relay information you found on the Dormant King, since I'm looking for him as well."

"Ah, yes," he confirms and clears his throat, drinking his piping-hot tea. How he can get that boiling inferno down his throat, I have no idea. "What has stirred you into your search, if I may ask?"

I'm faced with an internal dilemma. I trusted Calista enough to tell her everything; I had every reason to prove I could. But I can't say the same for Arthur now. Jael knew and trusted him, but it doesn't mean I have to. The way he studies me with such plans in his eyes, I'm leery. I've dealt with enough betrayal as it is.

"I thought it was time to see if he was real," I note with a shrug.

"A vague answer, but good enough," he acknowledges. He takes the tablet in his hands again and focuses on it. "I imagine that if he were banished, it wasn't somewhere he could come back very easily from."

"What do you mean? As in, he's in a cave with a rock in front of it or something?"

"No." Arthur's expression darkens, his gaze fearful and intense. "I'm speaking about a different version of our world. A dimension, if you will."

My eyes widen and I do my best not to chuckle. It's not my intention to mock the man, but the idea of another world existing beyond ours seems laughable. "So you're saying the Dormant King is in a . . . different world?"

"A version of it, yes. It's the only theory I can come up with, no matter how preposterous it sounds."

Preposterous is an apt word to describe this suspicion and the teacup is an apt object to hold in front of my face to hide my mocking smile. "A working theory is better than no theory," I say as I take another tiny sip of tea. "Can't say I'm not captivated, though."

Arthur sighs, his shoulders slumped in disappointment. "Havanna, I've been conducting research on the Ancestors for fifteen years. And during those years, the Dormant King has never been found. There have been many claims during that time, but none that I could count on."

I think back to Lavi. As much as I hate her and hope with everything in my being that I never see her again, this is the perfect time to see if anything she said had any value.

"I met someone who mentioned that anyone who claimed to see the Dormant King had to draw what they saw. Is that true?"

"Yes, actually. I even kept the drawings to see if it was some kind of puzzle that I could put together in layers, but all that did was create an unusual shape. I'll let you peruse and you can tell me if you see something in them." Arthur groans as he gets back up from the pillow. I continue to sip the tea to pass the time and cringe at its bitterness as he returns with different pieces of paper, all covered in lines and etchings in black ink.

"There are only a few," he informs me. "I kept hoping to find similarities between all of them, but none of them are consistent, so I don't know what I'm looking for. So either they weren't very good artists or they really only saw woodland creatures at night and thought it was something else."

I sift through the drawings, each page vastly different from the next. Most of them are just scribbles with no depiction of anything whatsoever, while others appear to be rough drawings of creatures I've seen wandering the land. I do what Arthur did and set the pieces of paper on top of one another to find out if it all comes together, then I shuffle the sheets to see if that makes any difference. All I come up with is a mess of scribbles and poor drawings.

"They must have thought the Dormant King could appear in any form he wanted," I suggest. "Hence the different shapes. But they look nothing like the Dormant King does on the tablet."

"I figured as much." Arthur sighs when he takes back the drawings .

I move on to the most intriguing rumor Lavi mentioned. "I also was told that people heard a voice talking to them. It said something along the lines of 'Come to me.' Does that sound familiar?"

"Fitting you mention that." Arthur shifts himself to get up again. His voice fades the farther away he walks in the house. "The fact that more than one person said the exact same thing gave me all the more reason to dig deeper."

He returns with a long, folded parchment paper with map lines all over it. The layout is exactly like the one I carry in my back pocket, except one specific part of Arthur's map is sporadically dotted in red, blue, and green inks.

"The red represents the areas where people felt the voice was clear. Prominent," he notes. "Blue indicates where it was still heard but slightly faded, and green means it was barely heard, but still heard nonetheless."

I closely examine his color-coded system. The colors appear in layers with most of the red dots on Luna Island in the Agura Ocean. The blue appears outside the red, further away from the island, into the ocean, and out to the shore. Around the blue are green dots that reach the shore and onto the expansive grassy fields between Cal-léa and Arythica.

"So most of it was heard on Luna Island?"

"That's what it appears to be. Then again, the voice was never identified. I keep the map as a reference, just in case more people come forward."

With a hand over my mouth, my eyes stay glued on Luna Island, on the area with the most red dots. "Has anyone gone to Luna Island to investigate?" I ask. "Or see if anyone else has heard this mysterious voice?"

"Yes, but as I mentioned, the source was never found," Arthur confirms. "There was no proof or indication of where the voice came from or any signs that someone had the ability to communicate their thoughts to others."

"There has to be an answer to this," I mumble behind my hand. "There *has* to be."

"I concur. Which is why I have yet to give up on this. The drawings may have no validity, but I have confidence that this does." He emphasizes his point with the map, then studies me with curiosity. "You seem to have experience in traveling about the kingdom. Suppose you should plan a trip to this island. See if you can find something my previous volunteers could not."

I stare thoughtfully at the map again. This meeting hasn't necessarily been the breakthrough I was hoping for. It's been disappointing, to say the least. All of these results seem to leave a hole. A very important, but giant, hole. And, for the life of me, I can't point out what it is. Arthur has been doing this research for almost as long as I've been alive, yet he has never found the Dormant King. All he can come up with are tunnels of clues leading to the answer, only to end up at a dead-end every time. It seems hard to believe that all of this time and effort was for nothing. My eagerness for having an answer is only growing by the minute.

I have to do something. I need to use it as a good excuse to make a hasty exit.

My gut tells me to stay far away from this man. Remaining here leaves me at risk for him to act out whatever plan he has in my most vulnerable moment.

If I'm going to travel to Luna Island, as he suggests, and create distance between us, then I need to leave immediately. But first, I need to take advantage of the resources Arthur has given me to the best of my ability.

"I would like to borrow this map, if you don't mind. And a couple colored pens. I just want to make some marks on my own map."

"By all means."

While he searches for the pens, I stand from the pillow; I feel I've been sitting for hours. I reach my arms to the ceiling and stretch my aching legs from being immobile after miles of walking. I move to a table by the window where I can get a full view of the camp, and Arthur hands me what he's found.

"Is it all right if I sit here?" I ask while taking a seat by the window.

"Of course. Take your time," he offers.

Both maps spread out on the table and pens in hand, I get to work. Clanging metal and yells from outside distract me, and I end up peeking out the window at the training grounds. Everyone practices a variety of skills, either in pairs or with dummies. It reminds me of practicing in Ketra, except the space here is about three times bigger, and it's smooth concrete instead of low-cut grass. I spent so much of my life honing my Gridlock ability when everyone else was sleeping, then meeting with Jael in the morning to work on my fencing, or with Aria to help her in hand-to-hand combat. Watching the men and women spar is a harsh reminder of what I've left behind, but dwelling on it now will only hinder forward momentum on the task in front of me.

With a deep breath, I turn my attention back to my map. I make red dots on Luna Island with one pen, then anything further away from the island in blue or green dots to indicate the strength of the voices heard.

Thoughts and questions flood my mind, as well as deep dissatisfaction that this meeting has only left me with such. There's no valid evidence to explain why Luna Island is the primary spot that these voices came from. Then there's Arthur's theory that the Dormant King was banished to another dimension. It may have been a preposterous notion, but he may be on to something. Fifteen years of searching for the Dormant King, people traveling to Luna Island to find the source of the voice and coming up empty . . . something about that doesn't click.

The Dormant King has Transform, the ability he copied from the Land Ancestor. With the reasoning that Arthur's theory is true, he had centuries to fine-tune his power from wherever he is. He probably created so many Dormants that they could appear anywhere I may be found. The Backers do his dirty work for him instead of doing it himself. How do the Dormants know when to attack? How do the Backers know to keep up their search, even though the Dormant King hasn't been seen in centuries? Why bother working for someone they can't see?

There's nothing I can find out for sure until I go to Luna Island. Perhaps my answers await me there.

After my map is marked accordingly, I fold up both copies and stuff mine back in my pocket. My mind is tired of thinking on repeat, so I stare back out the window. Just as I do, I hear the deep, round ringing of a bell above me. The trainees disperse from the area. Some shelve weapons on racks, others put their armor on hooks beside the racks. With the way they hang their heads and trudge along, they're exhausted from hard work—a feeling I can relate to.

It takes a few minutes to clear out. All the soldiers gather on the other side of the camp, taking seats at long tables and dining together. Again, I picture Jael partaking in lively conversation with her peers, a great way to end her day of physically demanding practice.

Bolt squeezes out of my pocket and climbs to my shoulder when I move to grab my equipment and pack. Arthur's footsteps thump behind a door, presumably a kitchen.

Just as I reach the double doors, I hear the kitchen door open behind me. "Leaving so soon?" Arthur asks in fake disappointment.

"Yes." My head whips between him and my exit point. I need to come up with a reason why I'm getting out of here without pointing the finger at him. "I left your map on the table."

He snatches the map, a somewhat dubious expression written on his face. "Report back to me when you can. I hope you return."

That uneasy, unsettling feeling I had when he was interrupted by the guard returns, sending a quiver into my hands. Something about the way he says that—almost in a way that hopes I *wouldn't* come back—doesn't sit well with me.

The betrayals I've faced have sensitized me to anyone I run into, but I still fight the dilemma within, and wonder whether I'm over-reacting. Jael trusted him for a reason. He trained her all those years ago and gave her the armband I'm wearing now. She must have known if there was something leery about Arthur; otherwise she would have told me.

My mind is playing tricks on me.

"I will be back," I assure him. "Hopefully with answers."

"A dream come true," he concurs. "I trust that you will find another hint or two."

"I'll try."

With that, I turn and practically rip open the door. Finally, I can breathe without the stress of being in his presence.

I can only hope Arthur isn't spying on me as I sprint across the camp and find my way back to the entrance. Seeing me approaching, the guards at the gate stomp the ground with the heels of their spears twice as a signal for the gate to be lifted, and I'm back out in the wilderness of Petros. After we're far enough away from Killios, Bolt changes to a horse and we continue the journey on horseback.

After about half an hour, we cross through the grassy field to the steep inclines of Solma Hills that sit between Cal-léa and Killios. From the vantage point on top of one of the hills, Cal-léa rests on the other side in its bright, peaceful splendor. Half circles of tall, concrete walls guard the city, one open end blocked by an iron gate and the other side only bordered by cobblestone houses and trees.

One of those houses used to be mine.

As I take my time ascending and descending the hills, I give myself as much space from Cal-léa as I can. I don't want to see how much my old house has changed. I'm afraid to search for Foss and Dahlia, maybe only to find that they don't remember who I am or didn't make it out alive. I don't want to come back and see that my parents are dead, even though part of me has always believed they were.

I'm still not ready to find out any of that. At least not yet.

This time, traversing through the vast land, I'm much more alert of any Swift Dingos that could spring up from the grass at any moment, now that I'm familiar with the sound of their snarl. Since that near-death encounter, I'm much more careful of my surroundings—listening to creatures within the trees and grass, to crackling tree branches and leaves underneath sneaky feet, watching for movement behind blades of grass—my eyes are everywhere.

Flapping bird wings and caws steer my attention to a pond within the trees. More Snapping Pelicans and Lime Geese glide along the water through spots of leaves that stay afloat on the surface. The thought of trying citrus-flavored meat makes my stomach rumble. I didn't get a chance to eat anything in Killios due to the need to escape, and now I'm paying for it.

Bolt halts as I dig through my pack. I have a few Pineapple Shells left, but I want to save those for more necessary scenarios. Another option I have can stun a human, but it might be strong enough to kill a small animal.

Electricity.

After hopping off of Bolt, I force electricity to travel through my arm and spark in my right hand. The ball gets bigger, then I throw it at the Lime Goose. An electric dome bursts on the surface over the bird, lasting for a couple seconds before it disappears. The Goose lies motionless on the water, along with a Carpie. Enough food to feed myself and Bolt.

"Can you grab those for me?" I ask when I motion to the pond.

Bolt transforms into an eagle, flaps his enormous, powerful wings, grabs the fish and bird with his talons, then drops them at my feet.

After collecting a few fallen tree branches, I figure out that the sparks from my hands can create enough heat for a fire. They make contact with the wood and flames grow. I take out my sword and cringe. It bothers me greatly to prepare a bird to cook, worse than when I have to prepare a fish. I do it anyway, holding my breath and hating myself with each cut. I don't have much of a choice, though. I'm in the wilderness. My Bennaru and I need to eat.

"Wow, this really does taste like lime," I tell Bolt as I chew on the tender meat that melts in my mouth. I toss some into his beak, which he guzzles down.

Once I feel full and satisfied, Bolt returns to the form of a horse. I rinse my hands in the water of the pond and use my clothes to dry them off quickly. The subtle breeze dries them the rest of the way. I leap onto Bolt and we continue onward until we reach the slanted cliffs overlooking Agura Ocean.

Luna Island sits about two miles off the coast. Stone structures dot the space, a civilization isolated from the rest of the kingdom. Palm trees and large boulders are spotted throughout the shore, sand lining the edge of the island.

As I'm admiring the expanse of the ocean, loud snapping blended with sizzling fills my ears and head, similar to the way a tree branch breaks mixed with hundreds of bees flying close by. I hold my hands over my ears to rid myself of the sound, to no avail.

A deep, ominous voice breaks through and speaks among the deafening noise. Someone on either side of me, talking directly into my ear in a muffled voice.

Go to the island. I need your help.

The sensation gives me chills, goose bumps erupting along my arms. I jerk my head side to side to search for signs of life around me, only to find grass, trees, and the cliffs below. With shaking hands, I reach for my map and look at the dots I made from Arthur's map.

I'm right in the spot where the voices are muffled but still heard. As creepy and chilling as that was, now I have proof that the claims about the voices are true, no mental illness involved.

Just when I thought everything Lavi told me was a lie, she had to be correct about this one.

I hop off Bolt and examine the position I'm in. Below the cliff is a wooden rowboat in the sand, the bow of it stuck in the shore and the stern dancing with the subtle waves of the water.

With the island in such a far distance, I may have to use the boat to get there, even though being in the open water with no protection—and no swimming skills—terrifies me to my core. I just hope the heat of the sun is enough to protect me from getting too wet. Having Bolt fly me there will increase his chances of getting shot down with arrows, if anyone resides there.

This is a tough choice to make. A choice that has me asking myself how important it is to risk being in open water or risk walking into whatever lurks on that island. The abandoned civilization there fascinates me. And even more interesting is that it is the one spot where people heard voices the most. I need to know what lies over there.

"Float me to the boat down there," I tell Bolt. "Maybe I can come up with a plan once I see its condition."

With a huff, Bolt changes from horse to eagle, and within seconds, he's flapping his wings. He leans forward for me to get on his back, then we're flying along the slant of the rocky cliff, faster and faster every second. The drop at such high speed sends my stomach to my throat along with a rush of adrenaline through my entire body. I can't help but gleefully scream, holding onto his neck with a fierce grip that doesn't seem to bother him. Once in the sand, I slide off with tremors all over, then find the adrenaline dissolving enough for me to relax.

The abandoned boat has windblown sand all over it, but is still in decent shape. An oar broken at the handle lies on the bottom boards, seaweed drapes over the gunwales, and algae covers the bow from long contact with the water. The only way to get it moving is to push it into the sea, which means I would have to step in the water to hop inside. The wind isn't strong enough to push the boat out for me or to dry me off from getting wet. The palm trees barely stir from what little breeze there is.

Then I'm struck with a memory of Aria and the day we met. Being on the beach, watching the waves roll in and out, admiring the open ocean and the miles of life underneath it, is the exact same scene I was surrounded with when she saved me. What she said to me when she pulled me out of the water has stuck with me to this day.

I know you're different, and that's okay. I'll still be your friend.

The way we left things still troubles me. I ponder over whether she's angry with me or if she wants to know how I'm doing.

If she even cares.

One day, I hope we can move past this and go back to the way it was when we were young and running a business together, when my secret was still a secret. My identity is known to the whole village, but I want them to care about me. I want them to care that I'm still alive.

Bolt softly caws at me to break me out of my reverie. On the stern, he turns around and flaps his wide wings with vigor. The gusts of wind cause the boat to tilt to the side, but not by much. He just gave me another idea, just as he did in Siro.

I pat his feathered head gratefully. "This is why I'm glad you're with me, buddy. Keep going."

Bolt gets back to flapping his wings. A little bit at a time, the gusts of wind he creates move the boat deeper into the water, just enough that I can get in. It wobbles on the surface as I step to the front bench. I hunker down and grip the sides so tightly my knuckles turn white. My breaths come out in rapid huffs in tune with my fast-beating heart, then I remember Jael's breathing technique. It was useful for tamping down the emotions that triggered my abilities, but it will be useful for calming down my fear of dying. I picture Jael sitting in front of me in the same black clothes I'm in now, her eyes burning into mine, gripping both of my hands and coaxing me to follow along with her.

Breathe in. Hold for five. Breathe out.

Since floating on the surface, water hasn't entered the boat and I haven't fallen in, which calms me down a little.

Breathe in. Hold for five. Breathe out.

"Okay." I sigh tremulously, swallowing down the vomit that wants to come up. I hold the oar for Bolt to see. "Okay. Give us a head start and I'll use this the rest of the way."

Bolt clasps his talons on the stern, flaps his wings again. The boat moves forward into shallow water, and we're in the sea, on our way to Luna Island.

The tiny ripples of the surface splash onto the boat and cause it to wobble in repeated side-to-side motions that makes me even more paranoid. The coastline is getting smaller the further we sail out in the open water, me still crouched on the floor. It would be the end of me if the boat capsizes, and that thought paralyzes me.

Breathe in. Hold for five. Breathe out.

I've always loved the sun and the warmth it brings. As someone who broke out of hiding and is now getting to know the kingdom I live in, I don't want to spend the whole time hiding from the scenery.

Steadily, I rise from my crouched position and scan the beauty around me. Besides the lonely island in the distance and the coast far behind me, there's not one speck of land around. The water is a clean, deep blue, enabling me to see the kind of aquatic life swimming around below us. The Ocean Hake's silvery scales glimmer with the rays of the sun underwater; the Salty Eel leisurely slithers its pale green, slimy body right past the group of fish. Salty Eel is another dish I've wanted to try. Supposedly, the flesh is salty enough that it doesn't need any other seasoning when cooked. Since it's an expensive dish, Arythica is the only place that sells it.

A warm breeze sweeps across my face accompanied by the heat of the sun. The water seems so refreshing in its clarity and shimmer. I yearn for the day I can dive in and simply float on the surface in perfect solace. Maybe the fish will be curious about the mysterious figure lying still in the water and swim around my feet.

Just a dip of my hand, to satisfy my curiosity.

I pull off my glove and drape my arm over the side of the boat. My fingertips skate on the surface at first, then I plunge my whole hand in the water. The ripples splashing and swirling up to my forearm as the boat keeps moving forward is a funny feeling. The sensation is soft but heavy. It's a peculiar combination of being massaged by moving rolls of cotton but weighed down by chunks of iron. This is nothing in comparison to rinsing my hand in the pond. Being above water and propelling forward brings on a whole new sensation.

Before I let myself get too attached to the feeling, I pull out my hand and promptly wipe off the moisture on my pants before my skin burns, then slide my glove back on. The heat of the day and the soft breeze dries it off quickly, along with my pants. I smile wide that I'm finally able to experience the feel of water without the consequences being fatal.

That glee is short-lived when the voice comes back to my head.

Good. Keep going. Someone will meet you when you arrive.

No matter how many times I shake my head or cover my ears, it doesn't erase what I just heard. It is much more pronounced this time; no snaps or sizzling to drown out his words, but no less ominous and frightening.

The buildings on Luna Island get bigger the closer we get. There are four tall cinder block watchtowers, all about four stories high, laid out in the corners of a square grid. In between the spaces of those watchtowers are small, one-story homes also made of cinder blocks with pointy red roofs draped over them.

"You should change to a mouse," I call to Bolt behind me. "I'll use the oar the rest of the way."

I dip the oar on either side of the boat and row while the weight from Bolt's eagle form lifts the stern slightly, and he crawls up to my shoulder as a mouse.

My arms and shoulders ache from pushing the oar through the water. My skin is pink from the sun, now tender to the touch. My burning muscles beg me to stop, but if I do for too long, the small ripples and waves will gradually push me back to the coast. I'm already so close; I can't fall behind now.

"Pain. Waits. For. No one," I enunciate to myself through gritted teeth. I keep rowing.

I look ahead for any signs of life waiting for me at the island, as the voice told me there will be. I don't see anyone waiting. The place is desolate. No one is moving around, no voices, and the air is whistling between the gaps and holes in the ruined watchtowers.

The boat digs itself into the sand; I hop out of it and leave my pack inside. One foot in front of the other, I scan the area around me. The eerie ambience is thick and hard to ignore. The whole island is stiflingly quiet, save for the soothing sound of waves rolling onto the shore. The palm trees don't hold anything conspicuous that I can see, and I still don't see anything moving within the buildings. I lift my hand behind me for my sword, wrapping one finger at a time around the handle.

A huge *boom* nearly has me jumping out of my skin. Before I know it, a large monster emerges from underground and crashes on the sand. The lizardlike Dormant that I estimate is the size of a small whale waves the tentacles around its neck in my direction and opens its mouth to release a giant roar, baring rows upon rows of sharp teeth. Its piercing red eyes hold all the evil that no doubt reflects the Dormant King's personality.

I unsheathe my sword and twirl it in small circles with my wrist. I'm ready.

The Dormant thrusts one tentacle at me while using another one to shoot icicles. I block an icicle with my shield while I cut off the tentacle aimed for my face. The Dormant screams in reaction, trampling toward me at full speed. I jump out of the way and slash at it in midair, only to scratch its back leg that has little impact on its actions. The Dormant dives into the ocean and swims a short distance away. I mistakenly think it's giving up the fight until it lifts its head above the surface. Water draws into its wide-open mouth and it's looking directly at me.

I find myself completely unprepared for what's coming because the Dormant shoots a flow of water so quickly I barely have time to react. I jump just as I see it coming, but the water catches my legs, soaking right through my pants and onto my skin. Before I can recover, it shoots more water and gets me in the face. I use my dry shirt as an attempt to quickly wipe off the moisture.

I'm already losing this battle. And I'm in the most vulnerable position.

This is not good.

There's no one around and I'm on a remote island far from the kingdom. I don't have a choice now.

I have to use Strike.

I trudge through the sand on my stomach and take cover by some palm trees. The Dormant roars from the water and swims back to shore, its feet pounding the ground and causing a tremble beneath me. I raise my hand in the air and focus on the creature as it searches for me. A large spot in the sky opens up as my right hand increasingly warms up until the electricity is sparking in my palm.

I come out of hiding and eye the monster. It spots me and charges at me again. I throw down my hand before it gets too close and the lightning hits the Dormant dead-on with a crashing *boom*. It convulses from the electrocution for a few seconds, then collapses in the sand just before it bursts into a cloud of dust.

As I breathe heavily from exertion, I evaluate my energy and pain level. My headache is minimal, but my eyes want to close and recover. Basically how I feel after using Gridlock for extended periods of time. I can get through that, I have many times before.

"Hello, Descendant!" a strong, male voice proudly announces.

What I see next makes the blood drain from my face and weakens my knees.

A crowd of people dressed in white step out of the buildings and spread out to enclose the space around me in a circle. The Backer directly in front of me pushes a button and extends his blade with its blue brightness I've come to recognize well.

"Wha . . . what—"

"Arthur told us you would be coming," he says. "Welcome to the Backers Fortress."

CHAPTER 10

*B*ackers Fortress.

The two words ring repeatedly in my head.

Arthur sent me straight into a trap.

And I fell for it. *Again.*

My reason for feeling unsure about Arthur was valid. He planned this all along. He fed me the information I needed that would stir me to action and encouraged me to go to the one place where he ensured a trap was waiting.

How did Jael trust someone who would steer me in the wrong direction? Did she know he was associated with the Backers?

Seeing my flustered state, the Backer cackles. "Finally, our years of searching for the Descendants will be made easier. The Dormant King will be pleased."

"Oh good, I'm glad you said that because I want to talk to him," I snapped. "Where is he?"

"You will find out soon enough," he says in a teasing manner.

"Where. Is. He?" I punctuate through clenched teeth. A slight burning sensation in my calves is present from the water soaking through my clothes.

"All you need to know is that he's in a place where no one can find him," the Backer answers.

I remember what Arthur said, along the same lines. *I imagine that if he were banished, it wasn't somewhere he could come back very easily from.*

This is the perfect time for them to confirm Arthur's theory.

"In a different dimension," I state plainly.

"Indeed."

All of these confusing emotions suffocate me. Arthur's claim to be looking for the Dormant King with supposedly no answers is because he knew where he has been this whole time. No one else who claimed to find him couldn't have because he was in a different place altogether. A place that wasn't in Petros.

I knew there was a hole in this entire investigation.

The Backers are closing in on me, inching forward bit by bit. Out of all of them, only one seems willing to talk. I need to keep him alive. The others, I can get rid of.

Their weapons are ready, poised for attack. Electricity in my hand sparks again and ignites the handle of my sword. I force the current into my blade, ready to use it as a tool to dispense my power.

"Get her."

One of the swords sweeps at me just as I jump. The blade catches air underneath my body, then I stab the ground with my sword. Lightning shoots out in all directions, striking every Backer surrounding me save for one. Electricity courses through their bodies, sending them into convulsions before they collapse. As fast as I can, I create a ball and stun the Backer standing in front of me. He shakes from electrocution. I march up to him just as he falls over and yank him back to his knees.

"How do you know where the Dormant King is?" The Backer coughs and makes a great effort to move his jaw around to talk. "I'm waiting!" I inch my face closer to his.

"He told us." His voice is raspy, still struggling to speak. "With his Transmission ability, he encourages us in our search from his dimension."

Time freezes as I process this tidbit of new information. "Wait. Transmission?"

"Oh, you don't know?" He smirks. "He has the ability to communicate to humans and creatures by sending messages to their minds no matter where he is."

He talks to the Backers with Transmission. At the Backers Fortress. The spot on my map that's red.

He spoke to me from the coastline where his words were muddled with background noise. The spot on my map that was marked in green.

The Dormant King is much more powerful than I was aware of.

But I fought a Dormant in the desert, on the other side of the land. Does the ability reach that kind of distance?

"What about the Dormants? Did he summon the Dormant at Sabbia Desert?" I counter.

"He always communicates with his lovelies," the Backer explains, loads of cockiness laced in his tone. "When he was aware of the trap we set up in Sabbia Town, he traveled there from the other dimension while maintaining communication with us. Then he created the Dormant and commanded it to attack. A simple plan, really."

My tongue runs over my teeth. The pieces click together and that eventually creates anger. I throw his body back to the sand, then grab his shirt and shake him with all my might. His head continuously hits the ground, so much so that I hope I make him go unconscious. When I bring him back to my face, the crinkles in his eyes show the cocky smile that I know he's hiding under his mask.

"And once we find all the Descendants," the Backer continues, "the King will rise and grant us all the powers you yourselves have claimed. Thank you for assisting us in our search."

I scoff. "We'll see about that."

I throw my hand in the air and let the Backer fall over. His legs and arms are still stunned, so he remains lying in the sand, unable to escape.

"Long live the Dormant King!" he cries out.

I bring down my hand. The lightning hits the Backer in the chest, and after a few seconds, he remains motionless.

I barely have time to recover when someone at one of the watchtowers shouts three chilling words.

"Release the cannon!"

White dots appear and disappear around one of the open windows, then a *boom* echoes so loud that anyone on the Petros coastline could hear it.

I thrust my hand out and focus on the large metal ball soaring with a trail of fire and smoke behind it, my headache intensifying with every passing second. With its weight and the speed it's going, Gridlock isn't working. Panic rises within me as I leap out of the way before it crushes me. The cannonball crashes nearby, sand fanning in the air and throwing me off-balance. I push myself up and run, my feet creating divots in the sand and making it harder for me to move.

Another ear-bursting *boom* reverberates. I try to find the place where the cannonball came from, but it crashes in the sand directly in front of me before I have a chance to spot it. I slide to a stop and fall, but I hasten to get up and go another direction.

Just as I'm about to enter the abandoned civilization, another lizardlike Dormant bursts from underground and blocks my path.

Staying in this position to fight makes me an easy target. The Dormant will overtake me if I run, so fleeing is not an option. Using Strike isn't either, as I need to save my power reserves for when I truly need it.

I'm trapped.

At least, that's what I think before something detonates on the Dormant, also destroying one of the small buildings behind it. It shrieks, waving its head and tentacles back and forth, losing control of itself. I turn to see where the explosive came from and how it struck the target dead-on.

A young man riding on a large grayish-white bird circles the small island. The bird is as big as Bolt when he's an eagle.

Is that . . . a Bennaru?

The bird caws a war cry once it's closer to the Dormant. I take this opportunity to step aside from the scene this man has taken over. He readies his bow with another Pineapple Shell arrow and leaps off the Bennaru. He releases in midair, finishing off the Dormant and turning it to dust.

The man, who appears to be around my age, lands in the sand in a way that makes him appear a show-off: one leg extended to the side, head hung low, one hand holding him up, and the other clutching the bow held at his side. The Bennaru continues circling overhead while the man readies three more arrows. Without taking the time to aim first, he shoots at the watchtower and makes a direct hit. The arrows detonate on the top floor, turning the cinder blocks to pebbles and causing the roof to completely collapse. The yellow powder floats in the air in a thick plume, surely blinding anyone in its proximity.

Lying in the sand, I stare in awe at this random person who just saved me. His archery skills are precise and agile. He hitches the bow behind him and runs toward me.

He's the most gorgeous man I've ever seen. More than Victor ever was. Dark brown hair pulled back into a high bun with dark, thick eyebrows and brown eyes that hold an intense smolder. The stubble on his face shows that he hasn't shaved in a few days. He wears fingerless gloves just like mine, beige trousers, and leather boots. The long-sleeved gray linen shirt is snug enough to draw any leering eyes to his muscular pecs and toned biceps.

"Are you all right, Zappy?" he asks in a deep, seductive, collected voice.

I nod, enamored with his skill and those chocolate-brown eyes examining me. We're in the middle of a battle, yet this mysterious savior has me frozen to the bone. The attraction is as fierce and instant as thunder. His musky, woodsy scent doesn't diminish that.

Suddenly, arrows stab the ground next to us. He grabs my hand and pulls me onto my feet, dragging me to hide behind some palm trees. He peeks at the crowd of Backers running between the small buildings toward the beach.

"Who . . ." I start softly. "Who are you?"

"Quill. Nice to meet you." His breaths quicken as his gaze switches from me to the Backers.

"Were you riding on a Bennaru just a moment ago?"

Quill holds up a gloved finger. "Hold that thought."

Like the brave warrior he is, he stretches his hand out at a tree, then I see his eyes turn a bright green.

A Descendant.

Quill is a Descendant.

I watch in astonishment as he makes the tree uproot itself and march toward the Backers. The moving tree bends and sweeps the Backers off their feet with its branches. While it fights the battle for us, Quill uses his other hand to aim his ability at the rocks by the beach. Like a moth to a flame, the rocks collect and stack upon one another to create a tall, walking form with arms, legs, and a head. The rock structure stomps over to the Backers and uses a limb to knock them all down.

Quill breaks focus on his creations once the attackers have been cleared. The palm tree buries its roots in the sand and the rocks crumble to a heaping pile on the shore. "To answer your question, yes, that was my Bennaru," he answers, indifferent to the fact that he just manipulated nature to do as he wished. "And yes, I'm the Land Descendant. So how about we hunt down the other Backers, I'll tell you when to use your lightning, and I'll call for our Bennarus when we need to get out of here—sound good? Good."

Before I can answer, he makes a run for it into the abandoned establishment. Flustered, I spin in a circle, wondering what just happened. Clearly, he knows I'm a Descendant. How he knows that is something I'm determined to find out later, if I ever see him again after this.

But first, we need to help him implement this spontaneous plan.

I move away from the trees and follow. Crouched low, side by side, we run between buildings and keep an eye on any movement in the watchtowers. Backers armed with bows aim at us from one of the windows in the tall buildings while others are preparing a cannon from another. I use my shield to block the incoming arrows. More archers are stationed on the roof of a nearby building. Quill pulls back on his bowstring and shoots the Backers on the roof, all in one smooth move.

"Get those ones in the watchtower, I'll take care of anyone down here!" he yells.

"How am I getting up there?"

As we keep running, he holds two fingers to his temple and his eyes turn green again. I wait for something to happen—whether it's a rock that comes to life and sends me up there or a tree sweeps me with its branches and throws me—but nothing does, and I don't know what Quill is doing.

Next thing I know, Bolt swoops in and grabs me by the shirt with his beak. He flies me to the top of the watchtower while I dangle in the air, screaming in fear that I will fall and I have nothing to hold onto. That moment doesn't last long when Bolt throws me through an open window. I somersault on the floor and come to a stand. The Backers, about ten of them, stop and turn. Evaluating my battleground, a few pillars are in the way and there's a table right in the middle.

Strike doesn't work in enclosed spaces, so that's not an option.

Well, I suppose I'm fighting ten Backers on my own. All at once.

Before anyone can act, I kick the table at some of them, then turn and work on the ones coming for me. I sweep my sword at a couple, followed by my shield, and send them flying out the window. A few more come forward. I lower to the ground and trip one with my foot; the other I spring to my feet and fence with. One on the ground tries to get back on his feet, which distracts me just long enough for my sword to be knocked out of my hand. My father's famous words ring true with my current problem.

Distraction doesn't look good on you.

A Backer almost stabs me in the torso, but I dodge his attack when I drop to the ground and roll. My fingers grab the hilt and

I'm upright once again. I jump and spin a couple times, getting both Backers with my sword.

I turn to an open window where a Backer has an arrow aimed at me. Before he can shoot, Quill's Bennaru drops him in between us. He takes his bow-turned-staff and shoves it in his torso, then after a few more hits, the Backer rolls off the roof and plummets to the ground. Another one shows up behind him about to stab with his weapon. I thrust my hand out and freeze the Backer, giving Quill a chance to yank on his staff and turn it back to a bow, then he shoots some arrows at him. I jump from the watchtower onto the roof to meet Quill and we run across it together.

"All right, let's get those ones over there." He points to a watchtower in another corner.

While he equips more arrows and shoots with outstanding perfection, I conjure my electricity. My right hand warms with my power, the sound of snapping in the sky in tune with the intensifying heat, then I throw down my hands. The Backers are electrocuted while the lightning punches holes through the roof.

"Let's get out of here before we're outnumbered," Quill says. "The other watchtowers are getting cannons ready."

He's right—flecks of white move hurriedly in the other buildings.

My head aches and pressure increases behind my eyes, but not as badly as it normally did. I keep following Quill as we make our way back to the beach, leaping down to roofs below us to get there. Just when I need him, Bolt appears in front of us as an eagle with my pack clasped in his talons. His flapping wings send grains of sand flying around me as he grabs my shirt with his beak and throws me on his back as if I weigh nothing. I barely recover from being tossed when Bolt launches back in the air, giving me little time to grab onto his feathered neck.

Quill on his Bennaru meets us high above the island. We take one last look at the destruction we caused. Adrenaline is spiked so high, and still reeling from the events, I don't even react to how far above the ocean we are.

"We need to get out of sight," Quill yells over the sound of large, flapping wings. "Before they form an all-out assault."

They get a head start aiming toward the Petros coastline.

One motivation moves me to follow closely behind: strong curiosity.

***

Darius has me on my feet while someone else has me by the arms as they get ready to toss me in the ocean. Their laughter as I squirm with all the strength I have has me in tears. This isn't funny. I can't swim. I could drown—and they're laughing. I don't understand how people, including these boys, can be so cruel.

They swing me back and forth, then toss me in the ocean like a potato sack. The water moves me in different directions while I flail my arms. More laughter at the beach rings in my ears, but it's not just Darius who's laughing at me.

Aria stands beside him, mocking and laughing right along with him.

I thought we were friends. I thought she would save me.

Instead, she's letting me drown.

I wake up from my nightmare with a deep gasp, the smell of burning wood filling my nostrils. For half a second, I fear that I'm back in Ketra, amidst the disaster of the raid. Instead, I find myself lying on a couple layers of blankets with a tent draped above me.

I wish the nightmares would stop reflecting my worries and deepest fears.

The vaulted "ceiling" gives me enough room to sit all the way up. Outside the open flaps, a young man roasts a bird over the flames, turning it with a makeshift spit crafted from a carved tree branch. His hair, once tied into a bun, now hangs loose as a dark, silky curtain framing his face, ending at his shoulders.

The one who saved me. The Descendant.

The extremely gorgeous Descendant.

My body feels weak, my arms a little wobbly as I hold myself up. Interestingly enough, I'm not as physically drained as I've been in the past after using my abilities to the greatest extent. Perhaps it's a sign that I'm growing stronger the more I use them.

"Well well well, she lives!" Quill exclaims, lifting his arm in presentation to exaggerate his announcement.

I blink to adjust my vision. Just as he was the first time I laid eyes on him, he's still a gorgeous specimen of a man. This time, I will myself to not let his flawless beauty impede my ability to talk. I crawl out of the tent into the chilly night air. "Have I been asleep for a while?"

"About a day." Quill's strong hands turn the spit over the flames.

"So," I begin, taking a seat on the grass and leaning my back against a tree. "You didn't sleep?"

"Not for a whole day."

"You don't get worn out after using your abilities?"

"I used to. But I've had years of practice away from wandering eyes. Living in a forest has its perks." He winks at me then turns his attention to the bird. "After a lot of practice, I only get slightly tired."

Then my original theory is correct. The physical toll my abilities take on me will get better with time.

I scan the area. There are trees all around us, but enough spaces in between give us a view of the land. Next to the fire, Bolt as an eagle relaxes next to a wolf, seemingly getting along.

No, they're *cuddling*. Rubbing their heads together affectionately.

I motion to the scene. "Why is there a wolf next to my Bennaru?"

"That's Koa. My Bennaru. He mostly stays in wolf form. They acted like long-lost friends that have reunited. They've been cuddling like that for hours. I have to admit it's quite cute."

I smile at our guardians who refuse to leave space between each other. These immortal creatures started off guarding the Ancestors together when this kingdom was created. They then separated when the Ancestors went into hiding. It makes sense that they would remember each other, even if it's been centuries.

"So how are you feeling, Zappy?" Quill asks.

I quirk a brow. "Why do you call me Zappy?"

He gives me a sheepish smile that flutters my heart and causes me to give him an equally sheepish smile of my own. "Because I still don't know your name."

"I'll help you out. I'm Havanna."

"Havanna," he repeats as he continues to turn the dead animal over the fire. "Interesting name."

"So is yours."

Quill shrugs while pulling out a knife from a sheath wrapped around his thigh. "I was born and raised in a forest. Everyone there has a nature-related name."

"Which one?"

"Arbol."

I pull out my map to see where that's at and compare it to where Luna Island is. The trip would have taken him over a day on foot if he traveled that kind of distance. "How did you end up all the way at Agura Ocean?"

Quill takes the bird off the fire and sets it on a large leaf next to him. "I was running away."

"Running away from what? Dormants? Backers?"

Quill avoids eye contact as he takes a bite of the meat. I see the wall he's putting up in his silence as he chews pensively, shifting his weight uncomfortably on his log seat. "Something like that," he answers, still avoiding my eyes.

I study him. There's more to the story than he's willing to admit, given his squirmy demeanor. The situation is serious enough that he fled across the kingdom to get away from it. Instead of pushing the subject, I fill my mouth with what I now know is Lime Goose.

"How did you know I was a Descendant?" I ask mid-chew.

"I saw lightning from the cliffside," he says. "I thought it was odd. Then I definitely knew something was wrong when there were explosions. I thought that was a good opportunity to put my impeccable archery skills to good use." He gives me a smirk that accentuates a dimple that would make any woman swoon. "You're welcome."

"Yes, thank you." I sit up all the way and cross my legs.

"So where are you from, Zappy?"

"You know my name now. Why are you still calling me Zappy?"

"It's just fun." His face falls in concern as he asks, "Does it bother you? I can call you Havanna. It's not as fun, but it's okay if you don't like being called Zappy."

Three things I know about this mysterious man: he's lighthearted, he's closed off about his past, and he's considerate. His worried expression softens my heart to him even more.

"No," I say with a reassuring smile, "it doesn't bother me."

"Okay." His shoulders relax. Whatever he's gone through in his life to worry about such a small issue has me feeling sorry for him. "So, where are you from?" he repeats, moving on from the tension.

"Originally from Cal-léa, but raised in Ketra."

"Why did you leave Cal-léa?"

I grunt as I reach for more meat. "Backers. My parents put me on Bolt and sent me to Ketra." I let out a sad sigh and motion to my Bennaru, who is resting his head on Koa's—they're both blinking their eyes sleepily. "My parents told me they would come find me, but they never did. I haven't been back since."

Quill shakes his head. "Backers always know how to screw up our lives."

I sigh again, this time much harsher. He has no idea how much that hits me to my core. "That they do."

"Is that why you came out of hiding? To seek revenge?"

"You could say that." Anger and frustration rise in my throat and are evident in my words. "They killed my mentor and mother figure. I wanted to kill the Dormant King to avenge her, along with Ketra, but all that has done is make me run around the whole kingdom like a Cluck with no head."

Quill leans forward and places his clasped hands on his knees. "I know how that feels."

"Is that why you ran away? You lost someone and you want to kill the Dormant King too?"

"Oh, I want to kill the Dormant King," he remarks. "But that's not the main reason I ran away. What has your journey been like so far?"

Since he leaves me no opening to talk about why he's on the run or why he wants to kill the Dormant King, I spend quite a bit of time rehashing my adventures. Ending up in Siro, meeting Lavi, walking into a Backers trap in Sabbia, going to Killios, and ending up on Luna Island where I walked into yet another Backers trap.

"And you had no clue you were headed into the Backers Fortress?"

"No clue."

"Why did you go there if you thought Arthur was working with them?"

I hand him my map. "I doubted myself and my gut feeling. I thought he might have solid information, even if I didn't have a good feeling about him. He had proof of people hearing voices in that area, so I wanted to investigate."

Quill looks at the map and narrows his eyes. "Wait a minute. I have the exact same map."

Thrilled, I get on my knees and scoot closer to him. "You do?"

He hurries to pull out a parchment from his pocket and opens it. The creases from being folded show its age, just like mine. "I don't have all those dots, but I've had this my whole life. Do you also have a poem?"

"Yes!" I shout and clap my hands. I pull out the poem and unfold it over the map. "What does yours look like?"

Without answering, he digs into his pocket again to produce another piece of paper. "'There is one who calls the storm, close to the ocean; a spark of hope is born—'"

"Yes, the same one! Ah! We're truly Descendants!"

Quill holds up a finger to keep me from being too loud. "I think our abilities alone prove that, but yes," he says with much more composure than I'm displaying at the moment.

"Did you ever figure out what the poem means?"

"No," he replies with scorn. "My father told me it was an heirloom for the Descendants that I needed to hold on to and guard with my life, no matter what."

I lay the poem over the map, letting the flames illuminate the markings and the stanzas that are written in an uneven circle on the paper.

Then I notice something I never had before. I reread the poem, starting at Cal-léa and reading each stanza clockwise, as my mother did:

There is one who calls the storm,

Close to the ocean; a spark of hope is born.

There is one who disturbs the sea,

Who, near the hollow of a cliff, spares themselves to a degree.

There is one in mastery of nature,

Within the green, they blend in with great measure.

There is one who curbs the flame,

By a mound of stone, they dodge the eyes of fame.

Lastly, there is one with the greed of a thief,

Once gone, the world once again lived in relief.

The first stanza sits on Cal-léa. The second one, regarding the sea, is placed over Macaphin Village, right on the coastline just west of Arythica. The third one about nature sits over Arbol Forest. The fourth one is placed over Vulca Mountain. And the fifth one is placed right in the middle of the map.

"Quill," I say with uncertainty, "can I see your poem?"

Confused, he hands me his copy and I place that one over my map. The stanzas are arranged strategically the same as mine. That alone tells me there was a strategy involved in the layout of the words.

"I can't believe I never noticed this before," I say breathlessly.

"What are you talking about?"

I straighten out the parchments and point to the stanzas, holding it up to the light of the fire. "Notice that each stanza is over a certain place on the map. That has to mean something, right?"

Quill shrugs. "Possibly."

"Isn't it odd," I begin thoughtfully, "that we both were told to never lose the map and poem, but we were never told why or what it meant?"

He wipes his hands on his pants and shrugs again. "I never thought much of it. I just kept it because maybe one day I would sell it and make a fortune."

My jaw drops. "Why would you want to sell something like this, especially after being told it was an heirloom?"

He hums before he answers in a scheming tone that disturbs me. "Let's just say it would be a wonderful statement of revenge."

The revenge he's thirsty for must be for one of his parents, since they were the ones that gave it to him. My best guess is his parents are the reason he ran away from home. But I know he won't tell me, at least not yet.

I clear my throat. "Well, I could never do that." My tone turns reminiscent when I continue. "My mother read this to me to calm me down when I was little. Her tone was always so . . . soothing."

I'm not looking at Quill, but I can feel his eyes burning into me. I look over briefly and give him an awkward smile, noticing a hint of sadness behind his own eyes. A sadness that seems desperate to relate to what I'm saying.

"Anyway." I shake my head. "There has to be meaning behind why the stanzas are where they are. I find it hard to believe it was just because the writer wanted to be creative."

Quill takes the poem out of my hands and places it over his own map. His brows narrow in concentration, a long, strong finger skimming over the words, then moving clockwise to the next stanza, then the next. I imagine those fingers clasping the end of the arrow and pulling back, his biceps flexing, aiming at his target—

I shut my eyes tightly and blink a few times. I need to stop with the fantasizing. I can't fall for someone else when it will only end with me getting hurt. I already know allowing the guard around my heart to crumble will lead to destruction.

"You said you're from Arbol Forest, correct?" I ask him to stay on topic.

"Yes."

I reread the stanza placed over his home. *There is one in mastery of nature, within the green, they blend in with great measure.*

I stay glued on three words: *mastery of nature.* Quill displayed mastery of nature when he moved the tree and created his own war machine by simply pulling rocks together.

Within the green, they blend in with great measure. A forest is full of green trees, just as Arbol Forest is.

My breathing quickens as I feel myself coming to a realization, and reread the first stanza set on Cal-léa. *There is one who calls the storm, close to the ocean; a spark of hope is born.*

There is one who calls the storm. A spark of hope is born.

I call down lightning. Electricity sparks in my hand when I use it.

A spark of hope. I'm the spark of hope.

Cal-léa is close to the ocean, as it shows on the map. As a child, the water was practically in my backyard. I was primarily raised in Ketra, but I was *born* in Cal-léa.

Finally, after having this poem for twenty years, I have figured out what this means.

"Quill," I mumble. "This poem is about us."

He tilts his head. "What?"

Excited energy races through my veins and forces me to spring to my feet. I run my fingers through my hair and pull as I pace back and forth. "This is giving the locations of all the Descendants. This poem . . . is about *us*!"

He shoots me an incredulous glance. "How do you know?"

I sit next to him and point at the stanza talking about him. "Look. Mastery of nature. You had that when you created weapons with trees and rocks! Within the green, you blend in. You did that while living in Arbol Forest."

"Okay," he draws out.

"Then this one over Cal-léa." I direct him with my finger. "That's where I was born. I can create lightning storms and make electricity spark in my hand. That's where 'the spark of hope is born' comes in. And I bet you that the Descendants are hiding in these places too!" I gasp for air and laugh excitedly. "This is about *us*, Quill! The Descendants! And where they're all hiding. I can't believe it took so long for me to figure it out."

"I believe you're looking too much into it," he states with doubt.

I stomp the ground. "You can't tell me that it doesn't make sense!"

Quill holds up his hands in defense. "I never said that. I'm just saying, what's the point in giving us the locations of the other Descendants if we were to remain in hiding?"

"Because one day, we will all have to come together to put an end to the Dormant King," I say while emphasizing with my hands. "And when that day comes, we will have this poem to tell us where the other Descendants are so we could find them."

"That also would make sense if our parents told us what the poem was really for," he points out with a wiggle of his finger. "Otherwise, why bother giving us the poem at all?"

My shoulders deflate at his question. He makes a fair point. My mother never explained what the poem was for, but I never asked either.

Thinking back to my childhood, my mother waited a long time to tell me the history of the Ancestors. So long, in fact, that it was to the point where she only told me because she believed I would rebel if she didn't. There was no point for her to explain the meaning behind the poem if her purpose was to make sure I stayed hidden. She wanted to make sure I wouldn't find the other Descendants before I was ready.

"Control," I say simply, but with a disappointed tone. "Our parents didn't want us to come out of hiding until we were ready." I shrug. "That's the only reason I can come up with."

Huffing angrily, Quill suddenly rises and paces the area. He grabs his hair and yanks on it harshly; even his breaths are angry.

The reaction is fair. There have been many times in my life that I felt frustration and anger toward my parents for not revealing the truth for so long, and only ever giving me empty excuses. Even going so far as to make me lie to my friends about why I wear gloves. Right now, I'm angry that it took me this long to understand why my mother never told me the story behind the poem.

But having two angry people won't get us any closer to our goal.

"Quill," I say calmly. "Are you okay?"

He stops in his tracks and puts his hands on his hips. "Yes. I'm fine," he replies softly, avoiding my gaze.

The whirls of emotions sink in as I sit on Quill's log seat. Some of the questions I've had for many years have been answered, but that still leaves a lot of other questions open. Those, unfortunately, will not be answered on my own. My entire journey since leaving Ketra has been proof of that. Betrayal, near-death experiences, clues leading me to travel all over the kingdom, only to come up empty . . .

Maybe I can't do this on my own anymore. Maybe I was never supposed to. Maybe all of this has been proof that, as hard as I tried—and ultimately failed—I need others by my side.

"I think there's only one way to find out if I'm right about this poem," I suggest.

Quill scoffs and takes a spot on the log next to me. "And what is that? Travel the kingdom and hunt for all the Descendants?"

"Yes, actually."

"Under normal circumstances, I would agree with you," he says with consideration, "but there're a few problems with that plan. You say you're originally from Cal-léa but you were raised in Ketra, yes?"

"Yes."

"Well, the poem wasn't rewritten to reveal your current location. So what if that happened to the other Descendants? Then we would, as you said, be running around the kingdom like a Cluck with no head."

I exhale and think about his argument for a moment until I come up with my own. "You make a good point. But, the stanza about *you* was accurate. That can still be true of the other Descendants too."

Quill nods while his eyes hold apprehension, staring at the dwindling fire in front of us, its flames turning to weak embers. There must be a way to talk him into finding the other Descendants with me. But that's not the only thing I want to do.

At last, I'm ready to go back to Cal-léa.

So much has happened since I left Ketra. I can trust no one, except Quill. That is, if he's an honest Descendant. Nothing has felt like home since the Backers raid, including Ketra once Jael died. I'm desperate to go somewhere that was once my home, and felt like such. And now that I've figured out the stanza placed over Cal-léa is about me, maybe it's time I go back to see what became of the place. Find out what became of my parents, of Foss and Dahlia.

The idea of going back home and finding the other Descendants brings nervous energy with a mix of excitement. I finally have someone on my side to help me during this journey, but the reality is hitting me harder.

We're gathering an army and we're going to war.

It's the only war I'm willing to risk my life for. My purpose for leaving Ketra will fall flat if I don't keep going. Calista's words ring in my mind.

See this through.

I turn to face Quill and implore him. "Listen. It's time that we band together. It's time to find them and fight the Dormant King. We've all been hiding long enough."

He watches me with those adorable eyes, the dying flames giving the chocolate-brown color dancing sparkles.

"Plus," I add, "I want to go home."

"To Ketra?"

I shake my head. "No. Cal-léa."

Quill leans back in surprise. "That's quite the step."

I roll my bottom lip between my teeth. "Yes. But it's time. I want to go back to the only place that's considered home to me. Maybe even find out what happened to my parents."

"What if you don't?"

The probability of not finding out about my parents during my visit to Cal-léa didn't occur to me. Someone in my hometown must remember who they are. Someone should have an idea of what happened to them. It's only been ten years. Then again, a lot can happen in a ten-year span.

I shrug in response. "Then at least I tried. And the mystery will live on."

Quill leans back, hands on his knees, restraining a side grin. "Let me understand your plan. You want to go back to Cal-léa, then run around Petros to find people that may or may not want to fight a war against the most powerful being known to man, then possibly die fighting it."

"That sums it up well," I confirm playfully, then use this opportunity to reflect the words he said to me when running through his spontaneous plan on Luna Island. "Sound good? Good."

He chuckles, laying a hand over his mouth thoughtfully. We sit in silence for what feels like hours, just watching the fire die down in front of us.

"Okay," he finally says. "I'm in."

"Really?"

"Really. The alternative for me is to go back home, and there's nothing I want more than to never see that place again." He turns to me with a teasing smile. "Besides, you've proven to be a walking death curse with all of your near-death experiences. It's probably best that I accompany you."

"Oh, how very kind of you."

"I know," he returns with a wink.

I giggle as he gets up and wipes the dirt from the log off his pants. He steps to his own makeshift tent hung over a tree branch, next to our now-sleeping Bennarus. "I suppose I'll get some sleep. Watch for enemies, and wake me when you want to go."

"You're placing guard duties on me? We have Bennarus for that."

"You slept for a whole day when we got here," he points out. "Your rescuer–turned–bodyguard needs his beauty sleep." He motions to his face. "It's difficult to look this beautiful without it."

If he wasn't being playful, I would think he was an exact replica of Darius, and therefore would hate him to the core. Because his expressions and body language make it clear he's not serious, and he showed some consideration before with the nickname, I can take it with a grain of salt. "Keep telling yourself that," I reply in between fits of laughter.

He points his finger and clicks his tongue. "I will. Good night, Zappy."

"Good night, Quill." Just as he is about to crawl into his tent, I quip, "One of these days I'll come up with a nickname for you."

"I'd like to see you try!"

As he shuffles around his tent, I try to remember the last time I had a good, hearty laugh, before Bolt hoisted me on his back when I least expected it.

It's been too long.

Meeting Quill has been a blessing in disguise. Not only is he pleasing to the eyes, I enjoy his banter. He made me laugh again.

He's made me feel alive again.

I think we'll get along just fine.

CHAPTER II

Quill woke before I did, shockingly enough. I left the night guard duties to Bolt and Koa. They were still attached to each other's sides, just as they were last night, which was so endearing to watch.

"I see you failed to be the night watch," Quill says jokingly.

"You're the man. You could've done it," I counter with a smirk.

"I told you, I needed my beauty sleep."

I examine his messy hair and the stubble on his face that has grown a little thicker, and his eyes are half closed in sleepiness. "I see it's worked wonders," I agree with sarcasm.

"I thought so too."

I shake my head with a giggle as I pack my things. I think about how kind he was to set up the tent for me and lay me down on the layers of blankets I had, then cooked food for us to share. I smile at the warm affection blooming in my heart.

No. I can't go down that route. You don't want romance. He's an ally. That's all.

"Ready?" Quill asks with a positive air.

I stand next to him and peer thoughtfully on the journey ahead. "Let's go."

With Bolt and Koa transformed into horses, we saddle on their backs and set off to Cal–léa, going at a steady pace.

"So what else do you know about the Dormant King that will be useful for the other Descendants?" Quill asks over the sound of clopping hooves.

"Well, there's proof that he was banished to another dimension."

"Another dimension?" Quill's face wrinkles in disbelief. "That seems a bit . . . far-fetched."

"Unfortunately, it's not. I have proof from a tablet I found in Sabbia that says as much. One of the Backers on Luna Island confirmed it too."

"A tablet that proves the Dormant King's banishment," Quill repeats incredulously. "I'll have to see that."

I chuckle lightly. "Maybe when we aren't on horseback."

"Okay, so we have a proven banishment. What else?"

"The Backers admitted that he communicates to them through this dimension."

Quill pauses in deep thought, then shrugs. "It makes sense. He copied Transmission and Transform from the Land Ancestor."

So the Dormant King *received* Transmission instead of already having it. That confirms one suspicion. The only thing that the Backer said about it, though, was that the Dormant King could send mental messages to humans and creatures. "What is involved with those abilities?" I ask.

"Well, you saw an example at the Backers Fortress," he states. "I can manipulate nature to whatever I want. And with Transmission, I can communicate with both humans and animals."

That explains why Quill's eyes turn green and how Bolt came so swiftly to throw me in the watchtower. Amazing.

"Tell me more about Transmission."

"I don't know how well the Dormant King can use it, but for me, it only works in a certain range. And I always, under all circumstances, have to be the initiator. Someone cannot communicate back to me unless I have communicated the message first. Of course, a creature cannot respond back to me. They just do as they're told. Any other person, though, has the ability to respond."

This fills a lot of gaps. People stopped hearing the voice at a certain range because that was how far the Dormant King could reach someone's mind. He knew to summon the Dormants and Backers in Ketra because the Backers saw my lightning and told the Dormant King from the Fortress. As the Backer said, he summoned the Dormant in Sabbia Desert because he traveled there from the other dimension, and the Backers were in communication with him. He summoned the Dormant on Luna Island because he knew I was coming. Because Arthur informed the Backers, who therefore informed the Dormant King.

The pieces are clicking in place. Relief blossoms through me, mixing with dread and fear. The Dormant King is capable of doing more damage than I was aware of and he's doing it from a whole different dimension. What else he is capable of is terrifying enough to make one shudder. What's more is the possibility of us Descendants not being strong enough to bring him down.

"You're thinking too hard." Quill's kind, deep voice interrupts my thoughts. "What's going through that mind of yours?"

I swallow hard and exhale deeply. "Nothing. Things are finally coming together now."

We reach the peak of Solma Hills in a similar spot to where I was while going to Luna Island. At the top, I take in the view from a distance. The town is a short walk to the ocean, buildings spotted sporadically among its borders. The clear skies and shining sun illuminate the bright, clean town that I remember so well. The well-maintained buildings tell me the people worked to rebuild what was taken from them so long ago.

One of the biggest changes I notice is a large gate at the entrance. That was never there when my father was a knight. It used to be wide open for anyone coming and going, and hospitality was a precedent for the town's culture. Cal-léa was strong enough to rise from the ashes and repair itself, even if I wasn't there to see it. I suppose it should give me a sense of pride that I come from a place that continues to exude peace, as our olive branch tattoos show.

My heart pumps in nervous energy on what to expect upon arrival. I've repeatedly gone over many scenarios in my head for when I had a chance to come back to Cal-léa. I highly doubt anyone would recognize me as a grown adult, ten years later.

Two knights stand on watchtowers on either side of the city entrance. This place is much more secure than it ever was before. A memory of my father flashes in front of me. Coming home in his metal-plated armor, sword and shield slung behind his back. A sense of longing fills my chest in the most overwhelming way.

"What exactly is your plan?" Quill asks as we trot closer to the gate.

One of the knights makes his way down the watchtower to greet us and opens the wooden door at the bottom. "Welcome to Cal-léa, travelers," he bellows with enthusiasm as we dismount our Bennorus. "What brings you here?"

Quill waits for me to say something believable. I stumble on my words for a brief moment since there are a variety of reasons why we're here and I don't know which to pick.

"I used to live here," I say, showing him the white–ink tattoo on my forearm. "We just wanted to stop by and visit. Memories and all."

The knight hums with uncertainty, then turns to address Quill. "What about you?"

I didn't think this through. He doesn't have the same tattoo I do, and now his face is showing his insecurity.

"I uh, uh, b—"

"He's a friend of mine," I tell him, breaking Quill's mumbling nonsense.

The knight examines Quill's arm for any hint of a tattoo, his eyes dubious. Then he inspects all the sheathed knives wrapped around Quill's legs, the bow hitched on his back, and the quiver of arrows strapped below that. Then he pivots his interest to me, inspecting the sword and shield I have equipped.

"Leave your weapons here," he commands, pointing to a room at the corner of the gate. "Only knights are allowed to wield weapons within the town."

"What?" My eyebrows move high up my forehead.

"You can bring your packs inside, but you can retrieve your weapons when you leave."

This request throws me off. Cal–léa never used to be this way. Weapons on display, or even concealed, were never a cause for concern. This would be easier to accept if I didn't have to give him Jael's sword. I haven't parted from it since I left Ketra, and I don't want anything to happen to it.

"Will you still have them when we leave?" I ask warily. I want to be certain that he means what he says.

"Of course." He points to the door he came from within the watchtower. "Anything in question is kept in that room there. I can assure you that your things will remain safe."

Quill and I look at each other with uncertainty. Neither one of us wants to trust a stranger with our weapons. My sword is precious to me, while I'm sure Quill's bow means a lot to him.

Eventually, though, Quill takes off his equipment, but does so hesitantly. I have a hard time trusting some stranger, even from my hometown, to make sure Jael's sword is safe. Besides the arm-band, that sword is the only thing I have left of her. However, not complying means I don't get to visit my old home.

Quill hands the guard his equipment when I finally start taking off mine. The knight holds out his hands and I lay my sword across them with the straps of Quill's belts. "This better be where you say it is when we leave," I warn him in a low voice, finger pointed at his face. "If someone takes this on your watch, I swear I will make you suffer so much, you will beg for death."

His eyes go wide in fear at my warning and nods vigorously. "You have my word, miss."

"Thank you."

Watching him walk away with my only means of protection is similar to stripping myself bare and handing him my clothes. It all feels so wrong, but we at least have our abilities at our disposal—and our Bennarus, if we desperately need something to fall back on.

After the knight stores our equipment, he claps his hands in an uneven rhythm, and the gate splits inward for us.

"Have a wonderful visit," he says with a dip of his head.

"Thank you."

I mount back onto Bolt. Steeling myself for what is to come, I take another deep breath, then lead Quill and our Bennarus through the gate. Immediately upon entering, we aim for a big building and dismount.

"They should change to smaller forms," I inform Quill.

Quill's eyes turn bright green as he focuses on Koa, then hops off. Koa, understanding whatever message Quill sent to him mentally, shrinks to a tiny blue bird.

"You're protective of your weapons too," Quill notes.

I fold my arms, eye Bolt's mouse form, and watch him as he climbs up my leg. "It was my mentor's. That and this armband are all I have left of her."

"I understand." Quill places his hands on his hips and shifts his weight. Koa flaps his wings and perches on his shoulder. "That bow belonged to my brother."

"What happened to your brother?"

Quill turns away from me and says softly, "He died right in front of me."

My hand immediately reaches for my heart, feeling empathetic for the pain he must live with everyday, as I do. "I'm sorry. I can imagine how painful that was."

"It was a long time ago." He shrugs with a sad smile. He heads back into the public eye without waiting for me to say anything more. But I have questions, which prompts me to catch up to him with a light jog.

"You didn't flinch when you had to give the guard your bow, though. Weren't you worried about something happening to it?"

"I was at first, but I don't think they'll do anything with it. I'm sure it's in good hands."

He's much more trusting than I am.

We follow the cobblestone path that leads straight to the hustle and bustle of the town. A large stone fountain sits in the middle—the center of the whole town and the very essence of my childhood. After all these years, that fountain is alive and thriving.

I stop in my tracks and allow the memories to return. I picture Foss and Dahlia, the way I remember them when we were young, running in circles around the immense structure made of carved stone, water gracefully bubbling from the top and cascading to the bottom pool. They were the only ones who accepted me despite my lie about the skin condition. That alone is a big reason why they have remained in the forefront of my memory for so long. And why I hope to find them while I'm here.

"What's wrong?" Quill interrupts my thoughts once again.

I weakly point a finger at the fountain. "I used to play in that area when I was younger."

Quill nods silently and looks in the same direction. "Let me guess, you were the one chasing all the boys, and because they were scared of you they all jumped in the water to hide."

"If that were true, I would wear that reputation with pride."

Quill chuckles and folds his arms. He takes the front of his shirt and flaps it against his chest to cool off from the heat. "Looks refreshing. Maybe you can act as my guard while I take a swim in there."

I swat at his stomach playfully and I don't miss how toned and muscled it is. "You're on your own with that one."

As we walk further into town, I search for anything that seems even vaguely familiar—the inn, clothing shops, the markets, and the alleys lined with dirt between the yellowish buildings. My mother used to let me play around the fountain while she shopped for the days' supper, but that's the only market I remember clearly.

I can recall how busy the town square was. People came and went, chatter permeating the air, yelps and gleeful laughter from children, and stringed instruments in the distance blending with the noise. The ambience hasn't changed.

Outside the food market is a stand with someone selling bowls of Conna Mondaña, Cal-léa's signature dessert. Suddenly, I'm taken back to the eatery in Ketra where I successfully replicated the recipe and it became a big deal when I introduced it to the village.

"You should try the Conna Mondaña," I suggest to Quill.

His brows knit together. "What in the name of Halivaara is Conna Mondaña?"

His remark sends me into a fit of laughter as I direct him to the stand with a long line in front of it. "See for yourself. You won't regret it."

We both buy a bowl of the dessert with its sweetened yogurt base, topped with chopped bananas and strawberries. We take a seat at the edge of the fountain and I hum happily as I scoop the dessert in my mouth.

"Tastes just the way I remember," I singsong, doing a seated happy dance.

Quill slowly inches the spoon into his mouth, the white, runny yogurt spotting his full lips. Once he laps it off with his tongue, I realize I'm staring.

He is an ally. A friend. That is all.

"You're right, this is scrumptious," Quill remarks with his mouth full, moaning in between bites. He gives himself no time between spoonfuls as he quickly chugs the whole bowl. "Mm. I could eat an entire barrel of this."

"Slow down!" I tell him through laughter. "Give yourself time to enjoy it."

He sloppily wipes his mouth with his sleeve and exhales. "Excuse me while I get myself a lifetime supply."

He comes to a stand, taking my empty bowl with him, and goes back for more. While I await his return, I scan the markets close by. While I recognize the ones selling food and clothing, there is one I assume is new with its wall-to-wall customers.

Paper lanterns hang in an arch above the entryway and all over the walls inside the shop. Varieties of olive branches are sketched across the paper surfaces, making them uniquely different from one another. People are crowding by the register to purchase their own lanterns; some are holding more than one in their hands.

Quill sits next to me with another bowl. With the same speed, he shovels the dessert in his mouth. If he keeps up at this rate, there won't be any Conna Mondaña left for others and he may not be able to maintain his muscular physique.

"I'll be back," I tell him, intrigued by the attraction of the lantern shop. He barely notices me when I get up.

I squeeze in between the throngs of people as I approach a wall full of colorful lanterns. One by one, people grab a lantern off the wall and bring it to the register. They are beautiful, I admit, but I don't fully grasp the craze for them.

An older female customer steps up next to me to grab one. As she turns it around in her hands, I muster the bravery to get her attention with a tap on the shoulder. "Excuse me. Can you tell me what this place is for? This is my first time in Cal-léa."

"Of course," she replies with a bubbly voice and a white-toothed smile. "This is for the lantern festival tonight."

"Tonight?"

"Yes. We have one every year to celebrate surviving another year after an attack on our town ten years ago. It's just a reminder of who we are and what we represent: peace and unity."

I find myself in shock. Tears prick my eyes and I'm unable to swallow. They're celebrating the event that changed my life and broke up my family. That was also probably the event that caused the town to hire more security and build a gate.

I dip my head at her. "I see."

"The owner spends all year making enough of them for the next festival. She's very talented, indeed."

I finally manage to swallow and hold back tears. "That she is."

She walks away to get in line as I continue to stare at the lanterns on the wall. There have been more changes to this place besides the gate and interviewing each traveling guest.

They came up with a whole festival revolving around a single attack. And I want to be a part of it.

Next thing I know, I'm snatching up a lantern to purchase.

I head back to the fountain and find Quill waiting for me. He holds an arm over his full belly, happy and satisfied.

"Oh good, I was wondering where you ran off to," he remarks.

I lift up the lantern for him to see. "I just found out there's a lantern festival tonight. To celebrate living another year after the Backers raid."

"The Backers raid?"

I sigh to hold back more tears. "Yes. Ten years ago. The day I left."

"Oh." He nods, then perks up, understanding the connection. "Oh!"

My sniffles fail to hide the oncoming sobs, and I don't want to do it in front of him. "I think I'm going to go for a walk," I say.

"Sure. I'll reserve rooms at the inn for us. Maybe I'll get a lantern too."

I nod. "Thank you."

Quill stands and tosses his pack behind him, then eyes me with concern. "You can fight without weapons, right? I just want to make sure you'll be okay. You are a walking death curse, after all."

I shake my head with a laugh, even though I'm crying. "Yes, I've lasted this long through my near-death experiences."

He winks with a grin. "Good. Meet me at the inn when you're done. Take your time."

Quill takes my lantern and retreats to the inn close to the gate, and I don't miss how his gait exudes confidence and strength with his long strides and swinging one arm beside him while the other grasps the strap of his pack.

My gaze veers off to the right and I spot an alleyway in between buildings that seems to click within me. I remember traveling from that direction to come to the square.

From the fountain, I retrace my steps. My boots on the path is the only sound breaking the silence of this isolated area. My mother and I always took the same route going home after she finished shopping; it should be familiar to me.

The businesses and buildings are newer, rebuilt within the last few years. The noise of the town died off the further away my mother and I walked from the square, just like it is now. It may have been a long time since I'd traveled this beaten path, but I do recall it was far enough away that the noise didn't reach our neighborhood, and the beach was walking-distance.

But I'm anxious that the house might not look the same anymore. I might find that my parents are still there and they simply abandoned me.

The beaten path converts into a cobblestone street where a lovely neighborhood starts. The way it curves to the left and how the surroundings go from buildings and businesses straight to a family-friendly area gives me the inkling that I'm in the right place.

I slow my pace and take it all in. Both sides of the street are lined with cobblestone houses. Behind each house on the right side is a view of the ocean, with no fence to block the scenery—exactly the way it was before. Flowers displayed on the windowsills, small patches of grass serve as front lawns while their backyards are as big as their houses, and curved walkways that lead right to the wooden door.

I missed this place. The tranquility, the waves rolling in from a distance, and the cutely designed homes all resemble a wonderful dream. Nirvana.

Then, a few houses down, a big tree towering over the roof from the backyard makes me smile so hard it hurts. Bolt used to perch up there. My friends sat at the trunk and watched my father and me fence.

The tree shows its age with cracks in its smooth, pale bark. I ruined so many of my dresses from climbing the gargantuan hunk of wood and thick branches. I used to climb it to see if I could get a view of the whole town from a higher vantage point without Bolt's help, but failed every time. Instead, I got a view of the ocean, where my interest in water was born. The tree became a landmark of the neighborhood with its monstrous height, magnetizing the other children to come and climb it.

The house itself is somehow brighter than I remember. The stones used to be darker in shade, which means newer, different materials were used to rebuild it. It must have taken enough damage from the Backers raid that it needed to be completely remodeled. The layout is still the same, at least.

I tilt my head to talk to Bolt on my shoulder. "Remember that tree?"

Bolt squeaks in response, rising on his hind legs to sniff the air. I fold my arms and we stare at the tree for a moment longer, reminiscing about our old life here, until a silhouette through the window makes me flinch.

A dark-skinned woman in a knee-length dress brings a platter from the kitchen to the dining room table, exactly where I sat with my parents to eat supper. A child around three years old runs in from the backyard, a flower-patterned dress flowing behind her and black hair messy from hours of play. I'm sure it's covered in rips and grass stains, just like all my dresses were. A man wanders in, kisses the woman on the cheek, and sits at the table with his daughter. The woman smiles brightly as she meanders back to the kitchen.

Those people are not my parents, but watching this moment feels like I've gone back in time. They're reenacting what my life was before I left.

Now that I look closer, I know those people.

Ducking out of sight, I creep to the front window and lift my head just high enough to get a clear view of their dining room.

The woman has black hair just like her daughter, her smile so bright it could improve anyone's day. The man has shaggy brown hair and a baby face with the smolder of a troublemaker, just as he did when we were young.

A tear trickles down my cheek as I watch Foss and Dahlia, who are living in my old house, enjoying a family meal with their child.

I can't believe this.

It saddens me that they're so blissful, and angry that they took over my childhood home. All those years of having them come over and play then suddenly never seeing us again, and they have the gall to swoop into our house when they had the chance. Clearly, I never meant as much to them as they did to me.

And with their blissful smiles, I can tell they've done superb without me. All they needed was each other and their child.

Cal-léa moved on without me. So did my friends.

Among the sadness and anger, I'm envious, particularly of the little girl. She still has her parents. She hasn't had to leave home and start her life over without them in a brand-new home in a whole other part of the kingdom. She hasn't lost everything because of an enemy that wanted to hunt her down and kill her to steal her abilities.

I don't resemble that little girl anymore.

Imagining everything—reuniting with my friends, maybe finding my parents and asking why they never came for me, seeing the house I was raised in—was all a waste of time. Of course Foss and Dahlia wouldn't remember me. I'm a distant memory for them. Their behavior shows no hint of grief.

My gaze shifts away from the happy family scene. The only thing I accomplished coming here was heartache and homesickness.

With nothing left to see, I walk away from my childhood, my heart breaking along the way.

Dusk has approached by the time I arrive at the inn where Quill reserved rooms for us. I don't feel any better than I did when we parted ways, so he asks what happened. Since the lantern festival is supposed to start soon, we follow the crowd going in the same direction through the alleyways between buildings. This gives me a chance to recap what I saw.

"It's definitely an odd coincidence that your friends live in your old home," Quill agrees. "But what were you expecting going back to your old house? That your friends would be depressed and miserable?"

"I suppose I hoped I would see some sign that they missed me," I grumble with a shrug.

Quill exhales as if he's about to deliver a blow. "Just because someone looks happy doesn't mean they're not hiding some sort of sadness. If they meant as much to you as you did to them, then they most definitely would remember you. Maybe they took that house *because* it's the only thing they have left of their memories of you."

"True," I agree. "It's just hard to accept that they moved on without me."

"Moving forward in life doesn't mean moving on. It doesn't mean they don't occasionally think about you or miss you. Living in your house is a constant reminder of you, if anything."

I regard him with a grin, amazed at his comforting words. "Do you have some experience in that area?"

His expression turns downcast as he reflects on how he claimed such knowledge. "Only when it comes to my brother," he says, voice low and pained. "I moved forward from it the best I could, but it doesn't mean I don't miss him or think about him every day. Quite the opposite, actually."

It brings him great sorrow to admit that, I can tell. His brother meant the world to him, as Jael did to me. One day, I hope he will tell me his story. For now, we have the loss of a loved one in common.

"That's how I feel about Jael, actually," I confess. "I miss her all the time. I have nightmares about her death almost every night."

"I hate to tell you this, Zappy," he says with warning, "but that will never go away."

His words hit me hard. I hoped that one day the nightmares and the guilt tied to it would dissipate. And maybe there would come a day where Calista replacing Jael in my nightmares would be a thing of the past. It's quite possible that I had unrealistic expectations there.

I suppose I have to learn to live with this side effect of trauma, just as Quill had.

We found that the only way to get to the beach for the festival was to sneak through a sandy path with trees between the houses of my old neighborhood, but beyond those obstacles is a gorgeous sight.

Most of the two thousand citizens have already pooled together on the shoreline, a school of fish squished together. One knight holds a torch to carefully light lanterns. I admire the dancing flames within each one, brightening the etched designs on the rice paper that flicker in the night. The glass and iron torches in Ketra did the same thing outside everyone's huts. The flickering of each person's lantern provides a truly magical ambience among the human sea that's reminiscent of my Twinkle Fireflies. My red ombre lantern changes to a dark orange while Quill's dark blue one lightens to an ocean blue.

I search the faces of the Cal-léans to see what their expressions are saying. With their chins held high, eyes closed in meditation, and holding their lanterns in front of them with dedication and seriousness, I see what this festival means to Cal-léa.

This event is more anticipated than I expected. The Backers raid impacted the city more than I was aware and their success in moving forward afterward means a great deal to the people.

And I'm honored to celebrate this moment.

A blow of a birdlike whistle silences the crowd. A gray-haired, light-skinned, middle-aged man steps to the shoreline in front of the crowd with a cone-shaped shell in his hands. I recognize him as Thomas, the mayor of Cal-léa. He used to have darker hair and obviously looked younger when I was here. The only time I ever heard of Thomas was from my father. Any direction my father received was usually given by him.

"Thank you all for coming tonight," his booming voice begins. "This is indeed a special night for us. On this day, ten years ago, we endured an unfortunate catastrophe." His tone turns solemn as he continues his speech. "Lives were lost. Businesses were ruined. And it took many months to recover from the damage. Despite all of that, let's not look back on that day as a day we fell. Let's not use this occasion to recall everything we lost. No. We will remember how we got back up. We will remember that we rose from the ashes and started over. We got back on our feet and we never forgot who we were."

Unexpected tears stream down my cheeks. His speech has unexpectedly tugged my heartstrings when I reflect on that day. Cal-léa did lose lives, including me, but in a different sense. Worst of all was that I had to do it alone. Jael made sure I wasn't alone, though. When she died and Ketra turned their backs on me, that loneliness came screaming back.

Now Quill is here, standing next to me in a place he's never been to and knows nothing about, going with the flow with the customs. His easygoing attitude means so much to me. I want to tell him as much, but I worry that will make him uncomfortable.

Suddenly, I'm very aware of how close our hands are. All he needs to do is stretch that strong finger and he could stroke my hand. I watch the movement of his finger closely in my peripherals, hoping—praying—that he will take my hand in his. Whether it's for comfort or for something more, I will take it.

"We are a town of peace and unity. That, my people, will never change." Thomas bends to the sand to pick up his ignited lantern and faces the sea. Everyone else follows suit, ready to release their symbol for rising above the damage. Quill and I take that as our cue to do the same. As much as I want him to touch my hand, just once, the timing doesn't call for it.

"We are Cal-léa!" Thomas shouts triumphantly as he releases his lantern.

"We are Cal-léa!" the crowd calls afterward, releasing their lanterns in the sky.

And away they fly.

The wind gives them the elevation needed to prevent them crashing into the sea right away. After a few seconds, the flecks of light serve as a whole set of stars as they dot the sky with their beauty.

The Cal-léans cheer in unison as the lanterns float farther and farther away from the shore, celebrating another year of recovery and another year of victory.

The beach has already started to empty as people head home. The chatter is a low mumble as everyone remaining reflects on the night, prideful they've made it this far. Quill and I stay a few more minutes to watch the lanterns burn off and disappear. The ones still ignited are so far away they can barely be seen from here.

He peers down at me at the same time I look up at him with teary eyes, and we break eye contact with an awkward chuckle.

"So, um," he says after clearing his throat. "We should head back to the inn. Figure out what we're going to do tomorrow."

I nod. "Yes. Good idea."

Our stroll back to the inn is a silent one, even though my mind is currently full of noise. I want to thank him for coming with me and doing this with me, but I debate on how to do that without it coming across that I have an emotional attachment to him. He may be a Descendant, but I have to be careful not to trust him easily. Trusting in a romantic bond will only end in disaster. I refuse to learn the hard way again.

I clasp the necklace Calista gave me and squeeze. She would have good advice on this subject. She must have some secrets if she and Malik are still happily in love.

Jael had words of wisdom too. Romance nauseated her, but she was usually open to talking about it with me and always seemed to know what to do in certain circumstances. She wasn't blind to how normal it is for people to have feelings.

Knowing both of them, they probably would reason the same way with me.

All you're doing is thanking him. That shouldn't be a big deal. That shouldn't give him the hint of any feelings you have.

Once we're almost to the inn, I realize I've spent way too much time thinking about this simple dilemma. All I need to do is say thank you.

I stop walking while Quill keeps on, living in his own bubble and not noticing I'm not next to him.

"Quill."

He stops and twists on the heels of his boots, waiting for me to say something while half facing me. His brow quirks in anticipation.

I clear my throat and rock on my heels. "Thank you."

"For what?"

"For coming here with me. For going to the festival with me. For being my partner." I pinch my lips together.

He gives me the shy sideways grin that I've grown to love seeing, still half turned, but says nothing.

"I know it wasn't ideal," I add to fill the silence. "We just met, yet you came with me to my childhood home without much argument. I'm just glad to know I'm not alone anymore."

Finally, he turns all the way around. "Well, we're Descendants. We have to stick together. After all, you are a walking death curse."

I huff a laugh, folding my arms as well, and doing everything I can to not look at the handsome man in front of me. "Will I ever be known as anything other than Zappy and the walking death curse?"

"Nope. And I'm still waiting for your nickname for me." With a wink, he turns and steps into the old-fashioned, outdated inn.

"I still need to think on that," I call after him as I catch up to his pace. "Something to match your personality as well as your abilities."

"I eagerly await your inventive ideas," he remarks with a teasing lilt, handing me the key to my room.

A warm smile takes over my face as we make our way up the creaky wooden stairs. I promised myself to be much more guarded if I came across a man I was attracted to. Try as I might, that guard is crumbling with each conversation with Quill.

Keep your guard up. You're both on your way to kill the Dormant King, not to fall in love.

Once I unlock the door to my room, I set my pack on the pristine bed and take in the room's features while I pull out the stone tablet and map. It's simple with just the necessities: small bed with thick blankets, nightstand with a mirror on top, bedside table, a chair next to the door, and an oil lamp being the sole source of light in the darkness. The only missing feature is a window. Bolt hops off my shoulder and converts to an eagle, scanning his surroundings too.

I'm just about to go across the hall to Quill's room to work out a plan when a knock stops me. Lit oil lamp in hand, I open the door and find Quill standing on the other side. My insides ignite a fiery passion at seeing him in a thin white shirt and loose black pants. I want him to be here because he can't resist me. Take me in his arms and show me what a kiss feels like.

"I thought we should talk about where to go next," he says softly, crinkling the paper of his map in his fingers.

I blink a few times to get my mind in the right place. He's only here for business. "Yes. O–of course." Beating myself up for stumbling on my words, I make space for him to enter. He takes a seat on the chair by the door and scoots it close to the bed. My palms sweat from our close proximity and I'm very alert to how close he is to me.

He opens the map and examines it. "So, it looks like the closest town to here is Macaphin Village, where the Water Descendant is. Or we can take the long trip to Vulca Mountain first and find the Fire Descendant, *then* go to Macaphin Village. In my opinion, it might take longer to go to Vulca then to Macaphin than the other way around. Either way, we're going to be traveling quite a distance."

Tracing the map with my finger, I realize he is right. Macaphin Village isn't too far away from Cal-léa. Because I don't want to spend time traveling that could be spent finding the Dormant King, my instinct tells me to take the shorter route first.

"Havanna," Quill says gently, his tone urgent and edgy. "What if we go through all this only for them to choose not to join us? What if we end up doing this alone?"

The thought occurred to me on more than one occasion. Understandably, the other Descendants might be too afraid to emerge from hiding and instead choose to remain in their safe space. Deep down, though, they must have a desire to break free, just as Quill and I had.

"We won't be alone," I say with conviction. "You and I will at least stick together. If they say no, then we'll have to come up with a convincing argument. Staying in hiding solves nothing. If my instinct is correct, they're just as tired of hiding as we are."

Quill nods, even though he still seems unconvinced. "I suppose we can cross that path when we get there."

I lay a hand on his shoulder and give it a shake. "Let's focus on getting to Macaphin Village safely. Once we know how the people are there, we can come up with a solution to get the Water Descendant to join us."

Hands on his knees, he takes a deep breath. "So. Macaphin Village. Tomorrow."

"Tomorrow," I confirm with a nod.

Quill rises from his seat and drags the chair back to where it had been. He takes all of two steps to the door, but stops just as he opens it. He peers back at me again, but with eyes that hold a world of insecurity. Eyes that silently beg me for consolation.

"Tree Mover," I encourage him with my warm smile. "It will be okay."

His shoulders relax a bit when he shakes his head and chuckles. "I think you can do better than that." He opens the door and takes one last look at me. "Good night, Zappy."

"Good night, Forest Boy."

"I still think you can do better." With that, he shuts the door behind him.

I crawl into bed and tightly wrap the blankets around me. The idea that we're finally banding together, as we should have years ago, excites me.

By breaking out of hiding, I started a revolution. I proved I was brave enough to leave the only home I was confined in to do what the Ancestors were never brave enough to do. Doing this will change everything. Not just for me, but for the entire kingdom.

It's finally time to find the other Descendants.

It's finally time to end the Dormant King.

It's finally time to go to war.

Thank you for reading *The Call of Thunder!*

Havanna and Quill's story will continue in *The Call of Allies*, book two of the *Hidden Heroes* series. Find out what happens when Havanna and Quill attempt to get the other Descendants to join their fight against the Dormant King. Will the Descendants win the war or will the Dormant King prove to be too powerful for all of them?

Dying to know what Quill's thoughts were upon meeting Havanna and starting this new adventure with her?

Sign up at www.sarahblynnewrites.com and get the story from his point of view!

Did you enjoy *The Call of Thunder?* Leave a review on Amazon, Goodreads, or Barnes & Noble!

Follow me on:

Tiktok: @sarahblynne

Instagram: @sarahblynnewrites

Facebook: Sarah Blynne Writes

ACKNOWLEDGEMENTS

ACKNOWLEDGEMENTS

Writing this book was so much fun! It took at least a year to come up with the idea, and another year to write the book. So I'm grateful this story ended up in your hands after all this time.

I want to send a big thank you to one of my closest friends, Andre, for having a wealth of knowledge about superheroes and powers to help me narrow down this story. Your input was more helpful than you know.

Thank you also to my parents, Alex and Francine, for encouraging me as I embark on my writing journey. Especially my dad for his artistic eye on the book cover and the map. I love you both.

And a *huge* thank you to Kasey Kubica for all the time you spent formulating this book to what it is, and helping me to come up with the right words to say what I meant to say. Your help is very much appreciated.

I also want to thank my other close friends—Megan, Amanda, Tally, Kirsie, and many others—who also played a part in supporting me on this adventure.

And, of course, a big thank you to my husband, Cody. You continue to be my biggest cheerleader and my best friend, and I love you more than you will ever know.

See you in the next book!

—Sarah Blynne

ABOUT THE AUTHOR

ABOUT THE AUTHOR

Sarah Blynne has written stories since she was a kid growing up in Tacoma, WA. She resides in Renton, WA with her husband and cat. In her spare time, Sarah likes to read, write, cook, play video games, go on walks, drink coffee, and spend time with her loved ones. *The Call of Thunder* is Sarah's second novel, with the young adult romance *Bloom* being her first.

www.ingramcontent.com/pod-product-compliance
Lightning Source LLC
Chambersburg PA
CBHW022122310726
48972CB00007B/2155